ON THE BRINK OF BLISS AND INSANITY

Love, Peace,

Lisa Tease-Dll

3835

On the Brink of Bliss & Insanity

Five Star Publications, Inc.
Chandler, AZ

Linda F. Radke, President
Five Star Publications, Inc.
POB 6698
Chandler, AZ 85246-6698
480-940-8182

Publisher's Cataloging-In-Publication Data

Library of Congress Cataloging-in-Publication Data

Cerasoli, Lisa.
On the brink of bliss and insanity / by Lisa Cerasoli.
    p.; cm.
ISBN: 978-1-58985-121-4

1. Young women – Fiction. 2. Man-woman relationships –
United States – Fiction. 3. Love stories. I. Title.
PS3603.E72 O5 2009
813/.6

PROJECT MANAGER: Sue DeFabis
COVER DESIGN: Kris Taft Miller
INTERIOR DESIGN BY: Koren Publishing Services

To order an autographed copy of *On The Brink of Bliss and Insanity*
or to listen to and purchase the groovy soundtrack featuring
"Fifty Ways to Leave Your Lover", "Wait in Vain", "Rebel Yell",
Newton's "Roses" and others, please visit:
www.LisaCerasoli.com
OR www.youtunespro/newtonsthereom.com

To check out the Star Dust Elite Venus Vintage Ivory Pearl Guitar
on the cover (and other cool guitars), please visit: www.daisyrock.com

"Not quite sure how Cerasoli jumped inside my brain, but you have to experience the refreshing for-once-in-my-life-someone-understands-me moment for yourself. It's one of the best damn books I've ever read!"

Tish Ciravolo, President/Founder – DAISY ROCK GIRL GUITARS

"Like J.D. Salinger for his generation or Bret Easton Ellis for the 80s, Lisa Cerasoli writes with a wit and frank honesty that cuts you to the core. This story about modern LA life amongst "frenemies" and lovers is just what everyone east of Palm Springs thinks life is like in Tinsel Town…and what everyone west of it is (almost) ashamed to admit is just a little too true."

Sean Madden, Producer
WALT DISNEY STUDIOS HOME ENTERTAINMENT

"Sex, music, tequila, religion, crime, *mary jane*…Finally, far-fetched fiction meets in-your-face reality in this sardonic, wry, laugh-till-you-cry artful work of prose."

Cory L. Schuelke, CFO – WINDSWEPT MUSIC

"*On the Brink*…is a quick & witty ride that takes you down a twisted tunnel with your best friend. When spit out the bottom, you find profound self-discovery and *blessed daylight.*"

Fredericka Deichelbor – A READER FROM "THE NETWORK"

"*On the Brink*…captures the riotous, unpredictable, self-loathing existence of a woman buried beneath her own low expectations of life. Drama and discontent have been Annie's security blanket for so long that wanting more and ultimately realizing she deserves it, is a touching, comical and entertaining journey that will resonate with both women and men. Cerasoli is a gifted writer who allows us to participate, almost as if intruding, in her character's heartbreaking and hilarious passage to renewal and love."

Sarah K. Blom, M.A. – SENIOR DIRECTOR OF DEVELOPMENT
MICHIGAN STATE UNIVERSITY

"Masterfully told through a flawed protagonist and irreverent cast of characters, *On the Brink*…is an exhilarating ride through a quarter-life crisis. The story makes you wince and laugh simultaneously at the brutal honesty of love, adulthood, and how *not* to handle them."

Bill Hinkle, Producer – SECRET LIVES OF WOMEN, WE NETWORK

"Cerasoli's writing is primal: It's all gut and even more heart. She's uncensored, wild and puts such a clever spin on true-to-life dilemmas that you find yourself laughing when you should be cringing, and vice versa. Mostly, she gets the point across while enticing you to read on and root for these unlikely, complex heroes of modern time."

J.Michael McClary – WRITER/DIRECTOR
SAM SHEPHERD'S *CURSE OF THE STARVING CLASS*

On
The
Brink
of
Bliss
&
Insanity

Definitely fiction, I promise.

by
LISA
CERASOLI

*I wanted to dedicate this book to my cousin, Bethany...
just for existing.*

*And then I considered dedicating it to my friend and
manager, Sandra, and sister, Lora. If it wasn't for them
telling me to "shut up and go write something," I would
have been too scared and too damned distracted to put
pen to paper.*

*And, of course, I'd love to dedicate this to my mother, but
honestly, my mother's got no business going anywhere
near this book.*

*So, after much consideration, I have decided this book is
truly meant for two very special people:*

*My father, Richard "Dick" Cerasoli. He suffered greatly
while cheering me on simultaneously as we laughed,
prayed, held hands and shed tears throughout his battle
lost to lung cancer, and mine won to On the Brink of Bliss
and Insanity.*

*And this book is also for the "average" American Girl.
Because, guess what? You're anything but that.*

AYN RAND ON WHY SHE WROTE
The Fountain Head

"This may sound naïve. But is our life ever to have any reality? Are we ever going to live on the level OR is life always to be something else, something different from what it should be? A real life, simple and sincere, and even naïve, is the only life where all potential grandeur and beauty of human existence can really be found. Are there real reasons for accepting the alternative, that which we have today? No one has really shown (today's) life, as it really is, with its real meaning and its reasons. I'm going to show it. If it's not a pretty picture – what is the substitute?"

LISA CERASOLI ON WHY SHE WROTE
On the Brink of Bliss and Insanity

"What she said."

On the Brink of Bliss & Insanity

Rock Bottom

Sometimes rock bottom is an accumulation of events. I think in one's life there could be a series of catastrophes, similar in theme, that when examined individually could all be handled with a relative degree of facility. But there may come a day, just one ordinary day, when something as simple as your cell phone dying in rush hour traffic, or your boss grabbing your ass for the tenth time at work and this time *really* holding on when you finally say, "That's it, that's all I can take. I can no longer be responsible for any and all of my actions… at least not for the next few weeks." And you hit, as they say, *rock fucking bottom.*

I get the feeling today might be that day, as I shove the pillow over my head to stifle the blare. *What is he listening to?* That blare is going to be the end of me. I'm going to kill him and his blare as soon as I get eight more minutes of shut-eye.

1

Blare!

Oh…my…god.

Shit! It's my alarm clock. Okay, say 9:48. Please say 9:48 because that would mean it's 9:10.

You see, I set my clock thirty-eight minutes fast and convince myself it's only thirty minutes fast to ensure my timely arrival at any event I need to arrive to on time – such as work.

I swing an arm haphazardly out from the covers to stop the unruly noise and it gets twisted in the alarm clock cord.

"Shut up!"

I swat at the dangling clock. Silence.

It's ten, um…I blow a curl from my line of vision; 10:17. That's um…oh, come on, 10:17 minus thirty-eight minutes.

You do this every day, Stupid.

Okay, that's 9:47 minus eight minutes. That's 9:37 plus two minutes. That's 9:39 plus ten to get ready and twenty to get there. That's…I'm screwed. Must have hit snooze four solid times without realizing it. What's the point of the snooze button when its use becomes an involuntary activity? That's my question to the world on this merry Monday morning (a mere six days from my big twenty-eighth).

I slip into my checkered work pants that look as if they haven't been washed since my *last* birthday, then dodge around a bit. No shoes.

Clearing throat…

"Are my shoes out there?"

No response. Hmm. Maybe he didn't hear me.

Weird, though, because I have one of those voices that carries. People say, "Oh, it's so sexy." Generally, I feel like I'm two days away from strep. Rumor has it "the voice" is an asset, although I consider my hair to be my première feature. Its shoulder length strands are a combination of copper curls wrestling with an equal number of feisty opponents the shade of a rose the day before it dies. I look at my hair, study it. It's the one

thing that represents me authentically. Plus, it's a great place
to hide. On Saturday, the dreaded day of the twenty-eighth
year of my unaccomplished life, I will undeniably be putting
my most faved feature to full use.

As the light through my bedroom window causes most
of my senses to climb back into my body after another night
of shifty slumber, the never ending illusion I've clung to since
forever creeps back in as well. It's like breath, this illusion; I'd
die without its constant presence. Most of the time, though,
I'm not even aware it's piloting my every move. This "hope" I
dream of daily should be as easy to catch as a dead butterfly,
as mindless as making a bowl of Jell-O, as achievable as tying
in tic-tac-toe, or as natural as telling an old friend hello.

It's that all I've ever wanted is a nice guy and a dog who
loves me madly – the guy, not the dog, no, the guy *and* the dog –
and a house where the sun always shines, and…well…shit.

When you spend your first eighteen years immersed in a
world that uses Margaritas as meal replacements, prides itself
on selective hearing or none at all, deals in lies, loose hands,
and tight hugs, and has perfected the art of religious subjuga-
tion, i.e., good old-fashioned brainwashing – things like getting
your hung-over ass out of bed to go to work is torture most
days. And ideals like the whole man-dog-house thing seem
like the recurring dream you know will never materialize, yet
won't stop frequenting your disillusioned subconscious. Yeah,
I definitely plan on spending Saturday night hidden behind
ringlets of gypsy gray smoke and rusty curls.

Clearing throat again, and hating cerebral Mondays more
than usual, I scream, "MP, are my work shoes out there?" and
race toward the sound of Pachelbel's or some other dude's
Canon.

And there he sits: Mr. Tall, Dark, and Handsome, perfectly poised in his matching blue-and-white striped pajama
set. A gift from Mommy that I'm certain he has dry-cleaned.

As designated laundry doer, I confess to never having seen it in among the more common clothing. Yep, there he sits; a lit cigarette resting in the ashtray to his right, a mug of coffee on the table to his left, the *LA Times* gripped evenly between his hands revealing a tuft of strategically disheveled hair – a freaking Norman Rockwell painting (insert hot guy behind newspaper).

I pause to take in the view.

Ladies and gentlemen, I give you Michael Paul Meadows, the most charming prick you'll ever meet.

"Have you seen my – "

I glance downward. There, being grazed by the black leather J. Crew slipper dangling buoyantly from his right foot, are my work shoes. I seize them in the typically exaggerated style used to illustrate boundless frustration.

He evades me with an even more masterful caliber of finesse, a skill that's categorically achieved *only* through years of diligently ignoring me. In fact, only one other man in history has been bold enough to reach such magnitudes of success regarding the *dis*regarding of my presence, and lived, of course, to *not* mention it. But it took that guy twenty years to finely tune his snub-Annie skills, whereas MP has stepped into the winner's circle in just twenty-seven short months. Bravo.

"You're going to be late for work," he states flatly, without removing an ounce of his being from the interests of his paper.

"Thank you," I reply facetiously while plopping the shoes onto the floor and jamming my feet into them.

A mad leap is made for my purse and then I double back with a genuine gravity-defying twirl to nab the nearby keys.

My poor forgotten keys. If they could only speak, they'd say, "Bitch, for the hundredth time, I'm right here in front of you. Open your eyes!"

I spin again – should have been a dancer – and point in the

direction of the door. As I take two steps forward and swoop to plant an automated kiss onto the cheek of the Boyfriend, he turns his perfectly chiseled visage abruptly toward me – which freaks my shit, truth be told.

"Is there any more coffee?" he says.

My eyes go wide, nose flares, jaw drops open. It's my I'm-totally-late-for-work-are-you-smokin'-crack look. Which is a subtle yet pleasant upgrade from the holy-shit-are-you-about-to-kiss-me-in-the-name-of-pure-affection look I was sporting the second before he spoke.

"Girl, I'm in mourning."

Girl, I'm in mourning; his latest catch phrase. Works like a charm.

I spin – dizzy at this point – bounce back into the living room with pot of coffee, fill his mug, bring the pot back into the kitchen, charge for the door.

"Cream?" he utters in his "small voice."

"Don't you have class today?" I knowingly inquire while retreating for the cream.

"Easy, girl."

He flips down a corner of the newspaper to examine my work, ignores the question. I put the cream back, dash out the door. Without lifting an eye from the business section, MP releases a whispery chant.

"One thousand one, one thousand two, and…she's back!"

I bust in and snag the keys that were tossed during the tending of his hydratorial needs, and then re-vanish.

So thirteen minutes late, I pull up to the restaurant in my pale yellow not-so-well-maintained '69 Mustang. Not bad. Took a short cut through Beverly Hills and managed to pull off a series of successful Beverly Hills stop techniques, shaving two whole minutes off the travel time. In terms those living outside the greater Los Angeles area can understand, I ran eight stop signs in a row and didn't get caught. Go me.

I'm about to bolt from my car, when the bossman screeches to an eardrum-popping halt and nearly takes out my driver's door. Paying careful attention not to scratch the slut-red paint on his new 80K Lexus *because someone has to*, I gradually wriggle my way out of the car. This prolonged battle forces me to peer into his car and bear witness to Antonio, the Chef de Cuisine, molesting his latest aperitif.

The term "molest" is used frequently when referring to any woman of the female persuasion Antonio happens to be fornicating with because they all look sixteen. Hmm? They appear to be struggling to switch places. And the look on her face clearly spells *agony*. But why wouldn't they just get out of the car and run around it clockwise, like everybody else? Wait a minute…

Gross.

Once inside, my T-shirt is replaced by the wife beater that lies crumpled at the bottom of my locker. Reaching for my chef's coat, I spy this cheesy little man perched against the now ajar door. A wave of energy shifts the room from pure disgust (my vibe toward Antonio) to undeniable sleaze (Antonio's vibe toward every female ever to exist).

He begs the question. "Why haven't you and I gotten together?"

"Antonio, I'm not your type," I state flatly.

"Oh, darling, whatever are you speaking of?"

"Well for starters, I'm old enough to be your girlfriend's mother."

"A sense of humor. Sexy."

Breezing past him awakens a trail of unruly scents. So stalking me all the way to the kitchen are swirls of day old Obsession mixed with last night's "house" Chianti (she doesn't know wine – no need to impress), and her perfume – Happy,

I believe. All that is topped off, naturally, with a mild hint of pussy – *young pussy*, thankfully. In a phrase, I'm being stalked by vomit-inducing aromas that span two very distinct generations. This is why I'm against daddy-dating. The scents don't gel. Trust me; we cooks have a nose for these things.

I have ten burners operating at once, creating a rumbling medley of sounds: crackle, sizzle, steam. I am mæstro, in control of this snappy aromatic concert. My show is conducted with grace and ease as I prance my way from stovetop to cutting board, not missing a toss or forgetting to taste. This gives me a real high. Between this and the joint I smoked on the way over, I am *one* content broad.

A waiter, the adorable, perfectly pressed, wrinkle-free, fat-free, perpetually twenty-something Bradley approaches.

"Oh, my god, girl! They've sent you straight from hell to fuck with my thighs." Taking a nibble of the seafood risotto, he adds, "Mmm, where's Wolfgang Schmuck?"

"He's in the back, beating his batter."

We giggle like the giddy worry-free school girls we had both dreamt of being as religiously wrought sexually distraught pre-adolescents.

"What's the special?"

"Fettuccini with wild roasted forest mushrooms, truffle oil, and prosciutto cream sauce."

Temptation will not get the best of Bradley. After all, his abs *are* at stake. He turns to exit, shaking his groove thang.

"Hey, come back in five to taste the pasta!"

He hooks around and points his finger while strutting backwards through the saloon style doors.

"Sweetheart, we're going to have to do something about this love-hate relationship."

"It's my specialty."

As soon as the words were spoken, a blade of air corkscrewed its way into my stomach. Can still feel it today, if I really focus. I cough to expel the thought – the virus – clear my throat to trample over its tracks. That wasn't about the food. I mean, whose specialty is pasta? Anyone who can rip open a box of mac and cheese, that's who. Emotional impulse had interrupted a delightfully blank moment between two wannabe vapid beauties in this City of Plastic Angels with the daring double entendre, "It's my specialty."

The love-hate relationship; I'd gone pro. Yet "don't think" was the only thing I could think to do to maintain my loosely defined version of composure. It was the only stipulation in my boundary-absent world that I possessed total command of. And let me tell ya, I spent a lot of time "not thinking" about it – up until October of '04, anyway.

So I force a grin to con myself into believing life is kosher, then reclaim blasé by yelling, "And your thighs are perfect! I'd kill for those thighs."

While reaching deep into the refrigerator, I hear my boss, Antonio, saunter into the kitchen. He dips two exhausted fingers into the risotto and licks them clean.

"Your appetizer is giving me a hard-on."

It is at this point that he makes a beeline *for my ass*, then resolves to *grab my ass*, and then chooses quite unnecessarily to hold indefinitely onto, yep, *my ass*. In the moment that follows, my neurotransmitters tell my brain to sense his hands on *my ass*, reach for the container of pâté in front of *my face*, and swing it blindly in the direction of, yep, *his face*.

Spuck is the sound it makes upon impact.

And from here on out there's but one choice, and I do it like the wind.

Thank God for the creation of the two-second delay. It takes Antonio that long to realize what's happened. It takes me about half that time to dive around him, swing back into the locker room for my keys, and jump into my ride. I'd like to also thank God that younger generally means faster. And that's probably about all I'll be thanking Him for today.

Antonio is at the back entrance as I peel out; a stout, fleshy caricature of a man propped awkwardly inside the steel door frame. And judging by the sheer amount of pâté draping his physique, he must have slipped several times in the splatter during his quest to pummel me (that's what he gets for wearing lifts).

"You'll never cook in this town again, bitch!"

And that's the last I saw of him, the restaurant, and my eight-hundred-dollar Henckels knife set – a gift from my most favorite human. Oh, and that pretty much blew a hole through my rising career as a sous chef. A job once deemed – to steal a term from a spine-chilling religious upbringing – *my calling*, was tucked snugly away under the category of "history" in a mad flash.

And that was all I could take.

To sum it up cliché-wise, it was the last straw.

It was my father making an art out of ignoring me, and then dropping dead a week after I turned twenty-one without ever having called me up on the telephone.

It was my Catholic schoolteacher fondling me inappropriately after band practice, making me miss my bus. And then me electing to loathe an oncoming inevitable that I should have embraced: my body surging uncompromisingly from girl to woman.

It was my high school Love taking my virginity and never speaking to me again.

It was me waking up in a college dorm room with puke in my hair and my underwear crumpled alongside a broken, used condom, my "date" nowhere in sight.

It was my mother with slurred words saying, "Don't bug me" every time I tried to talk to her about any of this.

It was MP disapproving of attire, detesting friends, and refusing to comment on my cooking, but mentioning all too frequently my lack of verbal finesse as if it were a three-pound goiter jiggling on my neck.

And, it was MP not touching me unless it was to fuck me. Or being even crueler; debasing me with centuries worth of pillaged witticisms just for sport.

The timeline of my life can be documented most orderly by the straggling stampede of men into it, and their individual, however vulgar, departures back out. A lack of love to an over-load of lust is how it would be graphed vertically.

That's my logic, and I can't see at all, so I hit the wipers, be-fuddled as plain fools often are. But this storm is on the inside. The wipers won't do shit to sweep away this self-produced tor-rential rainfall. I keep shifting hands to clear my vision, wiping one eye then the other. And I'm speeding carelessly toward the very place that needs to be abandoned once and for all if my life and dreams are ever to meet somewhere in the middle. A cruel cognizance is beginning to settle in, one that will later prove to be my benevolent hero. But at the moment, I need cold arms over no arms. Anybody. And that includes MP.

I have officially hit rock bottom.

And I'm on my way home.

Meet Billy

A jail cell door slams open. Officer Murry stands erectly – all five-six, two hundred and fifty-five pounds of him – foot a'tapping, keys a'jingling. A horizontal Billy, with feet casually crossed, glances up from *The Alchemist* and rests the book on his flimsy, white "T" sheltered under a faded, plaid shirt. He then glides his right arm behind his head, tilting it in the direction of the Law, and but one thing crosses his mind: *Man, give this guy ten more years, a glass of milk, and a one-horse open sleigh, and…* well, picture it.

Billy dog-ears the interrupted page of his book; a book that looks like it's a decade old, been read a dozen times, and maybe even laundered. He clutches it endearingly and twists upward into his version of Rodin's *Thinker* (what else?). Then, to rebel against his own mysterious silhouette, he swings an eye toward Officer Murray, and there it evolves: the stone figure's visage breaks into a melt-your-heart, leave-you-breathless, forget-your-worries smile.

As he rises, his free hand rakes through dark, untamed, jaw-grazing hair that hasn't seen shampoo since Sunday, and it's Monday – the following Monday. He then extends that hand, fresh with grease and sweat and stench; a hand that would drop a teenage girl straight to her knees if she were lucky enough to seize it but for one life-changing instant. Of course, she would then vow to her eight bestest friends to never *ever* let her Billy-devirginized-hand near the sight of soap. And she would keep that promise too, for like two hours, or until it turned blue from holding it above her heart.

Billy humbly holds out *that* soiled hand, oblivious of its super powers. Murry darts his eyes ninety degrees west, then back a whole one hundred and eighty degrees to the east before taking it in his and shaking it heartily. He then steps to his right, giving Billy permission to vacate his three-month habitat.

Cross this jailbird with every musician any chick's ever been hot for, had a wet dream about, or a fantasy they turned into a wet dream, and that's Billy: an alive Kurt Cobain meets a young Keith Urban.

While this Rock Star Extraordinaire waltzes down the too familiar racing strip of cold dirty cement, Officer Murry scurries to catch up.

"Billy," Murry says, nearly tipping over onto the guy as he digs for something lost deep in the cavernous front pocket of his polyester pants. Finally, he pulls out a palm-sized book and thrusts it between Billy's arm and waist, title face up. "Thanks sonny, good stuff."

Billy doesn't flinch, despite the fact that his space has been both invaded and violated.

"You dig it, Murry? You can keep it."

"Oh no, I couldn't," Murry disputes, maintaining the reach around.

"Sure, go ahead."

"No."

"Keep it."

"*Really?*"

Billy can't help but think, my god, it's *A Pocket Guide to Shakespeare*, not a Mercedes. How can the thought of owning it make this man so jolly? Oh, right.

"Sure, Murry, keep it. Didn't you say your lady friend loves a well-read man?" Billy knowingly hints.

"Oh, boy, she sure does," Murry beams, pulling the book back to snuggle it like a Teddy bear. "And she's a keeper. I got the ring right here to prove it."

He pats the bulge in his shirt pocket.

"You got the roses?" Billy says pointedly.

"Won't make that mistake twice," Murry reassures with conviction.

Two officers have stopped mid-conversation to veer toward the unusual commotion.

"Guess what?" Changing tunes, Murry resorts to his best version of gruff. "Today's your birthday. You get to go home sweet home."

"Yeah, right. What home?"

"As long as it doesn't go by the name of Best Buy, or Circuit freaking City, we don't give a shit."

Billy doesn't have the heart to explain to Murry that his joke doesn't make a whole lotta sense.

Rather, he chuckles. "That was poetic, man. You should write that shit down."

"Ah, screw you and the horse you rode in on."

"Did you just make that up too? I'm tellin' ya, officer, you're in the wrong line of work."

"But on the right side of the fence. Now get the hell outta my face."

They've reached the jailhouse entrance. This is where "father and son," or as close a parallel as either one of them has ever known, part ways. Billy bows his head, steadies a smile, holds back sentiment.

Even though he considers himself to be an average guy in the infantile stages of manhood, where one's mindset teeters pretty evenly between brazen confidence and undeniable ignorance, he's too aware that he's been the highlight of Murry's year. And it occurs to Billy that it's funny, or odd rather, where one can find solace. He and Murry found it in each other; converted loneliness and self-pity into humor and an improbable love of sorts. He's also deduced with a more than moderate degree of certainty that the next "bad guy" inhabiting his ex-abode probably won't warm up to Murry the way he did. But Billy doesn't let that thought linger. His future isn't going to be about loneliness or pity. Billy and Murry let basic *humane* nature dictate their behavior and as a result, pain detached itself from punishment and true pleasure was found inside a not-so-pleasant predicament.

At first, Billy thought it hardly seemed fair to experience bouts of genuine contentment while confined, while grieving the loss of his freedom and then the loss of something, someone, even greater. But then he realized he had discovered *The Point of Life*: Find your personal joy in every experience. And thanks to the last three months, he'll search for that joy in all future endeavors and work more wisely to evade self-destruction during the process. He's grateful for wisdom gained.

As Billy pivots on the worn heel of his leather boots, extending the distance between him and this sweet paternal impostor, a thick warm hand wraps around his forearm and pulls him back.

Murry leans into Billy and announces, "Once more onto the beach!"

Billy fires back with an enthusiastic "thumbs up." Then he

lowers his head and softens his voice, "Take care, Murry," and walks up to the counter.

Marge, the would-be androgynous policewoman working the front desk, gathers Billy's belongings. What separates Marge from other not-so-gender-distinguishable women of uniform is the sole fact that any remaining space between her neck and waist has been filled in with boobs. It goes: Marge's neck, Marge's boobs, Marge's waist. And her poor belt; it looks burdened by weight, and blue for lack of oxygen.

Marge extends a pen and a wink. Billy signs on the dotted line and reaches for the only two possessions that have graced his side for the last three years: a ragged, army-green duffel bag and a shiny, black acoustic guitar bejeweled by dozens of fingerprints smeared over a series of delicate random scratches. Billy pats his guitar, winks back at Marge, and jaunts toward the exit.

"Be careful out there, Romeo." Marge blushes and smirks. "That goddamned smile of yours knows no boundaries."

"Fear not, sweet maiden!" he says and then springs through the double doors, disappearing into the daylight.

Sunlight sprinkles across his face. He closes his eyes and breathes; lilacs and traffic, his new favorite scents. He finally raises his sun-toasted lids a minute, or maybe an hour later to realize his ride has yet to arrive. Thoughts nosedive from elation to desolation.

"I'm a free man," announces Ego.

"No, you've been permanently deserted, Fool," echoes Logic, Defeat, and Id.

"At last, a fresh new start."

"This is merely the beginning of another inevitable bad ending."

"No more mistakes. Not this time."

"Oh, c'mon, buddy, step into the spiral. It's a downhill ride – *and your only ride*, apparently."

Whistling a freshly composed tune and jaunting westward help bat the voices in his brain. Memories lull in the back of his mind, though. No song has been able to shed the memories.

Billy has spent half his life at odds with family and then the law. Looking back, anger expressed verbally or even physically probably would have served him best. His brother made a career out of being angry, and he's smart, successful, and *always* gets the girl. Billy could have opted to toss a couple of chairs across a room or lob a few punches in the direction of a random bystander, innocent or otherwise. Thievery shouldn't have been his emotional outlet of choice; he sees that now. But he's not clever like MP; never been able to pull off Angry Guy. In fact, Billy can't wipe the smile off his face long enough to make "irked" look believable. He's as genuine as the peace that consumes him when he's composing a new tune. And he bears a pain that is frequently submitted to like honor; the pain of growing up without a father.

And then there was his mother; the greatest friend any kid could ever ask for, if all that kid ever needed *was* a friend. His big brother was both father and foe, executing these roles simultaneously and tenaciously. So Billy got into stealing. He was a pretty slick thief, too, with a value system that paralleled Robin Hood's. That's how he validated his illegal escapades. Fast hands, a broad smile, and a conspicuous intimate style made his ventures in crime easy entertainment and also profitable. But he always figured if he'd had a real dad, he wouldn't have had to use stealing as a rite of passage; he'd have been given more direction, which would have been his resurrection. But he didn't have a real dad, and mother never truly got mad, and brother already hated him for simply existing, so once he embarked upon a life of petty crime, nothing really changed. Except after a while he got caught, and then ultimately ended up doing jail time.

Nope. There isn't a tune in the world that he can whistle, sing, or strum to obliterate bits of his past, so he accepts it and keeps on walking, steady and with purpose. Then, from a hundred yards away, he spots his first free-world opponent. Cold. Lonely. *Nearly* obsolete. Dirty from former use, but more recently from lack of it. Billy's savior or betrayer; only moments will tell.

He draws some change from his pocket, approaches the pay phone.

Tucked in among the coins is a crumpled corner of notebook paper with a number scratched across it. Billy dials with exaggerated effort, heart rate increasing, neck twisting and turning as he releases a kink.

"Relax," he catches himself saying out loud.

"We're not here. You know what to do and when to do it," a man's voice coolly states over the machine.

Not the scenario Billy was hoping for, but speaking to machine over man does induce an unprompted sigh of relief, mostly from habit.

"Hey, man, I waited outside for…I don't know, like an hour. You said you were going to be there. You promised her." He pauses. "I'm starting to get the impression you're avoiding me." Laughs. "Please come pick my ass up. And listen, if it's too much trouble, you could just drive by real slow and throw a bag of money out the window. I'd like to see you, though. Okay, heading down Santa Monica Boulevard in the direction of your area code, look for the shaggy guy with a Fender slung over his shoulder."

The phone is planted mindfully back into its metal cradle, though his grip around it remains tight. Turning again into the heat, he stares right into the edge of the world. Lyrics surface:

> *I should be able to choose my last,*
> *Exactly as I've mapped my past.*

On the Brink of Bliss and Insanity

> *How dare the Sun show its face,*
> *On a morning predicted without a trace.*
> *It goes against Reason to defy this light,*
> *To draw blood and mix it with so much white.*
> *So my anger erupts at a sky so vain,*
> *And I close my eyes and pray for rain.*

But Billy no longer slept with eyes fixed on a bedroom door as silent tears crawled down tender cheeks. He's not the child who prayed for a father he never met. Or the kid who hoped to be forgotten by the only brother he ever knew, and wished that the sun would go away for just one day so he could chase it into his next life. He orders those lyrics to be buried alongside that boy who wrote them and pries his hand – thumb to pinky – from the pay phone. Then he studies the grime newly lodged on his soulful sweaty palm – the lives of countless others now mixed with that of his own – and wipes it effectively down the front of his pants. As he increases his gait toward the not-so-benevolent sun, ready to wrestle with it if tempted, a thousand new little germs with a million old sad stories cling fast below the right pocket of his tattered hip-slung jeans.

And this is where they'll remain for the better part of his first free week.

Four Puppies
and a Real Dog

Smirking with satisfaction, MP sits half hidden behind a loosely held newspaper – half buried under a lifetime of strategically groomed father-loathing, mother-fixating predilections.

He folds it into quarters, rises, takes a final drag from his smoke, and with an air of supremacy, smashes it into its glass reservoir. I'm through with you, he thinks; now go to your death, death by suffocation. And he retreats down the hallway.

Standing before the bathroom mirror in one of a dozen finely tailored suits, this one a dusty slate, he drapes a red tie over his left shoulder and holds another one configured with navy and mocha diamonds up to his neck. He raises a brow, stares intently, chews lightly on the inside of his cheeks. The cheek-chewing is a habit *not* derived from nerves. It just so happens that with his cheeks sucked in and cheekbones accentuated, his looks shoot from "handsome" straight into "male-model hot." It's his tie-breaker move when deciding upon an ensemble.

While tossing the patterned tie over a shoulder, he lowers his brow and utters, "The Dominator will be highlighted in red today. Ladies, beware."

That cheesy phrase is the *coup de grâce* of his morning routine, which meticulously opens with an uninterrupted twenty-minute interlude between him and the *Times* and closes with a raised brow and self-enforcement mantra that bequeaths him with powers reaching godlike status.

MP, an intellect with the perfect spattering of wit, ambition, and charisma, finds little room in his very refined, expressly defined world for imperfection. To his credit – and in laymen's terms – this control freak has worked his tail off to get to where he is today: a semester shy of his PhD.

But to his discredit, he's been a zealous, sanctimonious prick throughout the journey. "The world owes me big-time" is a phrase he lives, breathes, and seethes. Being Number One has become his disease. And he's contagious, all right – that, above all else, is his greatest talent; that all his *other* talents make him somewhat of an addiction. It's nearly impossible to separate the musical, poetic, brainy, comedic, hunk from… *The Dominator.*

When involved with a guy like MP, deciphering whether he's the last chance at redemption or a straight shot toward destruction is a job that would be tasking even for an Einstein.

Like he said, "Ladies, beware."

He flips his collar up to slip the tie around his neck and fixates, as he does daily, on the lie he lives by: that he doesn't miss the father who left him as a kid any more than he misses the mother who dropped dead (literally) a few weeks back.

He also reminds himself to quit reminding himself of all this trivia, for if the thought causes a slouch that causes him to diminish in stature by even a centimeter, he's minus one vital centimeter with which to dominate his own world…or more precisely, crush somebody else's.

He hears a knock at the door.

MP glides toward it, red tie loosely draped about his neck. For a UCLA professor of music in training, he couldn't look more Republican (it's so weird). He turns the knob, pulls the door open, leans a cheekbone on its frame, grins.

"Can I help you?"

There, in all her twenty-two-year-old blonde glory, Starbucks in hand, stands the new girl from 3D.

"I was hoping to catch a ride to class, teacher, teacher. I've been practicing my scales," she whispers. "Wanna hear?"

Nothing turns on MP more than a girl speaking to him in her "library" voice. It's sexy, feminine, refined. Well, nothing except a great pair of tits. And this chick's tits are so fantastic, she could be screaming "Jingle Bells" off-key at the top of her lungs and he'd still want to nail her. At least once.

"Sure, I'd love to drive you…to work that is. Come on in."

MP escorts The Blonde inside and closes the door securely behind them.

Within milliseconds, The Blonde has managed to seize that red tie and wrap MP's arms around the leg of his upright Steinway. She does this using a slipknot the president of the Girl Scouts would be proud of. MP is also impressed on a number of levels:

1. That he, The Dominator, would let anybody tie him up.
2. That this woman – who could skate through life just fine using nothing but her cleavage to navigate anything from a secretarial position at any conglomerate to the mogul

himself who launched the enterprise – would know *how* to tie a slip knot.

3.   And that he, The Dominator, is letting anyone muss up his favorite power tie on behalf of an erection.

But damn those tits are hypnotic, he thinks. They're like the sound of Rachmaninoff's "Somewhere in Time," the soft flowing strokes in a Goya, a World War II documentary. In a word, *captivating*.

As The Blonde crouches over MP, a very tired pearl button bursts from her pink cashmere sweater, setting those puppies virtually free.

"Are you sure your students aren't going to miss you, Mr. Piano Man?" the proud mother of two inquires coyly, disregarding the fact that her tits have just disrobed themselves.

"I'll just tell them I was teaching you how to make beautiful music," he says directly to her left nipple, which is obstructing the view of her entire head, which is fine by him.

The Blonde grinds her pelvis steadily into his.

"You're a clever guy."

Speaking at this point has become a mere formality. MP's fully aware that this verbal game of cat and mouse has taken a turn for the remedial *and* the obsolete, but he tosses out a cheesy response nonetheless, "One of my countless specialties, baby."

"Oh, yeah? Let me show you one of mine."

And she undoes his belt buckle with her tongue, putting to shame anyone whose claim to fame has ever been tying that cherry stem in a knot with it.

And then the phone starts ringing. And ringing.

"We're not here. You know what to do and when to do it," MP's voice coolly states over the machine.

Through sigh and sniffle, a voice crackles into the machine. "Hi, I just left my job. Thought you'd still be home…"

"Shit. Shit! Grab that!" MP's flailing like a fish out of water on fire, trying to get this playmate off him.

All the while The Blonde's riding the wave with pure delight. Might as well be yelling, "Wheeeee!"

One, two, three, and four. Finally, she's tossed off.

"Boom," she giggles, then stands, grabs the phone and is about to answer it, when MP motions frantically for *her* to give it to *him*.

He mouths the words "*untie me,*" as she lodges the phone between his ear and shoulder and laxly attends to the slip-knot.

"Girl! Hi! You just left your job? Where are you? Okay, button up, baby – I mean, pull over, sweetie. Pull that car on over and talk to me." MP is struggling for words, a pair of free hands, and pleading like a madman. "Aaah...listen, sweetie, can't talk now. I gotta run or I'm going to be tied up all night!"

Sounds good, he deducts, not entirely a lie.

So I'm driving and crying and looking for a song on the radio that doesn't completely suck and calling to see if MP's left for work yet, 'cause damn, I need an "anybody."

Delusional on a number of levels, I dive straight into begging.

"Can't you wait five minutes? Please? *Please?*"

But, in anticipation of disappointment echoing on the heels of this miniscule request, 93.1 saves me with an oldie but goodie from Pat Benatar.

"I just can't. You know I've taken time off," he rationalizes through what sounds like...panting?

I pull the over-the-phone silent treatment, one of the oldest manipulative moves in the original relationship handbook of manipulative moves.

"But, hey," he musters up a little empathy, "I got just the thing to pick you up. Want to choose your birthday presents early this year?" Not bothering to wait for my response, he adds, "Okay, well I did a lot of soul searching and decided that this is the year of self-improvement. So, my lucky girl gets to choose between…drum roll, please…"

Upon hearing my choices for the dreaded day, I instinctively scream, "But I wanted a Chihuahua!" which is true, then dramatically fling the phone, blast the radio, decide must burn original relationship handbook of manipulative moves and invest in newly revised version, and deduce that MP really did *hit me with his very best shot.*

At this point, MP is shaking the ringing out of his ear and contemptuously eyeballing the receiver.

"Well, that's gratitude for you."

He slams the phone down, dives for his tangled tie.

The Blonde interrupts her enthusiastic drum roll mid-mime to shout, "I love small dogs! Have you seen mine yet?"

She reaches into her purse and pulls out a wallet-size photo of her in a string bikini and baseball cap, holding her Pomeranian, who's also in a matching doggy baseball cap.

Pointing to the dog, she squeals, "And this is Buttons! This was our first photo shoot. You can tell Buttons is a little nervous."

The corner of the piano that's been lifted to free one red power-tie is carefully set back in place. A wet-browed MP looks up from his save, dumbfounded, panicked, and increasingly frustrated.

"Baby, later!"

The Blonde proceeds to talk to herself while tickling the dog in the photo, "But not me, I wasn't nervous at all. Why? Because I love you, Buttons. I do, I really really do."

The phone starts ringing…and ringing. MP's anxiety level climbs at record speed. The machine picks up.

"We're not here. You know what to do and when to do it."

A guy's voice hesitantly speaks into the machine.

"Hey, man, I waited outside for…I don't know, like an hour. You said you were going to be there. You promised her." He pauses. "I'm starting to get the impression you're avoiding me…" Laughs…

MP's hovering over the machine like a fat chick over a bag of Oreos trapped in a room full of kindergartners.

"…Okay, heading down Santa Monica Boulevard in the direction of your area code. Look for the shaggy guy with the Fender slung over his shoulder."

"Jesus," MP exhales, then deletes the message and grabs the Blonde. "What can I say? I'm as wanted as the *Mona Lisa* in 1912."

"Mona from 4B?" The Blonde inquires inquisitively. "What about her?"

"No, the *Mona Lisa*. She was missing for two years. They even brought in Picasso for questioning."

"I just saw Mona at Ralph's yesterday. She bought a tofu turkey roll, Rice Krispies…and gummy bears!"

MP shakes his head, knowing his only option is to let this one go.

"Come on."

"God, I miss gummy bears," she utters lackadaisically as MP rushes her out.

Six minutes under my estimated time of arrival – I'm fully parked outside our apartment. I reassess my makeup in the rearview mirror and scratch a piece of dried mascara from under my eye. It leaves a tiny jagged welt, and I note: Must check into getting bags removed. They puff up so easily. I mean, with all the crying, maybe the insurance would cover it? Right. What insurance?

I knock off the inner monologue as my newly omniscient, and surprisingly cruel rearview mirror catches MP and Triple

D hustling out of the apartment. I refer to The Blonde from 3D as Triple D for obvious reasons: *she's wearing my ass on her chest!* Also, we haven't formally met yet, so I don't know her real name. But that's neither here nor there.

What *is* here *and* there is me – *here* in my car alone, and them – *they're* escaping from me together. My head snaps around. I crunch down backward in the seat and spy MP running around to the passenger side of his *newly inherited* black Beamer, help Triple D inside, close her door, then barrel around to the driver's side, and jump in.

They take off.

My helpless gaze strays logically to the bumper sticker plastered on the car parked in front of his: *Life's a Beach and Then You Die.* How stupid. I turn recklessly back around in my seat; my left knee collides with the stick shift, then, during re-adjustment, bangs into the volume knob on the radio. My fist punches the knob as if it's to blame for everything from the invention of the fanny pack to greenlighting *Waterworld* to my hurting my kneecap. The knob pops off and rolls under the driver's seat. Then, systematically, my hand swoops down into the cool cavernous darkness to retrieve it but recoils repulsively. The lame effort results in the radio knob becoming the newest in a surging troupe of small orphaned objects vanished forever into that strangely limitless black space beneath a car seat.

Well, that all took a generous amount of effort, more than was available to expend, so I close my tear-drenched eyes.

A minute or an hour later, my lids finally peel open, blistered from the unbiased autumn sun teaming up with the car window in an attempt to burn a hole through my brain. I squint hard, but not from dramatic daylight. I'm plugged in for the first time to the thousands of thoughts dancing violently, heed-lessly through my mind, needles stabbing every corner of every maze of tissue. My head hangs heavy from the sheer multitude of tiny flying metal shards. They won't stop and my eyes ache too much to function in any additional emotional releasing capacity, so I randomly choke one of these bastard imps up, hoping the others will exit along with it.

"Wow," I say. "He's never opened my car door."

But the others don't leave. They grow stronger, start traveling in clusters, and desert stabbing for the more rampant pounding.

He's never loved you, Fool. No man has ever loved you. Can a person die from loneliness? What time is it?

I can't breathe. Must call Foster. Maybe I do need boobs. Boobs, the key to happiness. The key to getting your car door opened. Can a person die from incessant thinking? From talking? From crying? I can't breathe in here. Babies die in closed cars everyday; why can't I? Please, don't cry. Don't cry!

Turn the key and fly. Fly to Foster's. Go, Stupid!

Drive! How did I end up here? Why did he stop loving me? Is it my breasts, my hair, the clothes I wear? My face, my feet, the way I eat? Cut the rhyming, Seuss! It's everything. Nothing's changed; I'm one big nonstop rerun and he got bored. Love is opening someone's car door.

The man didn't get bored; he's never opened my car door.

He never got interested enough to get bored. Never loved me long enough to have stopped. I loathe cerebral Mondays; they're ruining my life. And I hate MP. But why won't he open my car door? And what, by the way, comes after rock bottom? Oh, shut the fuck up!

My hands were pressed so hard into my ears they just might meet in prayer mode in the middle. This is why the strictly enforced *Don't Think* forum was originally adopted: I feared thinking. And after that, more thinking, and then constrained breathing and ultimately, pain.

It was just a car door. That's all I actually saw. It could have meant nothing. But it didn't. Instead, it sums it all up. One small gesture crumbled what was left of the wall protecting my self-created universe. And what is my wall? A paper maché shelter so soft and wet and new that it was dented by a single drop of dew. And then it folded down around me as if it were empty inside, as if it had nothing to hide. And me? I'm cowering, alone and naked, sunburned but cold.

I didn't ask for this kind of fame. Didn't ask for things to change, just someone to talk to. And now I've been hurled into a place I didn't want to see. And strangled silent inside a person I never thought I'd be.

I tremble, stare at the key in the ignition, crack the window, tilt my head back, take a deep inhalation. The air smells of rain. Then I remember something; Foster's birthday present from last year. Even when she's not around, she saves me. I snap open the glove box, grab the unopened, tepid glass bottle and hold it to my cheek like a child turning his face into his mother's hand for comfort. Not *me* as a child, or *my mother* as the comforter, but some child and some mother, like in the movies. I twist off the cheap gold cap and choke down a swig of its hot pale pleasure. It burns more than usual. Funny, the first swig never burns less than usual. The main thing is it works. I'm consoled temporarily. Thank you, tequila. Fuck you, world.

Another sloppy swig coats both my shirt and my soul, resigning me befittingly to this new place of residence. I'm just below the surface of rock bottom – which feels like suffocating, minus the involuntary struggle for air.

Memories

"*R*un!*" She screamed – I'm not sure to whom; we were already runnin'.

Chasing us was the oldest person I've ever seen upright: Mr. Harold Albert Ness, II. He was the manager of Kmart since the day Kmart was invented and fell somewhere between seventy-five and a hundred-and-ten. He wore a suit and tie that looked as if they'd been purchased for his 1921 high school graduation…*and he was gaining on us.*

Now, Fos and I had been borrowing shit from Kmart for a while. And to be honest, we assumed old man Ness knew about it, like there was this unspoken agreement between the three of us: We don't twist his name into anything crueler than his parents *and his parents' parents* had already done at birth, and we got free shit in return. But for some reason, Harry A. Ness must have had a bug up his butt that day, boy.

Fos kindly kept pace with me.

"Hang a right behind Happy Meadows Yogurt," she motioned.

School was only a block and a half beyond the yogurt joint. If we could make it to school, we'd get lost amid the shuffle and Old Man Ness would forget about this silly incident by tomorrow. I hung that right, while silently cursing the beastly desert. Oven-like powdered air slapped the roof of my mouth with increased fury upon every inhalation. A football field away from the main entrance, I turned my head sideways... and no Fos.

I stopped, wrapped one hand around a knee, and gulped some air that tasted stale, like unsealed crackers, but felt less cruel on my throat now that I was idle. Slowly, my other hand opened to loosen the death grip around a pair of red polka-dotted bikini underwear. I studied them. There they were; the cause of the drama. Looked around, still no Fos. So I stashed the undies in a bush next to the American flag on the school lawn. Yes, I stored stolen goods in close proximity to our country's flag; wasn't exactly weaned by a group of politically correct folk. And then I reversed my path.

Behind Happy Meadows Yogurt Factory there proved to be quite a spectacle. Fos was *grappling* with Harry A. Ness. This was new. He had her in a vice grip and was about to introduce her to his left hook, when she bit his thigh. Then he pulled her hair. Then she punched him in the...uh-oh.

"Ouch!" An ear piercing throaty wail gyrated from the old guy's mouth.

I think she was aiming for his stomach, at least that's how I've chosen to remember the incident.

"That's it, you little cunt. Take this!"

Then he got really mad.

That's about the time I jumped in, 'cause Ness just said the "C" word and this scuffle was taking a turn for the "disturbed." But Fos didn't care. She batted me away with a hand clean across the face.

"Get off me! Get the hell outta here!"

I went back to school as ordered. The cops showed up. Fos got charged with petty theft: a bottle of Nyquil, some diet pills, and her very own pair of blue star-studded panties. She got suspended – some bullshit about it happening during school hours. She also lost car privileges for two weeks, which ended up being more like two days – a minor bonus for living in a single-parent household.

Had that been me, "grounded for a year and a half" would have been branded on the bedroom door with the majority of that time spent on bended knees reciting Hail Mary's and polishing knickknacks, thousands and thousands of stupid ballerinas (Mother used to dance). And I would have been reminded of my soul-snatching sin for all of eternity. And at twelve, eternity seemed like a pretty long time. Thank you, Fos.

In regard to the day she became a "criminal" – a title she wore proudly for the remainder of high school; a title that replaced the "doesn't play well with others" stamp she boasted from elementary – she claimed that during the "escape" she tripped.

Let me tell you something about Cousin Cori Leigh Foster: the girl don't trip. She doesn't stutter, drool, stumble, or fall. She's never been a klutz, and she certainly does not trip. Not ever.

Don't know when the car started and sped off, or who dialed the phone, or at what point I mastered the art of guttural wailing, but all tasks are being juggled with artful proficiency. And I'm waiting for dear cousin Fos; "my life line" to pick up "her work line."

The machine comes on.

"Samsu Institute of Chinese and Alternative Medicine. You

have reached Cori Foster, please leave a message. If this is an emergency call 310–555–4382. Thank you."

Can barely deal with the sound of her professional voice – there's but a whisper of the ballsy, ball-breakin' bitch I know and love inside that feminine infomercial-like recording. But the mere fact that she answered neither her office nor her cell leads me to but one conclusion: Fos is busy with a patient.

I swerve my way into a meter. Scram from my ride. Then scram back to my ride and do it: dig my hand inside that ominous blackness under the seat, pull out a quarter, feed the meter, and dodge into Samsu Institute like some dude breaking through the double doors of a church cause he's late for his own wedding.

I breeze past a busy waiting room.

The woman behind the counter beckons, *"Escuse you? Mees?"*

She knows me. I don't know why she bothers.

I barrel down the hallway, popping open door after door, like in a stupid dream you talk about the next day to anyone who will "fake" listen. Lucky door #3 houses my Fos. I scoot in. She's hard at it.

"There are nine points along the meridian. The xiyan is right here where the electrical stimulation – "

Through random hiccups I announce, "Do I have 'Ba… bastards Prefer-ferred' tattooed to my forehead? Because th… that's all I seem to – "

"Let me see…" Fos turns, examines my forehead, then pops a needle between my eyes. "Nope. I'm sort of with someone. Go wait for me in my –"

"She's fine." The dude with the meridians and whatnots, utters in a sweet, unexpected Southern drawl.

Fos and I chime in unison, "No. She's not."

"I could use the company. Sit down, sweetheart. Take a load off."

I immediately take that "load" off. I mean, I was invited, right?

"Thanks. I lost my job, then MP, he took off in his car with Triple D, you know the Blonde from 3D with a huge…you knows. And…*he opened her car door!*"

Fos is all logic.

"Doesn't she have a class with him?"

"Yes, but he – "

"He opened her car door." Sweet, Southern Drawl says definitively. Then exhales and shrugs. "He's banging her."

"Thank you!"

I wanna hug the guy.

"I'll leave you two to discuss the erotic nature of the car door."

Fos is not a read-into-shit kinda girl. She exits.

Then Sweet, Southern Drawl adds, "Might as well have felt her up right there in front of you."

"Finally, an honest man." I'm so relieved someone's on *my* page, I could cry again. "I was beginning to think you guys were extinct."

"In the flesh, young lady."

"Annie."

"Annie, nice to meet you. I'm Elvis. *Thee* Elvis. You may have heard of me."

Yeah. So much for that theory. Meanwhile, I'm guessing Fos is kickin' it back in her office smokin' a fatty. Not too jealous. The needle lodged between my eyes has really mellowed my shit. It's like I'm swinging in a hammock at my gazillion dollar beach house, warm breeze on my face, and blah, blah, blah…*it's nice.*

"That sister of yours sure is fine." I hear off in the distance, hoping it's a cabana boy with a Long Island Iced Tea complete with umbrella. "I'd like to open her car door, if you know what I mean. Maybe you could put in a word."

Why, oh why, did he beam me back down?

"We're cousins, not sisters. And she doesn't date m – ." I take a long look at what could be the only living human more delusional than me. "Sure, *Elvis*, I'll put in a word."

"Thank you. And, Annie, no man is worth crocodile tears and sleepless nights. Unless they're a direct result of some good old fashioned lovin'."

Not bad for someone who thinks he's a dead guy. On that note, I smile softly and head out and down to Foster's office.

I'm met at the door by swirls of earthy, aromatic smoke.

"Do you know – " I start.

"He's obsessed with me?" She finishes.

"Does he know – " I add.

"I don't do dick?" She chimes.

"Do you know – "

"He thinks he's Elvis?"

Then she adds, "First time we met he was immediately smitten. Who can blame him? And the poor guy tried everything up to the last-man-on-earth hypothetical. I told him there's only one man on earth I'd ever do, last dude or not. He deducted it was Elvis, and has been acting this way ever since."

"Wonder how he came to that conclusion."

Foster's office, to under-exaggerate, is a shrine to Elvis. She's got the mugs, the velvet wall hangings, a stack of every CD ever released, a calendar, an Elvis paperweight, and the list goes on. To top it all off, she's wearing an Elvis T-shirt. It's one of those cool collages where like a thousand pictures of him gel into one really big picture of his face. She tosses me her Elvis key chain.

"I've got a few more hours. Meet you at my place."

I spin on a heel to exit.

"Annabelle."

She licks her fingers, puts out the joint, then approaches and yanks the needle from between my eyes.

I rub the spot.

"I love you, too."

And I'm gone.

Why Elvis? Well, other than the obvious, Foster's dad was constantly mistaken for him. He was the young, svelte King when she was a little girl. Then he became the tortured, overweight, pitied version of the icon right before he died. Fos was eleven at the time. Oh, and he died of a prescription drug overdose mid-August 1978. Her father left with a bundle of unspoken "I love you's" and a serious case of mistaken identity that should have vanished, but sadly grew exponentially the year that followed Elvis' death and preceded his very own.

I think the fixation is mostly like the rest of us believing in Buddha, God, or a soul mate. He's her last source of hope.

As I'm rounding corners aimlessly, my focus stays on thoughts of her. It makes the twenty-minute jaunt more interesting than if I were to concentrate on my own damned issues. I imagine Fos has flicked open her Zippo and drawn a fancy flame using that one-handed technique guys-you-should-definitely-sleep-with-but-never-date can do, and is finishing her joint. And I'm happy for her. Before marijuana, she was one mean bitch. And I was the annoying little bug she couldn't effectively flick from her ear. Thanks to her elixir, I'm still *me*, but considered quite amusing, mostly.

Now, who thinks marijuana should be illegal? Put up your dukes.

At a stoplight, the work pants become officially relieved of duty as I squirm my way out and toss them blindly into the back seat. Driving has become an activity that coincides more frequently than not with changing my clothes. So natch, there's an endless supply of wardrobe options scattered throughout my car's interior.

Feels like a red tag vintage Levis night, which I'll reach behind and snatch at the next stoplight. I once slipped into an evening gown (did I just say *evening gown* – I'm a freak) while driving up the 405 after a beach venture. What's-His-Name had some piano shindig. But between the meltdown and the acupuncture, changing has become quite taxing on this very unfair Monday. Another shot of tequila should accommodate my need-to-chill needs. And I think I'll retract my earlier comment and thank God one more time today. Thank you, God, for making driving a right-brained activity.

So I get to Fos' exhausted, overwhelmed. Stare into a dark kitchen that looks more like a hallway with appliances lined up along its walls. My destination: a stool at the bar table at the end of this corridor. Seems like a lotta work. I sway back, rescued from a fall by the inside of the door, then slide downward 'til my butt meets the shiny tiled floor. My wilted body molds into the corner, a cool cylindrical hinge from the door digs into my shoulder. The metal brings on a chill of relief. At least the flesh that's taking its impression isn't numb like the rest. Would like to reflect, but that never works when you tell yourself to.

Hmm? I remember his BMW peeling away from the scene of the crime, then *BIG LONG UNAPPEALING BLUR*, and now here I sit, lookin' at my feet. Could really use a pedicure, I think while staring immobile like an old doll propped on the dresser of a woman over sixty.

Her kitchen floor is a quaint distraction though; shiny yellow-and-black tile; a kickback to the seventies when drugs were in, bras were out, and men and women actually dug each other 'cause drugs were in. A trippy notion of slipping beneath the surface of this checkerboard materializes from my overstocked files of trippy notions. Makes me wish I was a mermaid, in control of my destiny, in pursuit of my prince. Imagine being a fish – something without a brain, a plant without pain, or a man, or the rain – then I'd be powerful and always the same. Someday crying will place second to not crying in my chronicle of daily occurrences. But my current dilemma: How many more smiles can I convincingly fake? My chin falls to my chest, creating a shelter of curls about my face. Some days you gotta hide…even when no one's looking.

Maybe sleep will erase the day; the last twenty-seven months. Aren't I fun? So melodramatic, as if someone just lobbed off a fucking limb. I suck. My wife-beater is scarred with tiny gray puddles, mapping the events of the day. If only I'd done something spectacular, I could go away like Janis Joplin. There's still six days left to exit like one of those tragically, infamous rock stars, but nothing spectacular for the world to inherit upon my tragic departure. I'm as boring as egg whites.

And the thing is, leaving doesn't seem to be an option. Not leaving the planet; that I consider once a day and twice on holidays – see boring. The thought of leaving *him* hasn't been entertained by any of my brain cells, sober or otherwise. What's to leave? I'm not flawless; he's neither the cause nor the creator. The scowls, the mockery, and the disgust can all be twisted into justified rational. His attempts to salvage what's left of the best of me don't go unappreciated just because they haven't been properly executed. I'm not MP and will never be. People don't look to me for the right answer; they don't hang on my every elitist word. I haven't a talent they could close their eyes to and feel trickle through their bodies like nourishment, like a dream they hope to never wake from. I search day and night for my own comparable magic trick – a way to hold the crowd – I come up empty. And all the reaching, the clinging, the reading, the scheming, the goddamned grooming – even that – is exhausting me into a translucent version of the person I used to be.

It'd be nice to identify the reason I still long for his next callous touch. But I'm too tired to expend more energy calculating that incentive. It's easy to fight for my right to internal pain, compliments of MP. It's better than starting all over with some other asshole. Instead of packing, I'll borrow a smile from our past and crawl home after dark. He may have taken *the last little piece of my heart now, baby,* but my face is still intact. There it is; my reflection, small but complete and untainted, floating about the surface of my drink. Why does everything seem so clear at the bottom of glass? Gulp. It's gone.

Pardon me while I pass out.

Lisa Marie's oral obsession rouses me back into reality.

"You know what you are? You know what you are? You're a furry little munchkin with a very serious foot fetish, that's what you are."

My best doggy voice is put to full use as the miniature ears of Foster's Chihuahua, Lisa Marie, receive the most enjoyable scratching of their hyper-alert lives.

Yes, I know what you're thinking. But Fos and I have an unspoken agreement: I don't give her shit about her obsession with Elvis, exclusive of the gyrating salt-and-peppershakers. In return, she doesn't give me shit about the obsessions I have with my boobs, my hair, my abs, my thighs, my bags, my ass, my hands, my pill-popping, my drinking, my boyfriend, my *ex*-job, my mother, my personality, and my goddamned life.

I must admit, though, to busting a gut every time Fos calls that little rat's name.

"Lisa Marie! LISA MARIE PRESLEY, YOU GIT YOUR BUTT OVER HERE!"

It sounds like she's about to beat some sorority chick simply for wearing pink.

But no one's screaming his name right now, therefore I'm not unraveling into a happy hysteria (and, yes, Lisa Marie has balls). Rather, Lisa Marie's foot fetish reminds me of MP's auto-foot fetish. I once sucked his toes until he orgasmed. It's the little things, you know, the memories that really get me. Time to cry again; this could be a record. Another drink should serve as distraction from the enemy – *myself.* Another drink it is!

P.S.

I'm not a drunk. It's just been a really bad day-week-year-life.

Oh, and double P.S.

If Foster's office is like a shrine to Elvis, her apartment is a museum.

Happy Hour(s)

My gaze remained glued to the reflections on the tabletop. "A boob job, or a year of therapy." There it is: the statement filtered into the consciousnesses of my two most devoted female peers. Looking Fos and Teri in the eyes would have been a redundant mental exercise. I know the expressions on their faces; have had them memorized since MP and I started dating.

"A what in the who?" Teri, aka Terbear, animatedly questions.

She always says something that makes no sense whatsoever when a lull in conversation requires a quick, quirky filler. She's irresistibly adorable, teaches fifth grade, dresses as if she's married to the president, and looks like a Dallas Cowboy cheerleader underneath all those sweater sets.

Fos sits quietly with fists clenched, as if she might be developing a temperature or possibly sprouting sideburns.

Shane, Terbear's coworker, husband and, above all, soul mate, strolls into the kitchen carrying a birthday cake. Did I just use the maxim *soul mate*? Yes, yes, I did. Well, that's the hope they've chosen to cling to. Fos and I figure as long as it works, we've got no problem letting them dwell in their love-sticky delusions.

The glimmering preservative-packed white entity, complete with twenty-nine candles, blinds me with light as it sways my way. In case you're wondering, I didn't lie about my age; the extra candle's for luck. They should've stuck about thirty more on there, now that I think about it.

"It's not my birthday yet."

"We're cheering you up. Now shut up and blow."

Shane grins and lifts a brow. We peer back at him.

"I've always wanted to say that," he shrugs apologetically.

And that's the thing about Shane; he'd only be crude in jest, and even then he has to apologize. Oh, the other thing: He's the last straight man *all* women adore.

"I gather MP doesn't have you torn between a Poodle and a Yorkie this year?" He can also read a crowd *of women* and isn't afraid to ask, "What's the matter?"

"A boob job, or a year of therapy," Foster announces.

But what I swear I heard her say was, "A boob job *die-you-prick* or a year of therapy *die-MP-you-fucking-prick-die-die-die!*"

No one else seemed to have noticed, though. Sometimes, when Fos talks, it's like I'm listening to *The White Album* backwards.

"Well…that's practical." Shane's got an unusual case of loss-for-words. He switches gears and tosses two gifts in my lap. "Presents? Presents! Drinks? Drinks!"

Then he reroutes to Foster's liquor cabinet, a cabinet that

appears closer in size to a walk-in pantry. Some people even call it that. Shane wrangles up a jug o' tequila and four shot glasses that bear more a resemblance to coffee mugs (Elvis branded coffee mugs). Basically, Foster's liquor cabinet is straight out of Alice's Wonderland.

Terbear claps her hands together as if she's about to play patty-cake. She boasts the title of "Designated Mood Elevator" and executes it proudly.

"Make a wish, Annie!"

I close my eyes and pilfer one from a thousand Cinderellas before me, then blow out the candles with all my might and wait to see if the sensation of my wish coming true rushes over me in a wave. As a disappointing second resort (the sensation did no rushing), I open presents. From Fos, a sterling silver antique cigarette holder containing twelve perfectly rolled joints. And thanks to The Happy Drunk Couple, the perfect-for-any-occasion-little-black-dress by *Betsy Johnson* is now and forever in my possession. This is more like it.

Shots have been poured. We clink glasses, say "Salud!" and the first in a hefty series of gulps barrel down our throats as our faces twist and cringe in unison. You see, we're too cool for salt and lemon to increase the pleasure of this tonic, tonight anyway.

Terbear downs her shot with an unusual flare of bold defiance.

"Sorry. No mommy-to-be news."

She shakes her head, smiles sweetly, holds back tears. Shane and Terbear have been trying to get pregnant since, like, forever.

Shane rises, looks for something – anything – in the fridge because he also knows when *not* to ask a crowd of women, "What's the matter?"

The Queen of Callous joins him. She's just plain uncomfortable.

"Shane, buddy, you might want to get the little defense attorney checked out. You know they say – "

"Hey, I've been wearing loose underwear and bathing in tepid water for months," he quips, "so leave the sperm donor out of this." Shane leans back from behind the door of the fridge. "But speaking of *gigantic pricks*, how much longer do I have to be civil to yours, Annie?"

"Baby, be nice. He's in mourning," Terbear scolds amusingly.

"Only for all of eternity, buddy," Foster snaps into his ear.

They really hate MP, no buts about it. And they've been referring to him as the "Master Prick" for so long, I'd wager the three of them together *sober* couldn't come up with his real name.

I rely on some bullshit medical data to answer – or *not* answer – Shane's rhetorical question.

"MP says the normal grieving period should be about six months but that he might take a little longer – "

"On account of him wanting to fuck her." Foster completes the statement ever-so-cheerfully. But to her credit, she is the "doctor" in the family. If anyone knows anything about medical data, it's her, no matter how disturbing the nature of the fact.

Without missing a beat, The Happy Drunk Couple chimes in, "Oh, yeah. Right."

"Hard to believe a guy like that even had a mother," Shane reflects.

"Yeah. Yep," they all respond in solemn agreement and fall momentarily silent.

MP and I had a *huge* fight this past Fourth of July – something regarding my lack of virginity.

"How long has it been missing?" he inquired.

Naturally, I lied.

"How many people have been in pursuit of it since?"

And lied.

And back and forth we went. Until, inevitably, it surfaced:

1.   Apparently, it would be preferable if I were a virgin, like
     somebody's mommy was when she got married – at eigh-
     teen. I was twenty-seven; that's so not fair. And…
2.   Every boy wants to have sex with his mother: The world
     according to MP.

The fight had taken a turn for the Freudian. People don't think.
He didn't even consider the impact his declaration would have
on me. Verbal abuse: the new not-so-silent killer of relationships and number one obliterator of the psyche. It's becoming
cruelly apparent why my parents never bothered with it (the
whole speaking thing). And then to massacre what was left of
anybody's privacy, I took the argument that ruffled me to the
point of hives straight to Foster and paraphrased the crap out
of it…over *and* over.

In the end, I'm the whore who lives with the dude who
wants to "do" his mother.

The lesson here is threefold:

1.   Control an argument.
2.   Don't allow people to scar you with words.
3.   Don't always run to your buddies with dirt on your boy-
     friend. 'Cause while you work on making it better, they
     focus on hating him forever.

"So what's it going to be this year, Annie?" the Chivalrous Ice-
breaker beckons. "Adding *to your chest*? Or getting everything
off of it?"

We laugh like a sitcom track, relieved that Shane was bold
enough to rid our brains of incestual images of MP and his

45

mother. Exhausted, drunk, and terrified of what might happen when the laughter dies, my head drops onto the table, dowsing it with curls.

Okay, I'll give you one opportunity to feel sorry for "the boyfriend." A few weeks back, his mother dropped dead. Literally. Brain Aneurysm. The funeral was the strangest. I didn't recognize a soul there, including the one of the hand I was holding. It was the warmest day of the summer. Everyone dressed way too casually, with the exception of MP and me. And no one made eye contact.

She lived in L.A., a straight shot down Sunset, east of us about eight miles. MP saw her all the time. Sometimes he'd be unattainable for hours. "We were playing," he'd say, him on piano, his mom taking over vocals and guitar. Rarely did I join them. He said she had no real interest in knowing me or any women he *merely* dated. That's what he said.

MP loved her madly. No one could live up to the image he'd created of his mother, certainly not me; I'm guessing not even she. But he didn't shed a single tear at the funeral. Have never seen him cry.

And I wore a red dress. He picked it out, brought it home like a present. But it wasn't a gift, it was an unspoken order to be followed instinctively. With a hat to boot. To this day, I don't know why.

Three hours, and a half-gallon of Señor Cuervo later, we're deep into Trivial Pursuit. Question was to Terbear.

"Um, I don't know...Vegas?"

Foster stares at her like she has seventeen heads – like she pretty much looks at everybody.

"Yeah, that's a state. Shane, roll to you."

Shane grabs the die. I stop him.

"Dude, your wife, soul mate, *the history major* just thought

Vegas was a state. What do you say we wrap this up? And, oh, as a side note; quit staring at my tits."

"Hey, if you want me to be involved in this decision, I gotta know what I'm dealing with."

Shane's eyes continue to bounce from my tits to my eye line (which is favored to just holding on my tits). Terbear slaps him.

"There will be no viewing of the tits. Your tits are fine."

She smiles, wrinkles her nose encouragingly.

Then Fos reassures, "Your tits *are* fine. And I've seen them plenty; could pick those tits out of a line up."

Then she points at them, dangling both index fingers an inch away from contact.

And I need for it to stop now 'cause, well, everybody's staring at them, and Terbear just copped a feel, cupping one of hers, then mine – you know, for the purpose of compare and contrast.

Looking back on that drunken delirious evening, I could've chosen any number of more auditory-friendly words to describe the female bosom. But no, I had to be a truck driver and say *tits*. Well, okay, not any word would have been appropriate back then. There were a number of synonyms that simply didn't apply in my case. For instance: I didn't have *jugs, melons,* or *hooters.* They didn't hang like *glands* or *udders.* They've never rubbed up against each other, so they weren't *knockers.* And they certainly didn't move under my clothes – even under the stress of a jumping jack – so they couldn't have been dubbed *sweater-puppies. Breasts* would have worked; *boobies* would've been fine; even *titties* sounds cute. My grandma used to toss around the word *titty* on a regular basis:

"I just love that Regis Philburn and tough titty if you're hungry, you'll wait for supper like the rest of us."

But I had trapped myself by saying *tits* at a time when I

hadn't considered that formulating a thought and having it fly straight out my mouth could be two separate activities, the latter being optional.

"They're boring, my tits. The nipples are really boring."

Yep, my nipples have just been lobbed into the debate.

"Boring?"

Shane's attention is dually piqued.

"I'm serious. The only time they come out to play is if I'm freezing, or hear Celine Dion sing."

"Wow that is boring. *My* nipples can cook a mean soufflé, recite the alphabet backwards and play 'It's A Grand Old Flag' on the recorder," Foster attests while groping herself.

"Too much information!"

Terbear has assumed the hear-no-evil position.

"It's those damned high notes; they send chills right through ya."

"Oh, yeah, yeah!"

Terbear couldn't be more excited about getting the nipple reference. Meanwhile Shane proceeds to serenade me.

"You were the strength when I was weak. You were the voice when I couldn't speak. You were – "

We ignore him.

Terbear quips, "I say you don't accept either of those fuck-up birthday gifts."

"Why the hell not? She needs both."

If you ever need someone to shit all over your parade, Foster's your man.

"Okay, my feline friends, let's finish this."

Shane pulls a quarter from his pocket.

"In the name of cleavage…"

He flicks it up. And there it goes, spinning upward. I wonder what's in store for my future. This could change everything.

One simple word is necessary to seal the deal, yet my lips refuse to give way to its escape.

And this is what didn't cross my mind: that it was a quarter,
and should only be used to purchase things like bubble gum
or to decide who gets to ride shotgun on the way to purchasing the bubble gum. It's not meant to shoulder the burden of
life-changing decisions. Yet I had somehow bestowed upon it
that power.

"Heads!" I clamor, only God knows why. Generally, I'm all
about the underdog. And, I know, it's 50/50. But c'mon, everybody knows 50/50 or not, *tails* is the underdog.

It lands.

It's tails.

All wide-eyed and stupid like, I secretly curse the unsym-
pathetic piece of metal for deciding I would take the hard way
out, the long way out, the talk-until-I'm-blue-in-the-face way
out. And did Fate just announce that it's okay for my *boobs* to
remain just the way they are? What's up with that?

My friends, comrades through thick and thin, utter one
small word in unison.

"Shit," they say, and lack for further comment.

Promises

"Are you sure you don't need this?" Dr. Lillian Schulman holds out a half dozen twenties as if she's offering him a tissue after a sneeze. "I worry about you, Billy."

Billy's lost in thought as he regards the address scratched across the note in his hand. A series of blinks preceded by a headshake revives his senses. Then, to further catch his mind up to his body, he blurts hyper-enthusiastically, "I'm all set!" and points at her with the note pressed tightly between his thumb and forefinger, offering it back as evidence.

"Thank you, Lily."

She smiles kindly. Billy relaxes in the familiarity of it. He's on a mission, but remains comfortably idle, glances lazily about the room. The décor still reeks of "shrink," with its soft lighting and humble yellow walls. The polyester foam-filled, mustard-and-wine striped couch looks the same; new, stiff, and light enough to pick up with one hand.

And while Mom and Lily spent hours chatting over lattés, Billy had picked that thing up, flipped it, too; it was his cave, his shield, even posed as a castle once.

He looks back at his mother's oldest and dearest friend. She's as conservative in dress as the majority of her protégés, but it's mostly her demeanor that makes her wholly human in a city that tends to generalize their shrinks as "not." She's soft-spoken and has always had an air of innocence about her. The twenty extra pounds she's sporting since Billy saw her last transcend the woman from "a real looker" to "matronly," yet oddly in her favor.

She has become the epitome of the type of person you'd want to tell a secret to, and that's the real reason Billy lingers. The comfort level in her office is intoxicating; he's steadied and warmed by the soothing energy enveloping him.

"You boys play nice now. Stay focused on your future – and if you need me, call."

"We will. I will – and I promise, I will."

Billy brands a smirk that's both boyish and grateful, then heads for the door. He stops in front of a bouquet of daisies, and then his eyes rise to study the Picasso above them, *The Three Dancers*. Has it gone without notice all these years? No, it must be new, he decides; a subtle but interesting choice on Lily's part. But *The Three Dancers* with its muted, earthy hues is no match for that batch of brilliant flowers. Not today, not with his agenda. Those daisies beg his attention, might as well be bending toward him. His tempted eyes drop back down.

"May I *borrow* these?"

His head turns and tilts like an innocent child asking for a freshly baked cookie, but his hand wraps around the stems of the daisies like that same child ready to claim his prize, with or without permission. A rush of emotion climbs from Lily's chest to her throat and into her eyes, revealing itself as delicate crystal beads skipping down her coral cheeks.

Billy senses the pain, too. They met when he was five and her look implies he's still that kid. She's privy to most of his legendary escapades, yet Billy feels safe in that knowledge. Plus, Lily misses his mother, too. So he holds his spirits as high as the sparkle in his eye and allows her a moment to file through her memories. Billy walks beside a past riddled with disappointment, not more than average if not for his youth, but he's never been the type to be seduced by pity to reveal angst. So the boy imprisoned by a grin has finally lingered long enough to make today's near memory lighter. He watches as resolve paints Lily's face.

"They're all yours." She sniffles, wipes her cheeks, and waves him sweetly away. "Tell her I said hi."

He nods.

"Thanks, Lily. You're the best."

Billy's wild on the inside. Final destination: farther away than he'd like it to be. He'd like it to be on the other side of the double doors as he exits the building, barreling through the one on the right. These flowers have him in a trance, as if they're staring back or made of glass. With neck bent downward and eyes rooted on his recent prize, he hangs a hasty left and *plows* right into someone attempting an equally speedy entrance. They bounce off each other and onto their butts. Daisies float up into the air in what seems like slow-mo, and then spill down like confetti.

In what can only be perceived as fast forward, Billy hoists the victim of the collision up while apologizing nonstop and scurrying to snatch flowers.

"I'm so sorry. Are you okay? I'm sorry."

Shaking off dizziness like a cartoon character, the

woman utters, "Well, this is the perfect beginning to a royally screwed-up birthday."

As soon as all the daisies have been rescued and properly rearranged, he turns to face her. They're nearly nose to nose, which places him unnaturally close to this female stranger. In fact, Billy and she are incontestably only as far apart as the flowers will allow. His breathing takes on heavier tones for various reasons – some more apparent than others. He studies his own breath rustling her autumn tresses, then wonders if those feathery strands of garnet and bronze are tickling her cheeks. He feels her breath, too. Then he considers writing lyrics about that untamed hair, kissing her as an apology, or incorporating coffee into his morning ritual. That's after, of course, he makes an effort to establish a morning ritual.

Damn, she's beguiling. Her face is angular but amiable, revealing the presence of both rage and innocence. Her eyes are slanted and sleek – but tired, pensive, and ironically wired. Her lower lip is perched in a pout that begs the question; *Hey, what about me?* She's pretty as if by accident, he surmises, as if all efforts to attempt otherwise have been utilized and proven futile. She's an antique that sparkles under years of dust and rust. A contradiction, like a smudge across a finished painting that ends up increasing its value. She's an anomaly, a homeless Persian cat that can disguise her matted mane behind a simple graceful strut, that's what she is.

She reminds him most of the place he's going, or rather a more naïve version of the person he'll be going to. But her careless hair, determined features, and smooth feminine frame do a mediocre job of concealing the storm that's brewing on the inside – and weirdly, the winds and haze are waving him in. Why she's still allowing this dissection, he knows not, cares less.

But logic ultimately overrides desire, so Billy takes half a step back. Then he lowers his eyes and meticulously separates a single white daisy from its flock of colorful friends. His eyes swim up her champagne-tinted flesh and scatter like those curls about her neck.

"Happy Birthday," he says, presenting the flower.

He does this as though he's been planning for her birthday all year, not because it was mentioned. Like she's a past lover he's been praying to run into.

"Happy Birthday."

He breathes those same words. They loom again in the space between them.

She seems to have either succumbed or gone numb from his peaceful examination.

"Happy Birthday," he whispers yet again, the phrase now symbolic of a gentle nudge to capture her token.

Okay, I stand there in wonderment; idle, stupid, stupefied. My eyes bounce down to check the time, then right back up to meet his. My wrist, of its own fruition, turns ninety degrees clockwise so my fingers can open and fold scrupulously, one by one, around the stem of that perfect white daisy.

"I gotta go."

In the fashion of skipping backwards, I awkwardly bail through the building's entrance, then make a mad dash for the elevator. Skim the directory for room ...803 *got it*. And now I've also got eight floors to try and figure out *what the hell that just was.*

Never been that close to someone without it ending in a kiss or a slap, and I reeked of a triple red-eye that was practically shotgunned on the way over. Gosh, I hope he likes coffee. How stupid. Why the hell did I think that? 'Cause I was breathing all over the guy – coffee. So what? So, naturally, I hope he's into it. Stop thinking that. *Stop thinking!*

This place is a maze of hallways and numbers and arrows, like a hotel casino minus the acid-trippy carpeting. Will definitely require directions to get back outta the joint. On the upside, after I get my brain pried open like a hammer to a pumpkin, I've got nothing pressing. Maybe I'll wander the building aimlessly for hours; spend my "big night" surrounded by a cold, stone structure. Sounds a lot like the plans I already have.

Wow – thoroughly distracted as I rake the building for room 803. That look in his eyes – the guy with the daisy – was so familiar I manage to pick a fight with my intuition.

"I know this guy," I deliberate.

Gimme a break. That's your vagina talking.

"You're a pig. Why would you say that?"

Because I know you.

My intuition thinks it's so smart.

"Why would he offer me a daisy?" I counterpoint.

He trampled all over you, dipshit. It's a gesture of kindness. People are supposed to be kind. They don't deserve bonus points for it.

"But the way he was looking at me? I recognize – "

Vagina talking – my intuition cuts me off. It can be a real bitch sometimes.

Check the watch again, 4:23. That's 4:13, minus two minutes. That's 4:11. I'm late for my very important date. Yeah, the watch is only twelve minutes fast, but I convince myself it's ten – naturally. Lost only six minutes in the grueling search for 803, so I give myself a little pat on the back and catch my breath. Sadly, this gives way to added contemplation.

I didn't bother to say thank you to that gallant stranger, didn't even say goodbye, didn't ask him his name, didn't think to tell him mine. Idiot. *And where the hell is the daisy?* I look down one corridor, then another, then the other and decide before trampling back down those endless tunnels it'd be best to self-impose a strip search. I pat myself all over, from hips to head. Phew, the little gem is nuzzled securely above my right ear.

Subconsciously, I'm pretty fucking bright. If I could sleep my way through life I'd be a goddamned genius; a Nobel Prize winner, a Lifetime Achievement Award recipient, or maybe the first woman president. But alas, I'm consistently buzzed, but nonetheless cognizant, and relentlessly illogical. The thought of it all is such a drag, but a drag that's readily smothered by a nourishing wave of "pretty" as I trace the outline of the daisy. It's a sure-fire reminder to wear a flower in my hair more often. A statement the whole world should adhere to at least once a year: International Flower Over Your Ear Day. Imagine the collective energy.

I later adopted the habit. Can't say for certain it's gone worldwide, but I can tell you it's as contagious as laughter or the chickenpox.

Knock…knock…kno-knock-knock…knock…knock.

"Come in," a voice calls from behind the door.

The euphoria is sucked from my body.

I lie on the couch, half patient, half centerfold style. Don't appreciate the calming ambience of the room, don't acknowledge her fantastic taste in art, even if it is only a print, fail to notice the vase below it half filled with water but absent of flowers – and choose not to recognize that the woman in front of me is giving off a pretty warm vibe.

What *is* recognizable is her poise, the Monroe-esque figure, the outdated "do" that actually works for her, and some rockin' gams. This woman has a pair of calves reminiscent of a dancer. She's a younger, most likely more sober, undoubtedly more educated version of my mother. If she speaks with a Minnesota accent, I'll kill myself.

"So, Annie, what can I do for you today?" Dr. Lillian Schulman says gently, articulately – no accent, small relief.

Before any worthy words are exchanged, I sense the serenity vacating her body. How? Well, it's being snagged and smothered by me and my misery – we sometimes work as a team – so Team Misery decides on an attack. We scratch the silent treatment and go for the tactic that's stored away for truly lethal times of trouble: we talk nonstop.

Propped up on an elbow that will surely go numb before the thirty-six remaining minutes of my first psychological analysis, I proceed to loosely paraphrase every pointed unpleasant occurrence in the history of my life.

"It all started to get truly fucked up for me in the fifth grade. My homeroom teacher, Father Philip, decided to molest me one day. *Who knew any of those dudes were straight?* Anyway, I went home and told my parents, like a good girl should. Well, that's not true. I told my mom. It went something like this:

"Um, Mom? Father Philip was touching me in a bad way today."

"Then she goes, 'No, he wasn't, sweetheart. He just likes you.'"

"And she stated it quite definitively, but not so much to me as to the red polyester-blend slacks she was ironing."

I remember leaning against the living room wall as if the whole house would fall to the ground if I budged even an inch. Meanwhile, dear Dad relaxed in that nappy, rust-colored La-Z-Boy hidden almost completely by Mother, the ironing board, and the evening paper – what's new? Yep, by fifth grade it was pretty evident that I'd never be able to pick that guy out of a lineup, not with a gun to my head, not by sight, not by sound. Maybe his profile, if while in the lineup he was holding the *Daily News* or the *Sunday Times,* maybe then I'd know him…by his profile.

"'No, Mom, he was doing bad things,' I said again."

"Then she interjects, 'No, honey, he wasn't'"

"And then I go, 'um, yes he was.'"

"'No, he wasn't. He Just Likes You, Sweetheart' Mom

snapped, emphasizing and over-enunciating every word while ironing those same red slacks for the second time."

That was the moment I became desperate, alone, and invisible. It's the moment I can't shake for even a day. Except the *invisible*, which goes away every time I open my mouth, whether to speak or drink.

"So now I'm pissed and I go, 'Yeah, well, I think he liked me a little too much today. He asked me to marry him while he had me pinned against one of those stupid wooden desks and was dry humping me with his Very Erect Penis.'"

"I capitalized right back for the first time in our eleven-year association – and attention was finally granted. Mom stopped ironing and looked up at me, mouth all agape and shit."

The scene is as clear as today is sunny – and, yes, it's pretty damn sunny out.

"I saw smoke rise, I swear, from what I hoped was burning pants – and I'm no dummy, so I blurted, 'um, if you'll excuse me, I'm going to go to my room now and hate myself for the next twenty years. Oh, and I'm also going to figure out how I can become a complete dick magnet. Bye!'"

The story was recollected with grace, ease, and a Minnesota accent that made me feel as if my mother was actually in the room. Oh, wait…it *is* like she's in the room. I peer at her replicate; she's evaluating me with either pity or disgust.

"You said that to your mother?" Dr. Schulman inquires.

"Sure."

"You used that kind of language at eleven?"

"Okay," I continue, irked. "I may not have phrased it quite that eloquently. This is a recap. I'm not on trial here, am I? You get the gist, right?" Pause. Breathe. Don't let her throw you, you're on a roll. "So that brings us to today. Hi, I'm Annie, president of Dick Magnets NOT SO Anonymous, at your service."

Okay, that was good, never been peppier.

"And by dick, I mean dick, as in asshole-prick-loser-motherfucker. But here's the thing; I told myself that by the time I reached twenty-eight, there'd be no more losers. That'd give me ten solid years of dating horror to weed through all the – *you knows* – and stumble upon my prince. Right? Right. That's how it's supposed to work. *Right?*"

"Love is different for everyone, Annie. It can't be predicted any more than it can be planned." Dr. Schulman shifts in her seat, recrosses those flawless gams. "I'm curious, was there any kind of resolution with your mother? After you ran to your room that day, did the subject ever come up again?"

Okay, Schulman's theory on love sucks almost as much as that bullshit follow-up question. But seriously, why is she talking? This is *my* thirty-six minutes – *mine.*

"Yeah," I manage to drag out, "It came up four years ago today, on a Margarita outing for my twenty-fourth. Mom didn't know *what* I was talking about. You people call that *selective memory*, right? Funny, though, 'cause my cousin Fos remembers the incident like it was yesterday, *like it happened to her* – but that's Mother, case closed."

I feel like I'm being side-tracked here. Must get a grip. Where was I? Oh, yeah…pervert, dick magnet, ten years of dating horror – MP!

"So then, like two years ago, I met this real tricky breed of asshole. This guy was gorgeous. Brilliant. Had two degrees; was working on his PhD. in piano concentration – *whatever that means*? Um, athletic, he was very athletic – "

"Have you two broken up?" Dr. Schulman rudely interrupts for like the gazillionth time.

"No. Why?"

"You keep referring to him in the past tense. Why do you think you're doing – "

"He *is* very athletic." I correct the mistake, evade the question, and continue my amazingly accurate and vivacious character description. "And, ouch, had – *has* a substantial amount of manhood. Even that was – *is* perfect. Perfect length, perfect girth, perfect balls. Who the hell has perfect balls? My boyfriend, that's who. Why am I mentioning all this, you ask?" I say to save her the trouble. "Because all this leads directly to my perfect orgasms…every time."

"Annie, a relationship can't be built around…orgasms alone. And nobody's perfect. The goal is to find someone who's perfect *for you*."

What? She must have a Daily Affirmations Calendar propped on that desk – that's all I can think.

"Nobody's perfect? Let me put it into perspective for you. We're talking about a guy who waxes his ass. Why? Because apparently ass hair isn't hygienic. His words, not mine. Me, I'm fine with ass hair on a man. I find it to be quite…oh, what's the word? Heterosexual."

I relax, wait for a response regarding MP's ass hair, or lack thereof. Nothing. Apparently, she wasn't prepared for a panel discussion on the subject of ass hair.

"So this is what I'm dealing with. Can't compete. I mean, my ass can – it's hair-free, as far as I know – but I don't play piano, have three degrees, or speak eighteen languages. I'm not an ex-college athlete; I'm an ex-college drop-out, know what I'm saying? But we're tied in orgasms. The playing field is pretty level in the orgasm arena. So I stick around, or he does, or whatever."

As a surprising relief overcomes me, something pertinent dawns on me.

"Oh, my god! Mom met him once like two years ago."

I jump up, kneeling on her putrid striped couch, let the blood flow back into my right arm, and proceed to re-enact another saga:

"She popped into my pad one afternoon to take us out for White Russians, her version of a midday latté. And things weren't going half bad until MP excused himself to the *loo* and I anxiously asked, 'So, Mom, what do you think?'"

"'Oh, honey,' she sighed, 'You've found yourself another asshole-prick-loser-motherfucker.'"

"So naturally I go, 'What are you talking about? He's been a perfect gentleman!'"

"Your mother used that verbiage?" Dr. Schulman disrupts the flow of yet another fascinating day-in-the-life.

"What does it matter?" I snap back.

"I'm trying to get a feel for the type of environment you were raised in."

"Well, you're killin' a good story."

Somehow, her inquisitive gaze yanks an honest answer outta me.

"Fine. She probably called him a fuddy-duddy. Tomato-tom*a*to. Trust me."

Dr. Schulman nods the nod of a person who's so over me. Hate that.

"So then my mom says, verbatim; 'Sweetie, I know these things.' Then, as if she actually *did* know something, adds, 'That man will use you and hurt you and drain you of your sanity. He will possess you, but he will never love you.'"

"She pointed her finger while she said it, too, and if not for the Minnesota accent, her fourth White Russian, and the fact that she never seemed to know *anything* worthwhile up to then, I would have taken her seriously. Maybe."

"Okay," I go on, beginning to care if Dr. Schulman sides with me. "So I'm thinking, is this the same woman who got scared of me when I started my period? Who came into my work when I was sixteen and in front of all my fellow employees, asked me what a blowjob was? Mother had just spent one hour with the love of my life and then proceeded to describe – with startling accuracy – the fate of my future if I stayed with this guy. You can't blame me for not taking her seriously."

She can't – but I can.

Deep down, I blamed myself for being so weak. As an accurate estimation of my circumstances evolved consciously for the first real time that afternoon, I worked extra hard to justify their presence just as rapidly. I knew whom the real love affair was with. It was Drama and Demise I made love to every night, fumbling along carpets and walls gritty from the indiscriminate L.A. air. Our bed had become an artifact, honored and ignored, but no longer serving half its purpose. MP was the vehicle through which I kept the plight of the Mad Martyr alive. I can look back now and laugh, sometimes. But Jesus, I was pathetic.

Lillian (we should be on a first name basis by now) has been writing feverishly.

She looks up and says, "So you agree with your mother, then?"

"Excuse me?"

"Your mother said, 'That man will possess you, but never love you,' and you said that she was accurate in her estimation."

"I said she was right. I didn't say I agreed with her."

"Are you in love with MP?"

"Pass."

"Do you think he loves you?"

"Pass."

"Would you care to address your mother's issue with alcohol?"

"She doesn't have an issue with alcohol. She liked it." As she pauses to consider me, I bring the rambling to a close. "I'm twenty-eight today. Jobless. Dogless. And my relationship? Well, let's state for the record; I'm way behind schedule."

My watch reads 4:02, that's 3:50. Time's up. My formerly

frenzied, presently drained physique labors its way toward the door. Lillian chooses, quite reluctantly I imagine, to speak.

"This might sound a little out there, but have you ever heard of the phenomenon of *Saturn Returning*?"

I fixate on the empty vase as though I've discovered a kindred spirit. Have I ever heard of *Saturn Returning*? What does she think I am, *stupid*?

Stumped is more like it – and, yes, stupid.

To cover, I get sassy. "Is that like hate fucking?"

"Excuse me?"

The honesty in her voice implies she's misheard me.

"*Hate Fucking*." I've become my mother and I'm talking to the deaf. "You know, one of the last few things on Earth that isn't overrated."

My feet drag into the hallway like two lead balloons; like the weight of my whole body has sunk into them. A phantom upper body swivels back toward Doc Schulman.

"Same time next week? Got this precious little date rape story you'll really get a kick out of. I, on the other hand, got chlamydia."

"Great."

She manufactures a stiff half-smile.

"Not really. Ciao."

I pivot on my heel to exit with synthetic, poorly executed confidence, and then pause, turn, and look this woman directly in the eye for the first time.

"Thank you. This was, I don't know...different. Different, like good, I think."

"You're welcome."

By the time the Mustang is in sight and the search for my keys well under way, regret creeps back in replacing the fast-fizzling rush of adrenaline. Sickness strikes flush and damp up the back of my neck, and I can't shake the thought of Father Philip's stupid army watch grating into my shoulder, flashing

15:13, 15:13, while another part of him pressed into me someplace else.

He was always talking about serving his fucking country. *What would your country have thought of you that day, creep?* Hate that memory. Fortunately, it only recurs when I talk about it, or some other girl talks about an experience similar to it. Or when I pass a Catholic church or a Catholic school. Or when I meet someone named Philip, or see an eleven-year-old girl, or a priest, or someone in the army. Or when I hear a joke about a priest or about the army. Or when I spot an older man with a much younger woman. Or when I see the number 13. Or when it's 3:13 in the afternoon. Fortunately, that's the only time I think about it.

What do women who have genuinely horrific sexual experiences clawing at the forefront of their cognizance do? How do they get through the day? How do they sleep at night?

What would I be like if my father had abused me rather than ignored me? If my teacher had penetrated me instead of grinded up against me? If I'd been conscious for the unsolicited sex on that stupid college date, as opposed to dead drunk? I guess I'd have to deal with it either way. All this comes with the territory of being a woman. There's no escaping most of it. It's life – or is it just *my* life?

I twist in the sticky car seat, searching for a comfort unlikely attained without a pale powdery pill and a shot of hot cheap liquor encased in hot cheap glass waiting loyally in the glove box. They're devoted solely to "the zone," so I rashly obtain assistance from both and relax in the swift false glory of their immediate gratification.

I knew enough to take responsibility for my quite deliberate circumstances. I had no right to blame my mother for incidentally fashioning me into her byproduct. There *is* such a thing as free will and MP had no right to blame me for not being more like a replicate of his mother, a woman I barely knew.

Doing something about this thorny situation was the obvious choice, but it was the outcome, the "unpredictable" hanging out there in space that was shackling any practical action on my part. Doing nothing resulted in an outcome I knew was manageable. I've been dwelling smack dab in the middle of "nothing" for a long, long time. Can trace the stagnant numbness throughout my body like it's a map of my chemical make-up. But doing something required, well…faith. And I don't have a grip around that yet.

Now watch how tequila, a sedative, and a place called Nothing unite with fear and idleness to produce this ridiculous rationale:

So I'm living with an arrogant prick who's recently added cheating to his list of *Things to Do to Endure Annie* – big deal. He doesn't beat me, and no one promised life would be bliss – not Mother, certainly not my father.

I was to blame. Lillian made me realize that much today, and my rationale was poetic, wry, contradictory, Shakespearean.

I was to blame: He was my punishment.

Problem identified, problem solved.

You know, I'm just a little girl living in a man's world, and I'm fine there. As long as I maintain a moderate buzz…I'm perfectly fine here.

Really.

THE SEVENTH CHAPTER

I Almost Brought You Roses

olding it in his fingers and catching the light, Billy can't take his eyes off the guitar pick. The move: a nervous habit that's helped him write a song, lose the time, and win the girl. Now he's turned to his loyal friend for one simple request: *Give me one purely profound thought that I can mold into verbal eloquence to define what she's meant to me. Or just help me encapsulate the meaning of life in a few sweet sentences. Is that so much to ask?*

His stare intensifies. Focusing on the shiny triangle disappearing and resurfacing between the folds of his fingers only escalates his apprehension. He's beginning to wish smoking and pacing were among his preferred habits. After all, they're two of the more renowned catalysts for problem solving and philosophy expounding.

What he's failing to appreciate is that the shoelace-bound daisies innocently grazing both his ankle and the obscure stone beside him have already completed the task that's stalking him.

Just outside the gates, Billy had put on his best – and only – black button-down. He'd left it untucked purposely to camouflage the "grime" on his jeans, and accidentally to disclose the "cool" on his person. He's had eight weeks and that many miles to prepare for this. What the hell's the problem? Marooned by expression for the first time in his twenty-three-year journey, he sits motionless, save for the rhythm in his right hand. As his eyelashes grow damp, he submits to the unsolicited exchange of "the man for the boy" and allows tears to burn his cheeks like January wind in New York.

This blur disrupts his focus and causes his tiny faithful friend to slip. The Fall: an inevitable signal to make his next move. Billy follows the rules of the self-indoctrinated game and looks up from the object he's placed his whole Truth in – *an object* that sits firmly erect between two flimsy blades of grass. He nabs it and dejectedly stuffs the piece of plastic into his pocket.

As if attached by string, his hand rises with his eyes and settles on the incision across the cold gray stone. No, it's not really an incision (although the absence of blood does little to dull the sting of it all), but the words *carving* or *engraving* have always corresponded with beauty in Billy's mind. This hurts to the eye and to the touch, and that, he determines, does not denote beauty. He traces each letter scrupulously, as if his finger is the chisel: Margaret Ann Meadows, Beloved Mother, Accomplished Lyricist, June 16, 1949 to July 22, 2004. When he completes the endeavor, his hand drops to his side and a surprising relief blankets him as shameless tears fall freely.

Just one more goodbye; that's all he wanted. One more time to say *I love you*. One more opportunity to tell her how beautiful she was. One more chance to proclaim that his second-to-the-last illegal activity was, in fact, going to be his *last* illegal activity.

A brain aneurism is something that happens to some unlucky old fellow you've never met, like your buddy's buddy's cranky great-uncle. Things like that aren't supposed to happen to your very own mother – your young, beautiful mother.

They never had to work at love, the two of them, never lacked for hugs. At least he's come to these conclusions and forgiven himself for missing *one last of everything*.

The time he's served has brought on a peculiar twist of circumstances he now recognizes as a gift. It's given him the courage to say there will be no more missed chances. Procrastination of the body, mind, and spirit will be unregretfully tucked away in yesterday. The desire to hold fast to this wisdom, especially in front of the woman who gave him life, feels as all-consuming as the scream that refuses to escape in the middle of the night.

He swipes the cuff of his shirt sleeve diagonally across both cheeks.

"So I know this guy, Murry. A friend – " He stops short, startled by the crackling of his own voice.

Billy presses his hand to the stone for support.

"Anyway, he told me he lost his first love because he *almost* brought her roses."

He laughs, thinking of Murry.

"Then Murry said, 'Failure never killed anybody. It's the *almosts* and the *should haves* that ruin a man.' Can you imagine that from such a funny kind of fellow? So anyway, I'm writing a song about it. Now that I know you can imagine."

His profile presses into the glassy gray smoothness with hopes of catching a whisper from the voice that's forever been his lullaby. A stone – the weakest of replacements he could dream of for his mother – is even icier than expected against his damp cheek. But subsequent to a shiver, a hopeful reprieve arises, so he relaxes into it and imagines he's being comforted by the beating of her heart.

Billy finally unwinds his arms and lifts the guitar gently into his lap.

"Okay, in honor of my newfound law-abiding persona – " The magnitude of the statement produces a yawn. "Boring. Ugh, I'm going to be so boring." He waves a hand in front of his face to shoo away any speculation about the future. "Anyway, Maggie, *Mom*, this is for you."

Billy reaches gracefully into his pocket to reclaim the pick that had been hastily dismissed, strokes the strings with a swift, soft motion, and then launches serenely into his latest creation, a song that succeeds at least a hundred others – a song he's tentatively entitled "I Almost Brought You Roses."

Happy Birthday to Me

As I walk up a hallway that grows ever more septic and suffocating and seems stretched like a rubber band about to snap, Doc Schulman's words play over and over in my head: *So you agree with your mother, then?*

I'd never agree with my mother. She forecasts my failures like the Very Merry Palm Reader.

On lucky attempt number seven, the right key squirms its way into the lock; the jingling and rattling of it all shatters what's left of the "common" part of my senses. I'm drained. I'm also a professional exaggerator, but totally drained, nonetheless.

On the Brink of Bliss and Insanity

No one should have ten keys attached to their key chain without color-coding them. And no one with ten keys should lose them twice a day. I've got serious, well-established key issues. Hey, I should get stoned and color-code my keys! Remind me later, will ya?

It's dusk on the first day of this twenty-eighth year of the rest of my life and the vampire in me should be revved up to play, but thirty-six minutes of therapy has me longing for a coma. I don't care whose birthday it is – this girl needs a couple more shots, a big-ass joint (fine...*another* big-ass joint), and some one-on-one time with her four favorite pillows. Of course, wishes such as these in *Life of Annie*, as it has thus far been scripted, generally prove pointless.

First of all, as the door swings open, I'm roused by the high-pitched squeal it releases. That noise crawls sideways through my skin every single time. Secondly, I'm involuntarily *aroused* by What's-His-Name. He's posed at the piano, stained by the glow of dozens of candles. This sight is foreground to a vibrant sunset comprised of colors yet to be named. They peek over the balcony like birds in a nest about to take flight for the very first time. This particular sky, with its crystalline structure and psychedelic tints, is reminiscent of any-day Arizona, but a rare backdrop for Los Angeles. It's exquisite.

God, the Prick looks fabulous in his favorite crimson shirt, intentionally untucked to look accidentally cool and unbuttoned twice from the collar, a move only a few guys can pull off without looking completely Guido – go figure, he's one of 'em. In fact, this particular cloak, which had to be tailored by the devil himself, lies unabashedly inches away from his pecs, coaxing me to find a curve of muscle just beneath the fabric and roll my eyes over and over it to the point of disinclined delight. As the temperature rises between my legs, a sensation slinks freely upward, forming an inner tickle that dances in carefree circles behind my navel. It's taunting me to jump the guy, and for that single impulse, another arises that hints I'd be better off scratching the epidermis off every inch of my body. You can see why I hate myself.

Upon assessing the situation from the safe but lonely vantage point of our dingy door, it's determined that this might be a six-shot shakedown, but I won't cave to this picturesque moment, despite its tempting blend of unusual and superficial beauty.

My gaze steadies. I could paint this, I think, if I could paint – and I would. I'd paint his portrait, stained in crimson, sandwiched between the heavens and his one true muse. Then I'd rip through the glossy wet canvas with a rusty, serrated, bohemian tool that's too heavy to hold with just one hand. The tear would be diagonal from top left to lower right. It would rip through his face, throat, and heart, all in one slice. That should have been my birthday present this year; a set of oil paints and a machete.

Hmm? Good to feel the therapy kicking in.

But to simplify in a much less graphic manner: I want him as much as I want to be rid of him. Is there even a name for that emotion?

My eyes travel down to his hands, which happen to be loosely draped across the diminishing row of shiny white rectangles. I hate that they're not on me. *Jealous of a piece of wood*; that'll go in my eulogy. Why not? It'll fit perfectly between *she drank too much* and *referred to her tits as 'tits' a lot*.

Why did I just look at his hands? Crossing my legs helps cease the imminent eruption of an uninvited mini-gasm and it gives the appearance of needing to pee (as opposed to needing to masturbate). *Why did I look at the hands?* I'm a hand chick, for Pete's sake, but why the hands? I'm a glutton for punishment, that's why. And a fool. Damn, he's beautiful. Every inch at any angle.

And now, Mr. Breathtaking is about to get melodic. I'm screwed, simple as that.

His fingers disappear and resurface, fondling those fortuitous keys. What the hell did they ever do to deserve his constant graceful touch? Whisper to me your secret, you selfish little toys. The various patterns his hands create across the magic keyboard anesthetize me long before their resonance registers and I detect his voice.

"Happy birthday to you, happy birthday to you. Happy birthday to *the girl*, happy birthday to you."

He rotates and bowls me over with a head-tilt combination grin.

"That was for you. Come here."

Understandably, I slam the door and go straight to my room – I mean – sit on his lap.

"Thank you. That's just what I needed."

Yeah, that and a swift two-by-four to the head.

"That's because I know exactly what you need, even when you don't." He traps a stray curl behind my ear, regards the wilting daisy foolishly, then captures and launches it onto the balcony. "How was it?"

I watch as the tiny flower sails to its freedom – which is cool. The move allows the memory of receiving it to rush through me and make me feel nice all over again.

"How was it, *girl*?"

MP doesn't like repeating himself; the brash inflection – a notorious trait.

"Um…" A fingernail loses life between my teeth. I'm nervous, like a child caught in a lie. Then my hand drops abruptly to my thigh ('cause I'm not a kid and am seriously considering not acting like one anymore). "She's not a woman of many words."

The soft, jagged, crescent-shaped fingernail jets out the

side of my mouth and rests in peace near the daisy. MP, smart cookie that he is, senses my apprehension toward therapy.

"This will be good for you, sweetie. It's just what we need."

We? *We?* How is *my* therapy a joint venture? That's it, he's gonna get a piece of my mind.

"I wish you'd come with me."

There. Take that you…man, you.

No response.

So you agree with your mother, then? Doc Schulman's question takes another lap through my mind, and this time it serves as a real eye-opener: He doesn't love me, and I don't love him. What I crave is some vague moment of delight I can barely recall to memory, and I don't know if there's a term for that sentiment, either. But what we have now is lonely and seedy. It evokes a self-inflicted harm that resurfaces in such perfect rhythm, its presence has become as common to my veins as…well, tequila.

His momentary passivity is stirring a notion of detachment and freedom, and despite the exhaustion and an inherent sense of worthlessness, I'm beginning to feel separate yet whole, an innovative replacement to separate and hollow. Now is the perfect opportunity to dump him like last week's trash; yesterday's news; like the nice guy for your asshole-ex the day before the prom; like…like the man who will possess you but never love you.

That man will possess you but never love you. So you agree with your mother, then?

Yes. Yes, Doc, I agree with my mother – but please don't tell her that.

This is my window.

"Can we talk?" I roughly murmur.

At least *something* was mumbled. The words were definitely mouthed. Here's hoping the dude's a lip-reader.

"Anything you want."

75

Of course he can read lips. Pick a talent, any talent.

Wow. He just invited me to speak. Is a breakup in the making? *Who am I?* The sheer idea makes the warmth between my legs blast straight into my throat. It explodes, inhibiting the passage of speech and air.

Just say it. Say good-bye to Mozart in the morning and ever finishing another crossword puzzle. Walk away from your live-in CNN correspondent, your Spanish teacher, karate coach, food critic, finishing-school tutor. Say good riddance to a partner with whom to sip Courvoisier at midnight and screw until 3:00 A.M. Slip away after dark from the most intelligent, diversified, talented, striking being ever to interrupt your predictably, disorderly existence.

MP is all the things I wish came naturally to me; all the things my mother claimed long ago to be. She once said that we could have been alike, she and I, but *someone* had erased the grace; that I was the girl who looked better with mud on her face. And she was right. I'll take Levis over Anne Klein any time – and embarrassment over the divine.

Then, one dusty day, grace – as I thought it was defined – walked into my life, and I've held onto it without considering whether I even wanted it.

He looks at me, this package of elegant male perfection, looks directly through me with empty, empty eyes. And that's where I find my voice – alongside courage, ego, and self-respect, buried deep inside those empty eyes.

As I formulate the ballsy phrase *I think we need some time apart, so I'm going to stay with Foster for a while*, lights from the kitchen concurrently spring on and an assembly of bogus, musical yuppie wannabes pounce out and systematically scream, "Surprise!"

Before my brilliantly concise soliloquy escapes my lips, I impulsively scream back. But my scream is a bit more primal, like a cheerleader being stabbed thirty times with a screwdriver

by her high school sweetheart for blowing his best friend behind the bleachers after football practice. Then I go blank and
land on my ass for the second time today.

When I reclaim consciousness (against my better judg-
ment), I focus in on a pack of genuine Republicans pretending
to be lax Republicans swarming around me – and *are those
Triple D's triple Ds looming over my head?* I've officially entered
the Third Ring. The night is young, but lookin' dismal, my
friends. Young, but dismal.

"Come on boneheads, open up!" Fos beckons with a knock that
could score an easy 3.1 on the Richter scale. She's at the door
of her premier hostages, The Happy Drunk Couple. They're
among a remote handful, not bound by lineage, who don't
mind spending the majority of their free time within a ten-
mile radius of her life-sucking aura.

The fire-breathing feminist is about to kick open the door
when the world's cutest dominatrix appears. Okay, so put Re-
ese Witherspoon's head on Carmen Electra's body and toss her
into anything Cher wore in the 80s, and that's what's happening
visually with Terbear. She's that exceptional breed of person
you feel compelled to either hug or fuck at any given moment,
but can rarely make up your mind as to which.

"Hey, Fos, what's up?"

"Annie's birthday party," Fos states while giving Terbear
the quick once-over.

She concludes that her bouncy blonde friend is wearing
her next Halloween costume and therefore suppresses a sar-
casm-packed rant.

"I thought he was kidding."

"Yeah, he's tricking us into hanging out with him 'cause we
bring so much joy into his life."

Shane enters the scene, pompoms in hand (imagine the
rest).

"Hey, Fos. What's going on?"

This is new and justifies a remark.

"Steal that from one of your students?" Foster leans back and cocks her head in bewilderment. "Are you sure you should be breeding?"

If either of them had anything to grab fabric-wise, she would reach forward and knock their heads together. But as she surveys them in their entirety; between the sweat sailing down the edges of Shane's brow, the pool of it resting in the crest of Terbear's cleavage, and the heavy breathing that's so exaggerated it's coming off vaudevillian, she decides it's best not to touch them.

Our crowd-pleasing transvestite does a cheer, "Go, Jefferson Elementary!" and he's good. "Rah! Rah! Rah?" and he's fading.

"Seriously, Fos," Terbear whines, "doggie-style's getting old, and taking my temp, and standing on my head – and I want a baby! Plus, Shane misses underwear."

"I do. At first I felt studly and liberated. Now I just feel sticky and cheap."

"Aw, baby. I didn't know that," Terbear sympathizes.

"What am I supposed to say, sweets? Sir Chub-a-lot and the dukes prefer to be shackled? We want a kid."

"Aw, baby." Terbear's all touched and teary-eyed.

Foster's head rotates mechanically to the side to catch a quick inhalation of cooler, less hormonally enhanced oxygen.

"Mm-hmm," she says, "Listen up. Hurry up and change." She reevaluates the scene. "Or don't."

Shane and Terbear look deep into each other's eyes. Fos waits with bated breath: The decision here is crucial. It would change the entire vibe of the party, but it could also get Shane's nose broken *again* – and the decision here lies solely in the hands of a poker-faced Terbear.

She finally chirps, "We'll change!" then taps the door shut with a five-inch, silver-spiked heel attached to her pleather thigh-highs.

Alone on the couch, I practice Zen in the art of catatonia. Don't bother me. MP's mingling like a bastard. That is to say, only with The Blonde.

"Your girlfriend doesn't look too excited about the party, Michael."

Triple D can read a person like the back of a peroxide bottle.

"She's fine," he says, staring at the back of my head – at least I hope he's staring at the back of my head.

A fierce series of pounds threaten the stability of the door. A familiar sound? Why, yes, it's definitely suggestive of a superhero I know. An eye pops open.

"Excuse me," MP says. "Why don't you cheer up the birthday girl while I go grab that?"

Cheer who – what? Shit, that's me. Suddenly, all my senses jump into hyper-alert, and sure enough, as MP saunters to the door, The Blonde approaches me. Uh-oh. Oh, no, play dumb. Wait, she's got that covered. Okay, play numb.

She bends over the arm of the couch and leans in like she's coming on to me – and I can't help but wonder: if I slid in a quarter, would she sing me a song? Jesus, I'm the straightest chick I know and still can't take my eyes off of 'em.

"Your boyfriend is the most talented pianist. You're one lucky girl."

I stare directly at the facsimile of my ass, which also happens to be her chest; it inflates, then deflates. Gain five pounds, lose five pounds, gain five pounds, lose five pounds. Yeah, yeah, I got it…you can breathe. As a side bar, I realize that if I were a guy, I'd definitely be a boob man. Hate that. Hate her.

Then she says, "I hear you used to cook. I used to eat."

Then with a giggle, she adds, "You know, before I moved here for my modeling career."

I'm speechless; my face may have atrophied. At least the numb thing's working. Please tell me she's being literal. I simply couldn't bear it if she were clever *and* stacked.

"I'm Summer."

Summer? No way. This really is too much.

"You know, as in, Winter, Spring, *Summer*, Fall."

My neck snaps upward. We're nose to nose-job.

"I'm going to be sick," I retort. "You know, as in, puke, vomit, *upchuck*, yak."

And the stare-off begins. Funny, though. She doesn't look too clever. She looks, well…pretty: pretty tan, pretty blonde, pretty young. It's pathetic when someone has to enhance themselves cosmetically in order to be confident. No crow's feet or puffiness around the eyes, either. Doesn't look as though she's shed a tear in a decade, so I guess that would make her pretty goddamned happy, too. I bet I look pretty tired. Bitch better not be checking out the bags under my eyes. Don't lose focus. Can't lose focus to this phony. I'll tactically search for something in my peripheral that looks distorted or icky, find relief in that. Maybe her earlobes connect to her head before they have the chance to form lobes. That would look weird. Maybe she has an outie; that could kill a modeling career. One can only hope. But all in all, she looks pretty perfect – and I'm shrinking, as if the cushion hasn't settled on the couch, except I've been sitting here for an hour.

The door flies open.

"Let the games begin!"

The voice shakes me from a near-psychotic episode. I leap up over the coffee table, single-bounded, straight into the arms of my long lost cousin. Thank God her mission on this planet is to rescue me at a moment's notice – or without notice, for that matter. The four of us dance, hug, and spew sentiment as if we've been reunited after a ten-year separation from various deserted islands and/or barbed wire-encased institutions.

Terbear bustles through the crowd to the stereo. Sorry, Rachmaninoff.

"Excuse me, excuse me. Hi, I'm Terbear. I love your tie. Hi, I'm Terbear. Are you a professional pianist, too? Gosh, that must be so exciting!"

As she dazzles the crowd with genuine charm; a trait considered scarce to this room and a feature deemed vintage to the city, I notice each of them secretly note whether they'd opt to hug her or fuck her. The four of us settle into a nook near the door, where Shane and Foster post watch while Terbear and I morph into dancing, giggling, teenage idiots for the next few hours.

"I just *luv* watching our babies dance," Shane reflects, passing a joint to Fos.

"Get a load of the Master Prick." Using the joint as a pointer, Fos singles out MP and The Blonde. "I bet he's fucking that chick."

"Nah, she's probably just blowing him. I don't see that guy taking any extra time out of his schedule to gratify someone else."

My people are perceptive with a capital P.

"Point well taken. Now explain to me again why we can't just kidnap dear Annabelle for the next thirty years or until she comes to her senses?" Fos says, flashing Shane her signature faux-smile.

"You know our role in this – to love her unconditionally until she learns to love herself."

"That's beautiful, man. I love you."

Fos embraces Shane like a mother would her son upon returning from the war. In the interim, MP is drawing a crowd

near the kitchen with his needle-sharp knowledge of abso-
lutely everything.

"Well, movies, like music, are subjective. It's my personal
tendency to examine an artist's unabridged body of work rather
than just one of his pieces."

A tiny clockwise circle of the hand swirls the dark liquid
methodically inside his goblet; with a raise and a tilt, a sip of
Merlot glides past his lips. He swallows and reassumes the
stance of a sixteenth-century philosopher.

"Bach can't simply be defined by his Brandenburg Quartets,
although a glorious achievement in and of themselves. Favorite movie, you ask?"

I abandon Terbear on the dance floor/coffee table to slink
through the crowd and slap an arm around MP because this,
I gotta hear.

"Jeffrey, I'd have to say anything by Billy Wilder. He was
one of the first of a dying breed of cinematic poets."

"*The Lost Weekend*," Adam replies, consumed with equal
amounts of pride and femininity.

"Ooh, cheers!" beams Jeffrey, Adam's darker-complected
archetype.

"I just loved *Stir Crazy!*" The Blonde says, bouncing on
her toes.

The crowd goes embarrassingly silent. This is Heaven!
Happy birthday to me! Thank you, God, for blondes and boobs
and for the world having momentary lapses of normalcy.

"A woman with a sense of humor," chuckles MP, rescuing
the bitch.

How dare he? See, now I have to turn into *me*. Bummer.

"Babe, your favorite movie is that Matt Damon action
thingy."

"Sweetie," he intonates "Everybody's a comedian!" Then he
leans in to further illuminate his posse, "She's had too much
to drink tonight."

"You're an action movie freak. *Spider Man*, X-Men, *Star Wars* – you own like all twenty of those. Want me to go get 'em?"

"No, but you can get me another glass of Merlot," he barks, locked in my gaze.

"*The Bourne Identity!*"

"I read that book!" Jeffrey announces.

"The book's always better than the movie." Adam adds all cute and casual-like.

Oh, boys – that *is* cute. Although, any attempt to placate *this* situation shall heretofore be dubbed fruitless. But thanks for playing.

"You didn't see it?" I'm aghast. "This is tragic. The movie's a real masterpiece. And Matt Damon…whew! He's one big, yummy stud that I'm going to thoroughly enjoy fucking later this evening." And to reinforce my lead in this vicious tête-à-tête, I add, "Say, babe, who are you going to be thinking about while you're doing me tonight?"

My beady, brown, bloodshot eyes burn a hole into the Blonde's Botoxed brow.

"Annie – " he orders.

"Because I really think you should set your standards a little higher. I mean, if I'm going to be with Matt…hey, you should fuck him, too! He's really good." I redirect to Adam and Jeffrey. "I'm speaking metaphorically, of course."

"*Annie.* I'm really sorry, everyone. Party's over," he apologizes, gentlemanly-like.

"Can you say *substance abuse problem*?" Jeffrey snickers.

"Can you say *freak*?" scoffs Adam.

The boyfriends have taken a turn for the snotty.

"Hey!" I scream. "You think it's easy being a basket case? I'll have you know I have to work twice as hard as the rest of you assholes to maintain this image!"

Whoa, I'm entirely out of breath and lightheaded – must

bend over and clutch knees. Whoa, blacking out. What's happening? Room's shrinking.

"Geez, Louise. Dial it down, will ya?"

Fos shakes her head, but maintains the vice grip around my arm as she and Shane carry me backward, then paste me against the far kitchen wall.

"You need to sleep over," she points out.

"Yes, I do, but not tonight." Then I wink, whisper, and elbow her like a prototype drunk. "Unfinished business."

Fos nods in rehearsed skepticism.

"Sure."

"Well, you call if you need us to come back and kick some ass."

Shane kisses my cheek and tugs Fos away. They reach the door, and as one would a subpoena, Fos presents her hand to MP.

"Call me. We'll do therapy."

They love to hate each other, I don't care what they say (actually, that *is* what they say).

Shane follows suit.

"Call me. We'll do…never mind."

Shane's got balls; they're just not wrought iron, like Miss Foster's.

"Aren't you forgetting something?"

MP motions toward a passed out Terbear, pretty as peaches propped against the edge of the couch. Shane and Foster nonchalantly hoist her into their arms and stroll back through the front door.

"Sweetie," Shane scolds, "I told you, never mix alcohol and fertility drugs. Never ever, *ever*. Oh, evenin', Ma'am."

The lovely Mrs. Greenblatt, our neighbor of the aging persuasion, is rubbernecking our state of affairs from a crack in her door.

"Mrs. Greenblatt!" Fos declares. "Are you still taking that Indian root for your bursitis, like I instructed?"

"How's the Mister?" Shane would tip his hat to her were he wearing one (and if both hands weren't occupied dragging his drunken wife down the hallway). "My wife sends her regards."

He jiggles Terbear's arm; she waves involuntarily. Mrs. Greenblatt shrinks back into her cave, a genuine virgin to fun.

MP slams my only portal to the outside world. Just the two of us. Yippee. As he reaches the bedroom door, he turns, skulking from the shadows. I feel frozen on my mark, but through a loose nest of fallen curls, my defiant eyes brave their denigrator.

"Is it something I said?"

"Go to Hell," he says, devoid of any specific emotion, and retires into the bedroom.

"I've been there for two years, thank you very much."

Alone, and like the painful rush of embarrassment, I'm suddenly sober; too sober for a midnight in my life, anyway.

Love: Los Angeles Style

Uh, oh. He's peddling backward and there's nowhere to run. All right by me. I'll press my feet flat into the floor and play chicken. Let's see, I'm lookin' at 195 pounds of impact lunging toward me from twenty feet away…it'll be fine. The alcohol will bury the pain of it all 'til morning, anyway. As they do in the movies, I raise my chin to face the enemy as he strikes, but the enemy surprises me and stops shy. Only his scent completes the collision, which is, above all else, his main drawing point, primal as it sounds. That beguiling stench envelops me and momentarily detracts from the original task at hand (which is *hating* him). I exhale hard through my nose.

"What did you just say?" he seethes, creeping closer.

As if being forced by a fistful of hair, my neck bends back

as far as it will go. Our lengthy silhouettes look stunning and eerie as they climb over the piano to scrape the ceiling. His face floats forebodingly over mine.

"What did you just say?"

Okay, *scared* and *shitless* come to mind, bumping out any previous thoughts that may have occupied the space. I know what I said was an insinuation that demonstrated a peculiar commonality between me, him, Hell, and the duration of our courtship – and it must've been good if he's this pissed. But repeating the statement is probably not a good idea, even if by way of loose translation. Times are taking a turn for the bizarre. Normally, he'd kill for me to develop an acute case of "mute."

With narrowing, darkening sapphire eyes and vascularization settling into his forehead *and* forearms, the heavy thinker has apparently kicked his gray matter into overdrive and placed his biceps on reserve; that much is apparent. As a precautionary measure, the same word reverberates over and over in my head: duck, duck. If he makes a move, it's my only logical defense.

Without flinching, he resolutely utters, "You're a little bitch" and walks away as if I've just been instantaneously erased.

The build-up has come to a crushingly anticlimactic close. Instinct tells me to shut up and set up (camp in the living room).

So I dodge past him and spurt, "You're the little bitch!" then stumble, one foot over the other, into the bedroom, a guaranteed refuge had I not unwittingly slammed the door – on his hand.

Ouch.

Oops.

Shit.

Time stops for me while I trace the outline of his fingers pressed so hard around the edge of the door they could very well leave an imprint. It's amazing how strong a man's hand is; stronger than my whole body flung against a wooden bar-rier (the door), and that hardly seems fair. But fortunately for my physical well-being, the only thing stronger than a man's hands…are his hormones.

He breezes through the door the way he would a Billy Joel song and threatens the wall next to my face with a fist. Fin-gers gather swift about my throat as a kiss ambushes me hard on the lips. My shudder stabilizes, a result of force as much as furtive relief.

The degree of initial pain this typically inflicts is directly in proportion to my blood-alcohol level. Thin skin at the center of my upper lip punctures from the crashing of our mouths, but it's surprisingly consoling, and the only true ache I have left in the whole wide world is for him to be inside me.

My jeans and underwear clumsily bunch inside-out around us. MP unhooks his belt and drops his boxers just low enough. Wherever the predator kills his prey is where he tends to feast, so he fucks me vertically against the very wall where I've been pinned; our lonesome bed barely inches away. No matter. My perfect orgasm erupts within seconds and trickles systemati-cally into his. Upon convulsing, he slides out, gathers his pants with his breath, and heads for a token shower. Me? I swiftly succumb to the role of nasty girl, peel off my top, and crawl into bed like a wounded animal seeking refuge in a ditch.

And that, my friends, is *hate fucking*.

I'm torn with respect to elaborating. If your experience in this arena encompasses solely what you've just read, I'm not here to recruit new members. The act itself is sexy and lonely, exciting and vicious, satisfying and draining, but it's lonelier than sexy, more vicious than exciting, and drains you beyond satisfaction. It's the kind of sex you don't muse over the next day in your head or celebrate with your girlfriend over Mojitos during a Thursday night venture to Chateau Marmont.

As for your partner in crime; don't approach him on the subject. Don't look him in the eye and even consider mentioning it. The reality of it is, you don't look him in the eye at all, especially when you're in the throes of it.

That's what I knew then.

This is what I know now:

I was, without fail, as equally surprised as I was sedated by an event so habitual that it ultimately turned ritual. Our only means of vengeance without actually drawing blood. The only time we both won; an indiscrete cycle of taboo victories and premeditated shames. The rest of the relationship was lax conversation and debasing looks no longer worth pondering. After the first episode, I naïvely anticipated a natural kickback to romance: eyes meeting, hands touching, voices beating long, breathy, rhythmic melodies into steamy ears – things that were rumored to be taken for granted. Someone might have pointed out the "No Turning Back" sign. The prospect of a little bit of gray in our new chronic black paradise swiftly became impractical.

The surprise: this wasn't a phase. So I caved, decided to will these cursed episodes into materializing. The drawback of my wiles became rapidly apparent: If you get that thing you hate to love you, and it does, the derivation of that love is still spawned from hate, and will be displayed as such.

Even now the topic is challenging. The passing of time begets neither tears nor laughter upon recount, but it could easily induce a one-way rap session with my toilet, if dwelled upon long enough.

My time with MP serves as an important reminder of what it means to live inside a lie. Each dark moment and, ultimately, its culmination symbolizes a time when I believed there was only one way to learn a lesson.

Like that cross someone slung around my neck once-upon-a-long-time-ago, the image of my past resides close, but walks next to me now so I'm neither strangled by nor forced into a slouch from the gravity of it all.

Three hours past midnight, moonlight sneaks through the blinds, jarring the REM right out of me. As a slave to its piercing beauty, my wilted body moves like smoke from bed to balcony in a quest to be near the keeper of my late night apparitions. Along this path, the items acquired are as follows: MP's crimson shirt, which I drape over my shoulders and button twice just below my breasts, a half-empty bottle of Merlot (yes, I'm a *bottle is half-empty* girl), and the remainder of a joint. As my bare toes hit the clammy cement, I step on what crushes like a bug but turns out to be a gift from a stranger a lifetime ago. Ordinarily, a move like that would make me want to cry, but at this point a move like crying would be redundant. I sit, press the skin together between the bridge of my nose to release a little tension, then strike a match and watch it burn; the perfect waste of time. The roach perched between my lips finally catches flame, and my wine-kissed eyes settle on its burning tip.

I stretch my neck back and shoot a funnel of chunky gray smoke straight into the dense cobalt sky, then examine the face of The Man on the Moon and allow him the same courtesy, too naked in his spotlight to mask any truths.

As its blue beam hits me and washes away the grime of self-deceit, I discover the moral of today's story: "Breakin' up is even *harder* to do while twenty loose acquaintances burst forth from behind curtains, walls, and furniture to surprise the crap out of you."

On the flipside, I did get laid, and that's always a good thing on your birthday, right? 'Course, on the flip side of that, the encounter itself can most accurately be described as *gruesome*. Then, on the flip side of that lies the most derisive of the questions: How does one sanction a breakup with their long-term live-in mere hours after copulation?

I had my window; it was finally two months since his mother passed and nearly a month since our last wicked grapple. Time had just finished shedding the residue from it, and I was feeling emancipated. That's what I should have recognized four hours ago. Instead, I broke a major rule in the pre-breakup codes. Now it'll be so untidy and I risk owning more of the blame – more than none, anyway. This wasn't how I imagined the end of the Annie/MP Era – disappointing and dirty. Man, nothing screws with a good, clean breakup like dead people and great sex.

I breathe in the cool blue air. It filters into my consciousness and my mind settles on the notion that everything will be okay. Accepting and generous are among the moon's most admirable traits. The sun has never allowed the same basking privileges. So, with the moon being the more forgiving of the lighted gods, it has always been my choice of worship. One of the few things worth trusting is the inner voice that this nocturnal creature inspires. I've always believed in the safety of its solitude.

It's okay, I exhale. It's okay that we did it. Tonight will be remembered as the crescendo in this off-key opera. I'll let the weekend quietly settle and tell him Monday. My mistakes will cease to overlap each other starting Monday. With that, one last swig of sure-fire-forget-my-life-'til-dawn-tonic barrels recklessly into my tummy. I rise. I'm full; the bottle's finished; a sure sign to end the chaos come Monday.

As I forcefully shift my body to go back inside, a dude adorned in a ski mask with a guitar slung over one shoulder bounds gracelessly into my periphery. My sore eyes bolt downward as this guy bends on one knee next to MP's Beamer and starts rummaging madly through the duffel bag he'd been towing over his other shoulder.

MP's Beamer: A final parting gift from Mommy. The license plate he purchased to embellish it reads *MPM* with a set of musical notes on either side of the monogram. My eyes loop up toward the sky, chagrined by the sight of it; the skin on the bridge of my nose is assaulted yet again by thumb and forefinger, and I think: Someday I'm going to smash in the faces of every owner of every personalized license plate in this ludicrous city. I don't know. Just a thought.

From my second-floor-balcony front-row-center seat, Dude in Ski Mask draws a book from his bag. *He's going to read to the car?* He approaches the driver's door and extracts a long flat metal object from between the pages of the book. A bookmark moonlighting as a slim jim? Not too educated in the field of thieving paraphernalia, but the hanger swinging from his other arm leads me in the direction of the bookmark's true identity.

The outfit, the stance, the focus, the slithering about the vehicle, and the metal gadgets in hand taper his peculiar escapades into one simple singular conclusion: Dude is going to steal MP's car!

Must wake MP! Have to. I *have* to.

I really should.

Of course, with curiosity fully piqued, tearing myself away from this sideshow is a much bigger undertaking than, say, *not* tearing myself away. He's about to set off the alarm anyway. Ooh, he figured that out and is backing away, frustration in his gait. Both items (the slim jim and the wire hanger) are launched into the air in the style of an imaginary slam-dunk – the duffel bag their intended target. They bounce off his bag and onto the lawn where they're buried in the shadows of the building. Now, with thieving gadgets nowhere in sight, he kicks the bag, hurts his foot, rubs it while hopping up and down on the other leg and utters a string of adjectives unfit for the more prudish ear. I must admit, the Dude is quite engaging at this stage in the attempted felony.

I lean forward, giving the majority of my weight over to

the railing while anxiously awaiting his next farcical feat. The empty green-tinted glass bottle loose in my grip vacillates freely above the head of this clueless, entertaining villain. He paces in circles until full function of his injured foot is regained. He then lunges vindictively at the duffel bag and takes hold of the culprit responsible for inducing the pain: a baseball bat. I've never seen someone so emotional over a piece of wood before. What a weirdo. Gripping and re-gripping eventually evolves into a move that in any other setting would be referred to as a *practice swing*. Nice form; maybe he's got a big game tomorrow. He creeps closer to the car, swinging with full force every couple of steps.

Uh, oh.

With no time to think, I balance on a toe and audibly whisper, "Psst! Hey, psst!"

Dude freaks, looks up, spins, trips over the bat, falls down, gets up, reaches for the bat, fumbles, lands on top of it with a knee – injuring both his knee and the hand he squashed between bat and knee. And to allot him a crumb of dignity, I'll knock off *my* description of *his* imitation of a bumbling idiot. But as a spectator, sheltered mostly by an olive tree I now regard as charming, my amusement is fully genuine.

I giggle. "Psst! I'm up here!"

He spins up to his feet again and like a child searching for the biggest snowflake falling from the sky, gazes open-mouthed until the outline of my figure becomes apparent through the leaves.

"Hi," I say, arresting his exit.

"Hi..."

The tiny word is dragged into a question.

Oh, boy. What to do?

"The key is above the rear left tire, in a little metal box."

Fuck it. He looks like he could use a car.

"What?"

What does he mean, "What?" He heard me. I'm known for my enunciating skills, famous in my circle, even. But just in case, I clear my throat to raise the level of my whisper a notch.

"The *key*. The key to that car is above the rear left tire!"

"The key to this car?"

"Yes."

He looks at the car, then me, then rests one hand on a hip while scratching his forehead with the other. Okay – playing charades – he's definitely doing *confused*, a gesture that would come off as boring and typical if not for the ski mask.

"It's where?"

His sincerity slays me, but honestly, how much assistance can one little amateur car thief need? Don't these guys practice dry runs?

"Above the rear left tire, in a little metal box!"

Man, this is exhausting.

"Thanks."

"Um…don't mention it."

I crank my neck back into the apartment, peer over at the bedroom window, then back at the Beamer. Dude is staring up at me, motionless. I'm not going down there to hand him the key. A few basic principals *are* at stake here.

"Go!" I yell, shooing him with my hands. "I'm on the lookout!"

Okay, good. He's finally scrambling.

Oh, Jesus.

"Try the other back left tire!"

This little dyslexic amateur car thief is toying with my patience, although the deviant in me is still cheering him on. Even when he barrels around to the right (left) side of the car and cuts too close to the bumper, I'm still a fan. Even when he smashes his injury-free knee and sets off the alarm, I still find myself pulling for him.

And even as a disoriented MP barrels from the bedroom in his boxers and demands, "What the hell's going on?"

And "Uh-oh" is all I manage, I still secretly wish the boy well and hope he escapes with both life *and* limbs.

MP is outside the building in a flash.

"What the fuck do you think you're doing?"

"Taking the car, man!" announces the little, honest, dyslexic, amateur car thief, and with every added inane choice, gesture, and statement, my fondness for this guy elevates.

The night air inflates with a clutter of unpleasant boy sounds: punching, swearing, stumbling, more punching.

"You promised her!" demands the little, disgruntled, honest, dyslexic, amateur car thief.

"Fine, you'll get your winnings!" MP threatens.

There's a moment of silence. I take it for escape or demise.

And then, as loud as an iron skillet slamming onto a slate counter, I hear it: *Smack!*

"That's for the car."

"And the first eight jabs?"

Ballsey but valid question, I'll give the dude that.

"C'mon." MP says definitively.

Suddenly, the racket shifts from below me to behind me as MP and Dude barrel down the hallway. I stand petrified in the doorway of the balcony forgetting MP's shirt is draped loose over my otherwise naked body.

Through a crack in their door, the Greenblatts angrily gawk, her head stacked on his. Yeah, she's a whole head taller than her crooked little counterpart.

"Go back to bed, Mrs. Greenblatt," MP shouts. "Nothing to see here."

He turns into our apartment, slamming the door for the second time this evening.

"Get off me!" screams the little, banged-up, disgruntled,

honest, dyslexic, amateur car thief, and with ski mask now in hand, he starts bitch-slapping MP.

Actually, they're both bitch-slapping each other, until a number of interesting conclusions become simultaneously obvious to them:

They look like chicks.

They look like children.

They also look as though this isn't the first time they've bitch-slapped each other. And...

Someone else is in the room, which, above all else, seems to be the driving force that represses the mutual, infantile assault.

Something's fishy. Behind dirt, sweat, patches of blood, and remnants of an acoustic guitar sticking out like gigantic splinters popping from his skin, the beaten-up, dragged-in Dude looks positively familiar.

A stray notion trails from my buzzed, bewildered brain before I have time to arrest it.

"You're the daisy."

He doesn't respond, but his eyes reflect, *Yeah, I'm the daisy*.

And if MP hadn't disrupted my trance with "She's drunk," I would have forgotten he was in the room.

He just apologized for my behavior to a guy he just beat the crap out of for trying to steal his car. Brilliant.

Then, as a means of introduction, he grabs his latest victim by the neck as if the guy were a puppy – the last of the litter, the runt that no one wants, and says, "I'd like you to meet my Machiavellian brother, William. Billy, Annie."

"I've heard a lot about you."

"Likewise."

A sly, sarcastic tone is followed by a smirk of similar origin. The sarcasm was for MP. The smirk, I sense, for me.

"Go put some clothes on."

Suddenly and strangely, MP's disgusted that I'm scantily clad in front of his long-lost brother. Oh, go ahead and act like a boyfriend, I dare you.

I sashay nonchalantly from the living room while holding my gaze purposeful and steady on Billy, hoping to taunt "the other guy." While gliding down the hall, my fingertips draw soothing waves that rise and settle across its walls. I discern two sets of eyes trailing my departure; one stings my back like a thousand bug bites, the other settles a little lower and sways with my walk.

Both are briefly satisfying.

Then the tension-consumed big brother shouts, "And grab some blankets for our guest!"

As I gather blankets – for our guest – too many thoughts to count collide. MP enters.

"You never told me you had a brother."

"We're not that close."

"Really?"

I can play stupid and blasé, too (in case you hadn't already noticed).

To validate the two-year lie, he adds, "He's not from around here."

"That matters. Where's he from?"

He mumbles something Spanish-sounding.

"What?"

I'm *not* a lip-reader.

"Los Feliz."

"Los Feliz, what?"

I sound genuinely confused – really good at that when I genuinely am.

MP stands face forward in the closet, staring up at the bedding, but not reaching for it. I jump onto my toes and grab the corner of a pillow. It hits me smack in the face along with

98

a compelling revelation: Los Feliz, the ten-miles-down-the-road Los Feliz?

"*Los Feliz, where your mother lived*?!"

My hand flies – taking on a life of its own – right across his head and shoulder half a dozen times, like an Italian grandmother.

"Hey!"

He puts an abrupt end to it with a block and a clutch.

"Michael, hello! You know, I don't know what it's like on your planet, but we humans – most of us anyway – have hearts and minds, and we actually care about the people around us like – "

"Settle down!"

The grip tightens with every attempt to release my arm.

"Like our friends and family, and sometimes little brothers – "

"I said knock it off! Keep your voice down."

With voice so-not-down, I continue, "And sometimes we talk about them. And when we're feeling really nutty we might even talk *to* them!"

"Shut up for the first time in your life!"

And for the first time in my life, I do. The decision motivated greatly by the pressure around my wrist and the nails digging into it. Also, MP's right. We do work diligently around here to keep manners in the forefront of all discussions. And I shut up because it's been rude of us to discuss the existence of his brother so openly and obnoxiously while the guy's bleeding, looking weary as hell, and possibly even starving in the very next room.

"I raised him."

He lowers his voice, waits for the medal. I can't reach it; my free hand is too busy turning blue.

"I had to stay here for school just so I could be on standby to pick his ass up from jail. Did you know that?"

"I don't know anything, Michael."

He laughs cynically.

"That loser can't even steal with any sense of finesse. Clumsy bastard."

"One question?"

There's like a million, starting with: Do you have any other family members that are MIA? Is your name really Michael Paul Meadows? Does your species even come equipped with the ability to love and be loved? And would you mind releasing my arm before permanent nerve damage sets in? But my single question must be strategically and cautiously selected.

"Why was he trying to steal your car?"

He just unwound his fingers – a good sign. The numb limb drops to my side. At least I think it did.

"He's after Mother's stuff, the money, whatever. Some of it's in my name."

Treading even more guardedly, "So give it to him."

"It's not that simple. It was supposed to be for college. Does he look like he's ready for college?"

With obvious permission, I picture him: A stranger holding a daisy, offering me a gift he deemed precious. Kindness consumed his eyes, but I couldn't speculate as to the color. The freedom of his spirit had swept over me like a spurt of hot summer air at the beach, but I failed to notice the guitar that must have been slung over his shoulder or the grime plastered artistically across his attire. It didn't occur to me that he might be homeless. I didn't spot the grease and confusion of a life harshly lived separating his hair into knotted sectored clumps. He didn't look like a thief. Or a beggar. Or someone's little brother. Or a scattered child wandering the Earth without a mother. I thought he was a whole hell of a lot cooler than me, and *way* more together – and I did college.

Now, I imagine him out cold on the floor in our living room, stained with blood, struck by harsh fatigue.

Does he look like he's ready for college?

"Sure. Why not?"

"Go to bed," MP says, disgusted with my reply.

Then he tugs the blanket and pillow from my embrace, drags them into the living room, and tosses them indifferently in the vicinity of Billy. And that's where they'll remain, folded near the feet of his forgotten baby brother until I get my ass out of bed and adjust them. 'Til somewhere around noon the next day I predict.

The Compliment

Billy's busy embarking on a siesta of marathon proportions – somewhere in the neighborhood of thirty hours. Impressive work.

I think this guy's the best thing that's happened to my relationship since Klonopin. Upon Billy's late-night arrival, MP and I have virtually stopped speaking (insert smiley face). One of us put a halt to banal household conversation so as not to *wake* our newfound buffer. The other has opted out of verbal communication so as not to *discuss* the newfound buffer. As an added bonus, MP's pretty much avoided the pad overall, which has granted me ample opportunity to study this peculiar new fixture whose mere presence has coaxed MP and me into shutting the fuck up in an environment that was otherwise inundated with sneers and tears and things that go screech in the night.

So this is the first time I've rolled out of bed and not felt like absolute junk since I lost/fled/ran screaming from my job – and I'm going for a run. With an imminent attack of cellulite only days away, I'm an embarrassment to this city of *unders* (under-worked, under-fed, under-weight, under-forty). It's Monday morning, I've packed a bag, I'm sticking to my plan, and I feel grand.

The plan: pack, cook, run, dress, shop, cook, end two-year relationship with long-term live-in, go to Foster's, and then, beg one petite but feisty Lisa Marie Presley for two weeks' worth of couch privileges while I reassess. I've revised the plan to include two home-cooked meals. This is partly because the recent intruder has put a small dent into lunging into promising new destiny, partly because I don't need to come off as an inconsiderate host over a little long overdue breakup, but mostly because I haven't cooked in a week and old habits die hard.

After having watched his stages of slumber quite meticulously, quite peeping Tomishly, I'm guessing that he'll without doubt be rising shortly, and nourishment has proven to be key for short-term survival in this joint.

I turn on a burner, then assemble in an orderly fashion various breakfast items in need of cracking, blending, frying, and flipping. There's two minutes to kill before the stove is ready to roll, so I decide to crack my own idea of A.M. nourishment – a *beer*, and plunge into the living room for one last dose of Billy T.V.

As I lean into him, I note the initial attention catcher is the deep dimple in his chin; the first of many physical distinctions between him and MP. His skin is tan and soft, but not too soft; temporarily torn between boy and man. And if one felt compelled to take a finger and trace his jaw line, it wouldn't be met by more than a dozen stray hairs. A tiny divot embosses the corner of his left eye, as if it's been eroded over the years by the same stagnant teardrop. Another scar that's thicker, newer, and assumingly more brutal in nature, jaggedly sketches its way from lip to nose. Strands of thick, black, shiny hair lay slick and tangled one over the other, like wet weeds framing a reclusive swamp. The structure of his face is oval, each individual feature more subtle than any of MP's – with the possible exception of his eyes, which I have yet to be fully acquainted. Overall, his imperfections make his regular features more prominent and rugged while still allowing a certain vulnerability to emanate – an openness that's absent from the faces of most men. Most men I know, anyway.

I take his pulse for a third time. Efforts like these are examples of my selflessness toward the preservation of mankind. In fact, I held off revising my work résumés all weekend to insure this guy's survival.

Subtle tracks of dirt embed the lines in his hands, emphasizing their musculature in all the right places. They're warm, calloused, beautiful. Damn, you know how I am about hands. My two fingertips-in-pulse-taking position feel for a beat. I'm crouched so close that instinctually, or maybe foolishly, I close my eyes and recall the day of the daisy. The breeze swipes my face, the heat of the afternoon sun lays its hand soundly across my back, and Time politely removes itself from this most original occasion. My eyelids reopen as I realize that if not for those hands, these two foolish men who call themselves brothers could pass for strangers.

Well, he's got a pulse, so I let go.

I'll cook this guy some chow before my run, but he better not take it the wrong way or want me to hang out and make small talk. Ugh. I'll be forced to watch those hands go from toast to juice to fork to napkin. I'll be a bloody mess on a day...no, on *thee* day I need to be the sole possessor of my convictions.

Ooh, the smell of burning butter jars me. I clumsily untangle my legs, slam my knee on the coffee table, kinda stifle an "ouch," and stumble toward the kitchen. My slick "combo" shakes and wakes him. He stretches – you know, one of those stretches that swiftly turns into a yawn that slides rapidly into a groan (sign language for "Hi, I'm up now"). I sense his half-open eyes before vanishing, so my famous spin habitually materializes. It'll look as if I'm coming out *from* the kitchen, I rationalize – and if not for beer sailing from bottle to blanket, it would've been foolproof.

My left hand slaps the wall as my body shifts its weight to the opposite hip (looking *very* cool and casual). What else? It's 9:00 A.M., I'm in one of my Kmart special: 3-for-1 boys 14L wife-beaters, army green yoga pants, and Corona in hand. I'm *cool* personified, right? Whatever.

"Hi."

He says nothing.

An alternative greeting occurs to me.

"Hey."

No response. He's staring at me as if I'm crazy, though. Now he's kicking his legs and rubbing the shit out of his eyes. No, this isn't a nightmare, asshole. Rub all you want, but I'm still going to be standing in front of you when you stop. *Or maybe he's just momentarily disoriented and all this stretching and facial massaging has nothing to do with me. That could be it,* but the silence, as always, is killing me.

"Would you like a cup of coffee?"

Silence.

Is this guy under gag order? A big old gulp of reliable beer kills a couple seconds of worrying about what to say next. Maybe *he* wants a beer. Stupid. Could've offered him a beer in the first place. I dive into the kitchen for beverages, receiving temporary solace from the shelter of the wall.

"Boy, that was some night the other night. Crazy!" I yell.

I'm getting dumb again. What is it with these two guys? One makes me feel as stupid as the other makes me act.

"Feel free to use the shower! If you want to."

Of course he'll want to, but I don't want him to feel forced. I'm all about free will. He should know that up front. Not that I care what he knows. I just don't want him to think that *I* think *he* thinks I'm difficult and demanding.

"You must be starving, due to that whole stealing-fighting-sleeping-thing you had going there."

It's also important for him to think that I have a genuine knack for placating serious situations. I mean, I certainly don't need him to think that I wouldn't recognize a serious situation if it blew my boyfriend on the living room floor the week before my birthday. Things like that don't bode well for the sensibility I feign in front of folk I've just met.

To put my belief of free will into action, a beer and a cup of coffee are set down on the table in front of him. And for the first time in the history of my cohabitation with coasters, one is placed under each beverage. His vocal capabilities have yet to resurface, so really I'm just using the coasters as a lame attempt to bide time.

Attempt fails.

"The coffee's decaf, by the way." An afterthought on my way to cover. "Hope you don't mind. We don't use caffeine around here. That shit'll kill you."

The third crepe hits his plate: Add fresh blueberries, roll, smear butter along top, sprinkle powdered sugar: Perfect.

"You like eggs? Everybody likes eggs. Pancakes? Well, they're not really pancakes – they're better. Well, not better, more interesting. Well, not more interesting as in pancakes are boring, 'cause they're not! These're simply – " Oh, *shut up*. "I think you'll like 'em!"

I cascade pepper sparingly over the omelet and set the shakers diagonally in the center of the table. Upon review, I decide a bud in a vase would really tickle my fancy, but I bet *this* brother will be okay with his five-course *petit dejeuner sans accoutrements*, at least for today.

Next move...my exit. My Corona and I meander in the direction of the door.

"So, like I said, you can shower, eat. I made you a little something. It's on the table, if you're interested. You can watch TV." I move the remote one inch closer to his beer (in case he didn't spot it – and because I'm a freak). "You can shower...oh, I said that. You know, whatever. I'm going for a run."

I chug the rest of my beer and realize, although I'm growing coolly comfortable in his deadened presence, the pre-workout beverage may require explanation. Some people don't understand the value of combining carbohydrates and exercise. He doesn't come off as one of those, but you never know.

"Carbs," I say, jiggling the empty bottle before setting it on the catch-all table thingy by the door. "Yep, going for a run. Figure I should do at least one thing to keep my free radical count down, so I picked running. It's fast, relatively painless, and plays an important role in the battle of the body parts."

The battle of the body parts? As a man, he hasn't a clue as to the nature of this saga. Must expound.

"You see, I haven't exactly been..." looking down at my breasts, "genetically gifted."

I'm truly disturbed that my breasts must be discussed with every Tom, Dick, and Billy I meet, but relieved – no, *ecstatic* – that they've been referenced without using the word *tits* this time (small miracle).

"So I have to work twice as hard as the average chick to keep my, um, butt in shape – to look proportional. Know what I'm saying?"

Please don't answer. Nodding would be all right, but please don't answer. Screw it, this guy's been stifled indefinitely. Just turn and exit.

I stare at the outline of his body, too nervous to make direct eye contact, too curious to turn away.

Just turn and exit already.

Billy did one nice thing for me – not for me, actually for a stranger he slammed into. MP did one nice thing before, too. I mean, it doesn't recall to memory, but I know it's what propelled me into my current saga. All I know about Billy is that he's the brother of MP. They share DNA. Billy shares DNA with a guy I dream of stabbing with rusty kitchen utensils on a daily basis. Is there anything else I really need to know?

"Turn And Exit, Annie," my Intuition orders, imitating my mother.

With keys in hand, I wrap my hand around the door knob.

"You've succeeded." Billy nonchalantly indicates.

"*What?*" My head whips back around.

"You've won your battle. Your ass; it's perfect."

And he says it like it's common knowledge. Like the weatherman says it's sunny and 70. Like a fact, absent room for opinion.

I'm speechless, but not entirely paralyzed, so I leap through my portal to the outside world, then exploit the aperture to hold myself upright. As I lean and breathe and fondle my own ass, an easy smile replaces the shock. I may even be blushing as I spring into a full-on run, foregoing my routine warm-up.

On a day like today, what would be the point? My heart is hardly at rest.

... and the Kiss

J'm rambling up the hallway and won't cop to paying a considerable amount of attention to where
I'm going – which is home. I mean, generally a considerable amount of attention isn't required to get
there. Also, my outside persona (woman on the verge of a
nervous breakdown) caters nicely to people kindly stepping
out of *my* way. So with a bag of disassembled dinner in one
hand, a six-pack of Bohemia in the other, a six-pack of Negro
Modelo in the other, and a stack of résumés in the other; I'm
jam-packed with fun.

While cruising and minding my own beeswax, a thunder-
ous rumble of angry unedited voices traipses into earshot. The
sound? An altercation restricted to a specific group of people
recognized by most as "family."

Please don't break anything (like a nose), I hope as I hug

the wall and forge toward the friendly fire. Then suddenly, BAM! Résumés fly everywhere. Everywhere!

MP has run into me – *as if he were me* – blindly confused, unapologetically scattered and in a raging panic. He catches me hard around the arms to stabilize the both of us, and thank God, 'cause the well-being of twelve beers were at stake. Résumés zigzag to the floor like flimsy tissues, blanketing our feet.

"I'll be back," he announces (but not exactly to me), then releases his grip and proceeds to stomp all over my flimsy white life. The bundle of tattered papers trails him like they're craving his stamp of approval. So, as he hop-scotches his way to the exit, his polarized feet attract each and every piece of card stock (*linen*, I might add – splurged on this lovely shade called *linen*), until they're all branded, all but one that gets crushed in the swinging glass door while attempting to tail him straight through it.

There are about a thousand excuses for me to cry right now:

It could be days (more likely weeks) before I psych myself up for another afternoon with a computer.

MP plowing into me like that was just plain scary.

Seeing MP hastily destroy my work without remorse or even awareness hurt my iddy-biddy feelings.

MP hastily destroying my work without remorse or even awareness is yet another sign from the Universe to leave him and I hate it when the Universe does that.

All the beers nearly met with their death; there's that.

There's a brother around the corner that could easily treat me the way MP just did.

There's a brother around the corner who may be violent, distraught or mentally disturbed. He may be popping pills or canvassing the joint for sharp objects.

There's a brother around the corner who surely requires immediate counseling, and I'm way too sober for that job.

There's a brother around the corner who might spot or hear my entrance when my immediate desire is to slide past him undetected.

But above all, it's noon and I have yet to shed a tear. I'm obscurely behind schedule.

If you don't think these are tear-worthy events, tell that to the stock boy at Ralph's who dialed the suicide hotline the last time I was PMSing and they were out of Chunky Monkey. Nine hundred and ninety reasons to go, but you're probably over it, so I'll bring this particular stream of bullshit to a close.

I hold my breath (an attempt to feel invisible) and quietly shuffle into a room cluttered with a vast collection of fresh and ripe combative energy.

His back is to me, head bowed – a chance to dart into the bedroom *or* to ask if he's okay. As the former choice moves guiltily into finalist status, Billy slams a book against the wall, then falls onto the couch, cupping his head in his hands. A slackly hung picture of MP and me tumbles to the floor. Big surprise.

"I hate that prick." He exhales a phrase that should be inducted into our Hall of Slogans, then wipes the corner of his eye with the cuff of his thermal and regurgitates the idiom. *"I hate that prick!"* Then he catches my image. "Sorry," he snaps, and regretfully drops his head back into those beautiful hands.

Well, shit. I'm the Freaker-Outer, not the Freaker-Outer-Fixer.

Evaluating...exhaling...debating...

"Master Prick," I finally say, correcting him.

"What?"

Billy's eyes target mine.

"M-P. We like to refer to him by his full name around here: *Master Prick.*"

Billy nods slowly. "Empty."

"What?"

"We used to call him Empty, *M-T,* instead of MP. Because he was completely devoid of emotion."

"We?"

"Me and Mom."

Spontaneity takes over. I pull a Foster and look at him like he's got seventeen heads.

"Not to his face," he explains.

"Right."

My head drops, a smile intended for my feet gets lost in the bag of groceries. Now would be the perfect time to put the food and drinks away. He's soothed; we had a moment. Exit while the exiting's good. A choice rare to character envelops me and I adhere to the whim of my intuition and scram.

"You want a beer?" I shout from the kitchen, busting one open for myself.

"No, thanks, Rosie. I'm going to head out for a bit."

"You do know my name's Annie, right?" My laugh dissolves into a tiny string of chuckles as the groceries find their designated homes. "That's the second time I've heard you call me Rosie. I mean, you can call me Rosie if you want to. Maybe I remind you of someone you know named Rosie, but the name is officially Annie. I know that much."

When I duck back out of the fridge, Billy is standing virtually on top of me; my shoulder blades impulsively hit the wall. And you know what I'm going to do? Patent a rearview mirror designed specifically for refrigerator doors because *startling the fuck out of Annie while she's dealing with perishables* is really getting old. So this guy, the anomalous other brother, has me cornered and rendered inanimate.

"The night we were *formally* introduced," he starts, ignoring my shock, "You were standing on the balcony; that spicy hair all tousled; cheeks flushed…probably from an evening saturated with spirits." His body angles closer. His voice dips, resonates scratchy. "And that shirt draped over your body, streaked ruby by the light, blowing gently from the breeze, moving like waves over and away from your legs and back again…" A grin takes shape as he revisits the scene. "You looked like a rose."

And just when I think he's going to walk away, he takes one steady step forward and immerses his entire being into my zone (you know, that-very-personal-space zone). He raises a hand, catches some curls. One of them winds delicately about a finger and springs back as his callused fingertips swoop softly, diagonally, down my cheek. I study him. He draws a delicate trail to that space at the base of the throat designed to cup a charm on a choker, then fixates on it, sketching and caressing its outline. He's so considerate to ease into eye contact. How he knows that's not my forte, I can't begin to grasp. The time can only be gauged by heartbeats. There's maybe three to go before he looks up, and but a single strand of hair (the one he separated from the pack) to save me from full disclosure.

One, two…my God, his eyes are black. They're black, like those flat silk-surfaced stones glistening at the bottom of a koi pond. His pupils are discernible solely due to our pre-kiss proximity.

"You *look* like a rose."

He breathes this truth right into me as his lips merge into mine. A hand glides around my neck. I'd shiver if I thought I could move. We maintain this perfect union as I drown in his scent. When I'm finally blue (sans any need for resuscitation), Billy opens his mouth and intertwines his lips with mine. One sweet stroke of the tongue concludes his kiss. A daring finale – mostly because it was his finish, and not the conception of an act soon to be arrested through bullshit rationale.

I guess he left via the door. Don't think he vanished into thin air. Can't imagine I dreamt up the entire incident.

He must have had a previous engagement.

Me? I've got nothing pressing. So I close my eyes and let the memory multiply.

Help Wanted?

His mommy always told him that if you want something bad enough, you'll be left wanting it. But if you believe that the thing that stirs you awake at night *is* yours and live in a state of grace and thanks as if you already possess it, your highest dream will escort itself right into your reality.

Mom also instilled a number of other ideologies:

Respect your elders, unless they're irredeemable assholes.

Family always comes first, unless they're *total* irredeemable assholes.

Sometimes kindness is the best policy and honesty should be the last resort.

Don't talk back to me – ever.

If you do something wrong, don't get caught. And…

If you're smoking the best stash on the block, have a block party – *'cause karma's holding all your aces.*

Billy's had no problem sharing any primo herb that's happened to drop onto the path of his mercurial travels; that axiom's been adopted with humble obedience. He has, though, had difficulty bidding adieu to an enduring "familiar" reality for this supposed "illusory" existence filled with granted desires. Up until now, that is.

Because this week, an angel; an apparition in the shape of a skittish, self-doubting, borderline-lush, beyond-the-line-neurotic redhead made him cognizant that the fairy tale starts now. He simply has to seize it. As a former expert in the field of duck-and-dodge when it comes to life's ludicrous responsibilities, he finds himself now galloping merrily toward them.

Raised by a woman who traded in guilt for passion the day she was born, he was instilled with the idea that everything happens for an absolute reason, making it really simple for him to rationalize twenty-three years as the brother of MP into the reason he met Annie. He sees in her the boy he used to be. Sees her glimmer, dim as it is. Despite popular belief, she's not in need of a net, he postulates, just some good lovin' from the right man. And Billy's decided to obligate his soul in that direction. To be that guy. To be with her.

On behalf of his mother, destiny, this sunny day, and, of course, his penis, "Life of Billy – " a life he's been postponing the commencement of, for like a decade – is officially open for business.

Confident, charged, and drunk with an enthusiasm for a future he's in the mood to nab, he saunters down one of a hundred L.A. boardwalks and stumbles upon the sign: HELP WANTED.

The day just keeps getting better.

He steps inside a small dark bar: Anywhere America.

Three faded dart boards, two scuffed pool tables, a wobbly foosball table, and a dingy jukebox total the accessories of this establishment. Oh, there is one more counterpart of sorts. There's the owner, a big spooky guy named Joe who's dressed like a butcher with Popeye forearms and big spooky everything else. And judging by the way he's juggling two keggers, he's very likely a former member of the WWF who never got his last hoorah.

Billy moseys on over to the jukebox, blows some dust from the corners of its silver buttons and strategically selects, "I Shot the Sheriff," "Don't be Cruel," and "Sexual Healing." Billy figures the first two will cover the musical gamut. As for "Sexual Healing," anybody who knows anything about music should revere it like they would the National Anthem. Plus, music cheers everybody up, right? Not that big spooky guy needs cheering up. Possibly the frown is a permanent result of having one too many Frankensteiners pulled on him in the ring. Could be, but it certainly can't hurt to try and turn that frown upside down. This is Billy's first thought. His second is that only a true dork could come up with the phrase "turn that frown upside down," and he temporarily feels awkward and *nine* for having had it.

He stands opposite this fifty-year-old bear of a man (on the patron side of the bar) and starts singing along to Bob Marley.

"Problem, buddy?" Joe growls.

Be smooth, Billy convinces himself. He smiles just long enough to gain the undivided attention of the formidable being, but not in a good way. He loses the grin.

"No, no problems, sir. I wanted to inquire about the position. I've done plenty of bartending. Yep. Served *a-llllotta* drinks." He mime's spinning a fifth in his palm and splashing a shot into a glass, a move that immediately works to his disadvantage.

"Plenty, huh? What are you, *nine?*" Joe rests an empty keg on his shoulder.

No, I'm not nine, Billy thinks. I just feel it, and it's an obscure drag that you picked up on that.

"Okay, maybe I haven't mixed plenty of drinks, but an ample amount because we used to have Jazz Night at our house when we were growing up." Billy stuffs his fists into his pockets, sways to and fro on his heels. "Yeah, Mom would break out a little Stoly's and a lot of Ella and my brother and I would grab the olives, shakers, bongo drums, her favorite tambourine, and…it was…great…"

He fades, fearing he just rambled like a girl, or worse, like a girl trying to conceal a long-standing crush. To shake away a mass of unwelcome nerves, Billy yanks a fist from his pocket and instinctively taps the refrain to "They Can't Take That Away From Me" on the counter. The move pulls him briefly and contentedly back into one of his family's more memorable Jazz Nights.

Our friendly bar owner interrupts, "Sorry, buddy, you're a day late and a dollar short. Just hired a bartender. Forgot about that sign."

Joe jumps over the bar and tears it down.

"What about the kitchen? I've been known to cook a mean…" He scans the place. The pub seems to be of Irish descent. "Corned beef hash."

"Don't need the help."

Billy's head drops along with his heart. Unaware of the full influence his modest, endearing character has on others (those super powers), he decides upon a discreet, sullen exit. Then Joe blindsides him with an act of kindness.

"You want a beer?"

He cracks a Budweiser before Billy even answers.

"Sure."

Joe treats the Bud like a puck and his bar like a shuffleboard as he eyeballs the distance and shoves the beer toward Billy. It comes to a perfect, faithful halt directly in front of him. Billy watches as Joe basks in the splendor of his bottle-sliding abilities. Billy's dually impressed. He toasts Joe's athletic achievement, then ceremoniously downs the first quarter of it.

Relaxed somewhat, it's only minutes before Billy's creative wheels start spinning. Music and alcohol are notorious breeders of many things, *more music* ranking in the top two of his list.

"Excuse me? Do you have a pen I could borrow, please?" he asks while reaching for the official rock star's manuscript – a cocktail napkin.

The phone rings. Joe grabs it, sails a pen over his shoulder.

"Yeah? Yeah. So your girlfriend dumped you. I'll send you some fucking flowers. What's that got to do with your set tonight?" He pauses. "How the hell do you survive in L.A. without a car?"

Billy looks up from his budding composition as an agitated Joe continues.

"Oooh, she drove you everywhere. That's real nice." Joe's eyes roll up behind his lids and back down again with added edge. "Oh? You think you'll have another girlfriend by the weekend? Well, you know what's easier than a musician finding a girlfriend? Then what looks like actual steam flies out of his nose. *"No, it's not a trick question – a bar finding a musician!"*

Slam.

Joe checks his watch, shakes his head, grumbles, "Just wasted thirty seconds of my life with that idiot."

An obvious light bulb, accompanied by a flashing neon sign that reads: "Subject must be broached cautiously" looms over Billy's head.

"Excuse me? Um, I'm a musician, sir. Yep. You know… singer, songwriter, guitarist."

"You don't say? Don't suppose you got a girlfriend?" Joe demands with a cynical sideways glance.

"No, not quite, but I live just up the street. Walking distance."

"No such thing in this city."

"But there is. I'm at – "

"You take drugs?" Joe interrupts, thank God. Billy was blanking on the address.

"No, sir."

"You a criminal?"

"No."

Joe steps closer. Billy sits rigid while Joe uses "evil-stare-tactic" as truth serum. As Billy anticipates, it works.

"Not anymore. I made a promise to my mother."

"She a criminal?"

"No." Then he reluctantly confesses, "She's dead, sir."

Joe maintains "evil-stare-tactic." And Billy realizes that when you could pass for Cro-Magnon Man at a glance and handle kegs of beer like gallons of milk, "evil-stare-tactic" is the only approach you'll ever need to get whatever you want from whomever you want. Billy is as static as a sculpture as he submits to Joe's evaluation for whatever else it may disclose.

"It just turned into your lucky day. Be here tonight at 10:00 sharp."

Billy springs from the seat and extends a stiff arm yielding a handshake that explodes with genuine gratitude; a handshake snagged from that moment in time when one man grants the other permission for his daughter's hand in marriage; a handshake Joe had filed away under "extinct."

"Thank you, Sir. Thank you so much."

Joe releases his grip and turns away. Billy wonders if he

just saw him blush from the unforeseen surge of vulnerability they just shared.

"Joe, the name's Joe. Now get the hell outta here." Joe looks over his shoulder, waves Billy away.

"Thank you, Joe. I'm Billy Meadows. See you at 10:00 sharp."

And he gives Joe a thumbs-up as he takes a step back.

"Hey, the beer's not free until you're technically hired. And it ain't free then, either."

"Right. Sorry." Billy smiles wide and slams some crumpled bills on the counter, then backtracks and waves.

"And don't play anything that hurts my ears." Joe's hands jiggle loose on either side of his ears to demonstrate a reaction to loud, frustrating clamor. "I don't like it when my ears hurt. Get *real* moody when my ears hurt."

"Right. I wouldn't think of it."

As Billy reaches the bulky wooden door, Joe punctuates one final thought, "Don't forget your guitar!"

Billy's smile gains attitude upon hearing that and releases a bellow bold enough to squeeze through the door before it slams in his face. It sounds terribly exaggerated, that laugh, but the truth is, it isn't. That's the best punch line he's heard in a while.

Don't forget your guitar. The words reverberate over and over, like an echo in a canyon. That's quite a joke.

Too bad the joke's on me, he thinks.

He counts a ten, three fives and three ones. If he could reach into the reflection of the glass and swipe that cash, too, there'd be fifty-six bucks. Still not enough for a guitar, even with the imaginary dough. But his reflection has proven good for one thing; making him feel foolishly aware of his predicament.

"Oh, brother." He leans in to erase the image staring back, his head tapping the glass. "Oh, brother," and the subtle bang-

ing takes on a steady rhythm, leaving a more prominent imprint on the glass with every consecutive rap.

He closes his eyes, bucks up, stares deep into the glass
one last time. Too close for his own image to stare mockingly
back, he sees instead his brother, MP, inside the store stroking
a beautiful guitar with one hand and something close to *Miss
California* with the other.

"Oh…*brother?*"

Both hands press flatly, firmly onto the glass; the tip of his
nose joins them. He's back at the pet shop window, immobile
and desperate, begging for the little Lab he knows he'll never
get. When tears turn to anger, it'll be time to bolt. That's what
he told himself then, that's what he's repeating now.

The antics in-store are as follows:

"Can you hear the wood vibrate, man? This one here's
your girl. She's a real beauty. Mm-hmm." Rob, our laid back
sales representative, trails off, mm-hmming to himself and
bobbing his head in the direction of the Blonde. "Mm-hmm,
Mm-hmm."

MP eyes Rob, a guy he quickly deems to be the store's
couldn't-give-a-shit-less sales dude, then surmises quite readily that this guy probably wants nothing more out of life than
to regularly play guitar, occasionally get laid, and perpetually
remain stoned. This efficient evaluation drives him even faster
into the doggedly patronizing prick he so enjoys portraying. A
little labor, combined with some sly verbal demeaning, is just
what this dude needs. And MP loves discerning who needs a
good kick in the pants almost as much as the thrill he derives
from executing it.

"I like it. Sounds warm, has a built-in EQ. How much,
Robert?" MP asks in the tone of a snob, seeing clearly that the
name tag says "Rob."

MP's also aware of the price of the instrument; it's dangling from one of the machine heads. And, of course, the built-in EQ is an obvious feature, but the technical jargon is spouted forth on behalf of impressing the Blonde.

"Oh, dude, this goes for a smooth $1479, plus tax, you know. She's a steal, man. And – " He takes a break from talking as if to think, or breathe, or both, or neither. "And I'll throw in the case – red velvet interior."

Rob raises a brow toward The Blonde, a hazel eye becomes visible for the first time.

"Okay, Robert, buddy. See if you can find me something similar in tone but half the price."

"But I've already brought you like – "

"Go see if you can do it, Rob, my man."

"O...kay."

Rob mashes his eyebrows together in the middle.

MP chuckles at the gesture, a clear byproduct of frequent confusion. He motions with his own eyes to move along, so Rob strolls deep into the store in search of another guitar.

"And I'd like it in blonde!" MP yells, then turns to The Blonde, hiding a hand up her skirt. "I really like 'em blonde."

"Are you *thee* Prince Charming? Because you're so sweet buying a guitar for your little brother. The best men are always taken, *which is why I have to date them.*"

She sings that last part as if she's sporting pigtails, then takes a freshly painted bubble gum pink fingernail and runs it right up his rod. MP cringes with delight.

Billy watches in paralyzed awe as two men who are visually, intellectually, most likely religiously, and undoubtedly politically worlds apart work feverishly to wow Miss California with their vast knowledge of this obscure enigma of an instrument that certain less annoying, low-browed types refer to as "a guitar." Man, Freud threw parties over shit like this.

Billy feels for the poor sales guy, knowing his chance of

getting into Miss California's pants is as likely as the proverbial Hell freezing over. And he particularly bums for him because he knows full well that *the other guy*, his brother (having already been in her pants even as recently as a few minutes ago), could still get that blonde to blow him even if he had blood spewing out of his eyes, worms crawling out of his mouth, and his dick ripped off and hand-stitched accidentally back onto his elbow.

Billy shakes his head in an attempt to shoo that last visual. But the thing is, he knows MP, knows how smoothly he operates with women. Also, every night wasn't Jazz Night at Chez Meadows; that he knows most of all.

At the very least, Billy's relieved that his "figurative tears" evaporated back around the finger-fucking incident between guitar number four and guitar number five.

As he grows more lost in thought, he refocuses his gaze through the sweat-smudged, breath-smeared window and spots his brother staring right back at him. After a delayed anchored panic, he bolts.

Rob returns with another guitar.

MP lunges at it.

"I'll take it."

"Don't you wanna feel her vibrate between – "

"No. Ring it up. There's someplace I have to be. Just ring it up now, Robert."

MP's sudden frenzy is palpable to all near-dwellers.

"All right, dude, sure thing. Be cool."

Rob momentarily picks up pace. But as MP helplessly watches, coming slightly undone, the-couldn't-give-a-shit-less sales dude slows to a snail's pace and lackadaisically rings up the instrument like he's chosen to dwell in the sweet satisfaction of MP's current turmoil.

And MP can do nothing but wipe his sweaty palms down the sides of his pants, and wait.

The Joy of Cooking... and Scheming

O kay, if I were bound and blindfolded I couldn't be traveling more leisurely about the kitchen. Bound and blindfolded? Mmm. Nasty ideas are bouncing all over my little brain. Stop it. No wonder it's taking fifteen minutes to peel and dice a single carrot. Although, in my own defense, it is a *really big* carrot. *Stop that*. I'm such a guy.

They say cooking is meditative. But I've always appreciated the spell that *eating's* induced in others more than any pleasure the task of preparation has provoked in me. But today is new; I'm lazy in love with the art of it. And I'm daydreaming of a whirlwind romance of magnificently ridiculous proportions. I mean, if you're gonna dream; might as well make it ridiculous.

So, once upon a time, Billy and I traveled to far-off lands, became one on white silk sands under the painted moonlight on a beach in Morocco.

Then we danced until dawn in gay Paris as a tornado of auburn lights, drumbeats, and unburdened faceless figures spun about us. And then we made love all afternoon as drizzle caressed our chateau window. The flavor of our hot bodies working so seamlessly together sunk forever into the room's velvety, jade sofa, then branded the silk damask bedspread, and eventually left the Oriental rug separating bed from sofa in frayed disarray. He set a new curve on the stamina scale that particular excursion.

After that came mad, passionate animal sex outside dirty rest stops and inside musty Motel 8s as we drove cross-country the summer after we wed.

And finally, we were missionaries, stealing intimate moments on earthy floors of abandoned box houses and in cargo spaces on rickety planes while we forged across South America playing redeemers to those less fortunate.

Basically, we saved each other, saved the planet, and screwed everywhere conceivable.

But by the stroke of midnight, a shoe cracks on a nail protruding from the carpet rail dividing Eden from Abyss: a sign that the time has come to slither back into the damp, pungent cave – my bedroom. It's time to remove my ball gown – sterling satin splashed with pearls – and slip out of the one unscathed glass slipper that's useless now for lack of a partner.

As I lie stiff under crooked half-stolen covers next to a creature that crawls close to the ground and is cold to the touch, not unlike myself, the fanciful summoned fable of love (as any love affair worth remark) takes a turn for the doomed.

Daisy or no daisy, Billy is, after all, the brother of the man I loathe. And it should be no shock that they share commonalities in regard to character, their attitude toward women and, ultimately, a wily disdain for me. Logic could have presumed this outcome, but as an alternative, I commit to being stunned by the realization: Call me Stupid.

Eventually, even in this fantasy-gone-jagged, my only option is to leave. But I'm not an easy leaver. So, instead, the relationship disintegrates day by day until we cultivate an actual sickness from the sight of each other. Then one bleak morning, a morning that's somehow murkier than its myriad of predecessors, I awake…and Billy's gone.

I'm idle with hopelessness. But time moves unforgivingly forward along with my embittered indifference toward love, men, and my own dismal destiny until the memories of this romance couldn't replace the space a whisper takes. And Billy becomes a mere acquaintance from a past life. And that, at least, is sufferable.

It's pathetic really; even in my dreams I lose the guy.

You know what I need to do? Control, curb, or, better yet, destroy my parasite-like attraction to every mysterious creep that demonstrates an ounce of kindness. I need to stop tossing my whole world at the feet of strangers before any real dialogue has been exchanged.

I am desperation personified, conning myself into believing that any sweet gesture from a male passerby aligns them further with this lifelong conception of the prince inside my head. It's like I decide who they are for them and don't allow them to stray by rationalizing any move that doesn't suit the fantasy.

In truth, I never really know them at all – these men who have traipsed through my life. Some have skirted around the periphery, leaving me famished for affection. Others stampeded right over me like a bull, then vanished before the dry dust settled and the bruises surfaced.

Stop thinking.

I reach for a cucumber and release a sigh that is widely indicative of post-coital festivities. Because, although Billy and I didn't last, didn't even stand a chance, my active imagination had a blast on the world tour. And we were gorgeous in the beginning, boy. Just gorgeous.

As I lay this phallic *edible* object on the cutting board and speedily dip my sharp edge in and out of its waxy green skin, creating tiny uniform geometric discs, a unique rose-combo-wildflower bouquet is thrust in my face. This adversely produces an inhalation specifically reserved for pre-rape encounters.

A situation that would normally have reached heights of hyperventilative proportions is speedily diffused as my senses are captured and calmed by the aroma and beauty of this unprecedented batch of flowers.

Adrenaline surges through my body and surfaces as a giggle.

"Okay, now you're getting a little carried away. I almost believed you earlier with that whole Rosie story."

My face falls into the plushy eclectic arrangement, eager to swim in its fragrance.

"What are you talking about, sweetie? A *rose* story? I never give you flowers."

The pitch of MP's voice shoots into my brain, then slithers down my spine. Or, in my lingo; he startles the living shit out of me. My hand jerks and the knife splinters haphazardly into the cucumber, leaving it in the shape of something a first-year culinary student would be embarrassed to present to his mother. And, oh yeah, sliced into my index finger, too.

I shove the blood-spotted finger into my mouth and turn to face my peculiar suitor.

"That's what I mean…you can't just – out of the blue – buy

me flowers. It's creepy. I got creeped." The seductive bundle draws me back. "They're gorgeous."

They are gorgeous. I adore flowers. Sometimes ache for them, like a journal desires a memory or an old man craves a nap. Can't imagine what I've done to warrant them twice in a week's time.

MP kisses me.

I'm not receptive.

But I'm not receptive because I was making a big stand on behalf of all women, and a stupid batch of weeds won't make up for months of emotional mistreatment. And it's not because I'm on the verge of breaking up with him. I'm *not* receptive because I was simply distracted, prey to the charm flowers possess. They could obliterate every bad day ever survived with MP and every other man – if I felt compelled to bestow upon them that power. But in truth, it'd be nice if they'd just erase two long years of tears and tummy aches. If only temporarily.

So I'm not the woman whose greatest concern is to rid the planet of sexism – just a girl who'd love for every yesterday to escape permanently from memory, and fool enough to let some silly flowers hasten the process.

MP doesn't realize this as he proceeds to address "the bigger issue."

"What? Look, I haven't exactly been living up to my… Prince Charming reputation lately. *These*," he studies the bouquet to make his point but without any genuine regard. "are a token of my appreciation for the space you've given me. It's been an incredibly challenging year. You know that, girl."

His words fall somewhere in the vicinity of what one would consider an apology. But in case this half-ass attempt (free of the words "I'm sorry") doesn't qualify, he pulls out one final trick: his dazzling smile. "Now clean up this mess so I can take you out to dinner."

Here's an example of one nice thing he's done – that nice thing I couldn't think of earlier – that one nice thing that can throw me off course for months. Still, I'm leery.

He opens his hand, the flowers pour onto the counter, then that same hand sweeps around to the small of my back and presses me into him.

We kiss. And this, quite frankly, is easier than talking for the time being.

Billy enters. Stops. Then he studies the single rose dangling in his grip. Impulsively, it's stuffed into his pocket like crumpled old bills and a chunk of change.

Closed-eye kissing has never been my thang. And thank God, because as I pan the room, Billy is presently "going on." Abruptly, I disengage. Strangely, MP doesn't detect that as odd – which I find odd – but also a relief. I don't need to be branded "the bad guy" when all this is said and done. I especially don't need MP whittling down the pitiful two-year disintegration of our relationship to one meaningless moment in the kitchen with a practical stranger. And he would do that, too.

These two dudes turn and look at each other as if they don't speak the same language – probably the most profound observation of my life up to that point. I don't recognize its profundity, of course. What's clear is that a lot more is going on than meets any of our eyes or understandings, but no one's quite ready for those suspicions.

So they're in the midst of some kind of intra-family mental telepathy thing when I glance down and notice MP's been holding a guitar in the hand that wasn't gripping the bouquet (or more recently, my ass).

Huh?

Wow. These two have developed a severe case of beady eye-*itis*.

Wait. MP just looked down at the guitar he's holding.

Now Billy glances at it.

Now they look back at each other.

Now MP nods and leans forward so that the guitar is within Billy's grasp.

Billy remains motionless.

Still not moving.

Wait, he just nodded back. He reaches for the guitar.

They make the exchange.

They go back to that mental telepathy thing.

Now Billy pats the guitar and then nods.

Now MP nods in agreement.

Now they nod again in unison and twist their lips into what could loosely be construed as closed-mouth smiles.

The tension in the room dissipates. Sort of.

Ladies and gentlemen, we have just witnessed another precious moment in the history of male bonding.

And also, ladies and gents, I've never been more relieved that my pants don't house a penis.

Men: They really only have two emotional avenues to traverse when communicating among themselves. They can react by *not* reacting – or they can jump on each other like members of a socially accepted gay football team that just won the Lotto. These two guys, like countless before them, know better than to dive on top of each other for this particular shining male moment. But they both seem temporarily at ease. A nice start for two strangers who call themselves brothers. And a strange one that leaves me curious.

That guitar holds hidden meaning, undisclosed scheming. Its manifestation is as unlikely as, well…flowers.

The blindfold that has faithfully braved me into the majority of tomorrows is growing frayed and sheer like my favorite pair of underwear.

Something's definitely up with Billy and MP.

Mostly, something new and unusual is up with me.

I reach into a drawer for a bandage to protect the one boo-boo in this room that's visible to the naked eye.

Ritalin, Chips, and Salsa

My family moved from Minnesota to Arizona when I was a kid. I'd like to say we were *all* shell-shocked to go from snowballs to tumbleweeds, but in truth, it was only me. Dad's biggest hurdle was re-acclimating from the *Daily News* to the *Phoenix Gazette*; he pouted for about a day and a half. Mom fixated rigidly on maintaining her Midwestern style of living and dress. Our peach stucco house, the twelfth in a row of forty-two matching peach stucco houses lined up like Dominoes, was an interior mishmash of macramé wall hangings, plastic plants, ceramic roosters, and those goddamned porcelain ballerinas. It has remained absent of terra cotta pots, Kokopellis, and desert driftwood to this day. She also clung to that Minnesota accent like she did her virginity.

Everyone knew it was gone, or should be, but erroneous nostalgia kept insisting on recalling it to memory, especially during liquid lunches and mordantly overdone holidays.

But my life…was over. Left a school I adored with an abundance of buddies crucial to my adolescent development, but chiefly, I was without my lifeline – cousin Fos. The move separated us for the next four years. The bitch – Mom – basically made mincemeat out of my perfectly choreographed tree-climbing, doll-decapitating, tap-dancing existence. And I was pissed. There was no other choice than to act out. I screamed, whined, threatened to hate her, vowed to run away, you know…pulled the basic seven-year-old temper-tantrum crap. I also may have spray-painted some of her favorite heels a lovely shade of farmer green, broken a ballerina or two (or ten), and regretfully poisoned our dog, Scruffy, one night when we (Scruff and I) decided to rid the house of Mom's second favorite pastime: chocolate. After that, it came down to Ritalin or bust. And there were days, too many to count, that I couldn't bring myself to ingest that vicious "Annie alternator" without appropriate incentive…and chips & salsa were my Southwestern weakness.

To this day I can't pass a Mexican restaurant without hearing the overly-enunciated phrase beating through my brain: *Sweetie, if you take the goddamned Ritalin, you'll get your goddamned chips & salsa. Now grab your mother a cigarette and quit making me nuts.* Then she'd dig inside the pill bottle and snatch one of those white chalky villains between two blood-red fingernails filed pencil-point sharp, lodge it between my tonsils, then crack a Coke and shove half of that down my throat (which even then I knew defeated the purpose). And off we'd go to spend a buck ninety-nine on chips & salsa and eighteen more dollars on four Margaritas for her and a second Coke for me.

I said it before and I'll say it again: Caffeine – that shit'll kill you.

Had I been aware of a little phenomenon called "retrospect," that fabulous concept big people abuse to explain inexcusable past behavior, I wouldn't have made such a stink. I mean, look at me now – a proud card-carrying prescription-drug-o-philiac. But how was I to know my system would take to Ritalin like a sunset to crimson?

A few years lapsed before I acquired the gumption to secretly deplete the house of Mom's first love: booze. But by then, I was too angry and she was too listless to catch up with me.

So approximately every other full moon, when our minds (MP and mine) teetered on the brink of eruption via guilt and our bodies clung to a dizzy exhaustion specific to hate siphoning out any remaining trace of humanity toward each other, *or more literally*: When I'm one floundering rational thought away from grabbing a paring knife and scalping him in his sleep, then drawing a nice warm bath, popping thirty Zanax, and using that same bloody edge to slice lengthwise into my femoral artery while "Silent All These Years" plays faintly on repeat, MP and I hit the town, get creamed, and fake nice. And we really live it up, too, knowing it'll be sixty more days before we're compelled to reassess whether to stay in the ring for another round or exit in a fashion to be retold as some botched *seriocomedy* that would be cataloged directly between the departure of Romeo and Juliet and the exodus of Sid and Nancy.

So, here I am, out for Mexican, brothers all around. I pensively force the imminent breakup plan to remain present in some layer of my mind, like one makes themselves sit up straight on a day when all efforts are already focused on simply sitting up at all. Meanwhile, I concurrently *fend off* another plague: memories.

.Mother's reprimands spiral out from every recess of my

brain *not* housing the phrase: *"End relationship with long-term
live-in and end it now."* Of course, the alcohol is slowly dilut-
ing both her bickering and a bit of logic. And so is Billy, who's
here, I've concluded, because life is that interesting – don't ever
let it fool you into thinking otherwise. Boredom is a rest stop,
not a residence. If you dare dwell in careless contentment or
take refuge in shoddy remorse, life will inevitably happen as
it always does and screw up your comfy pattern of perpetual
nothingness.

Take me for example: Just a week ago I had lost my job,
perfected a mild drinking problem, conceded to stay with
domineering, disappointing, disloyal boyfriend, and succumbed to the notion that there's enough will left in me to get
my ass out of bed in the morning, but not enough to accom-
plish much else beyond that. And now, one small week later:
Still don't have a job; the drinking problem's graduated from
mild to moderate; I've decided to leave domineering, disappointing, disloyal boyfriend; and have recently accumulated
enough will to not only get my ass out of bed, but to also "bluff"
accomplishing oodles of other tasks in the hopes of impressing
some guy named Billy. Why? I can't begin to imagine. Revenge
maybe, boredom, curiosity, defiance. Maybe it's love. Maybe
I'm just plain twisted.

We lick salt off our fists and slam our fourth shot.

"We met two years ago in the Bahamas. He was searching
for the woman of his dreams – "

"And found the one of my nightmares," MP smirks.

I crinkle my nose.

"Same difference."

I love that everyone I've ever met, befriended, slept with,
dated, lived with, lived by, shared in the same gene and/or car-
pool with also loves tequila. This clearly validates the theory
that like attracts like, but not necessarily in a good way.

"And I was on a break from school."

A lemon wedge bursts between my teeth.

MP tosses back a Margarita. Ice spreads over his flawless visage. A cuff catches residual droplets rolling toward his jaw line. When he's drinking he sometimes joins the rest of the world – playing the role of a carefree slob with startling precision.

"A permanent break. You were on a permanent break, sweetie."

"Fine." I play along, getting way too buzzed to suffocate the tingly just yet. "I'm a few credits shy of my master's."

A reluctant admission.

"Really?" Billy follows with the exact wrong question that everybody follows with. "In what?"

"Never mind."

MP sits back.

"Psych," he says, then leans forward and rests a salt-sprinkled grin on a set of knuckles, anxiously anticipating his little brother's reaction.

Well, the only thing bigger than Billy's initial shock is the secondary effort he produces to try and bury it. *And MP is thrilled.*

Familiar with this response to the point of boredom, I exhale, "Oh, please, I'm a textbook psych major."

MP smugly adds, "The most fucked-up group of people you'll ever meet."

"Second only to tortured musicians," I fire back.

Sometimes our banter flows so smoothly, it feels rehearsed.

"Your little brother asked how we met. Do...you... mind?"

"No, no, I love this story. Just let me grab a drink to get through it." MP flags down the waitress. "Hi. We'll need three more shots of Silver and another pitcher of Margaritas. Do you two want anything?"

We laugh. We can't help it.

"What? Can't a man enjoy a couple twelve drinks while he's forced to relive the Beginning of the End?"

This *is* the beginning of the end. *Do you not see my intent? Can you not taste it through this bit, this act, this routine that seems way too normal*?!

That's what I'd like to say, but what comes out is, "I don't see a leash around your neck."

I believe it's easier to be left than to be the leaver. I wish he'd just get up and walk out – no explanation, no regret, and no money for the tab. Please don't make this harder by paying the tab. Just get up and go.

But MP bypasses my lame comment entirely and holds up a finger to help direct the tray of shots that were already barreling our way. They're distributed. The brothers slam theirs. I spin mine between thumb and middle finger and revert back to story.

"Anyway, we were *both* wasted out of our minds, and we were at some dance club."

"The Bamboo Shack."

"Good memory."

"I know my dance clubs."

"That you do."

MP pauses to relish in the glory of knowing his dance clubs pretty much the way he relishes in the glory of knowing everything else.

I turn to Billy to close the first in a series of *Twisted Tales of the Life and Times of What's-His-Name and Yours-Freaking-Truly*.

"So your bastard of a brother asked me to dance. And by the end of the night…" the shot stings my palate, swims down my throat hot and prickly. "I was madly in lust."

142

"By the end of the night you were puking in my lap!"

"That came after the lust, actually, as a direct result of it."

Which we all find hilarious because that's how it works when one divulges intimate information to the point of awkwardness. Laughter is by and large the immediate by-product. And let me tell ya, there's a whole lotta laughter going on here tonight.

Through staggering residual snorts and snickers, Billy surmises cynically, "Match made in Heaven."

Quite fitting; the newcomer's a fast learner. I make an unlikely, anti-controversial choice to change the subject before anyone announces where in fact the match of What's-His-Name and Yours-Freaking-Truly was more likely spawned.

"So, did you inherit the gift of groove, too, Billy?"

"I may have a move or two." He relaxes into a sweet shy smile, then darts his eyes at MP. "No thanks to you."

"Don't tell me somebody finally let you lead in juvie?" he teases.

Their lips form into identical half-moons, mirrored images that reveal their shared bloodline for the very first time.

"Oh, man, it was beautiful. Mom taught us the rumba, the cha-cha, tango, salsa, swing, you name it. But William here didn't appreciate it like I did."

"That's 'cause you never let me lead!"

"Not my problem. Somebody had to be the chick. If the shoe fits…"

MP throws his hands in the air, waives responsibility.

"If the fucking *shoe* fits? You're like thirty years older than me, asshole. You could've cut me some slack."

"Slack never made anyone president." MP slyly remarks. "Where's the gratitude?"

"Well, then, before I get too ripped and divulge my campaign strategy, I'm gonna kick it." Billy stands and bows to MP as if he's royalty, then downs the rest of his beer. And just when I feel as though I'm no longer in the room, Billy adds, "But before I go, I'd like to ask the lady to dance."

"Be my guest, little brother."

MP relaxes back in the booth, stretches his arms and attempts feebly to pull off amused. And I realize that they knew I was here all along. I didn't disappear; this whole show was for me.

"Annie?"

Billy offers me his hand. I readily take it.

While dancing, I examine Billy's nose as he gets up close & personal with my eyebrows. This alleviates eye contact, so as not to give anything away. Give what away? Who the hell knows? But in my world, a look can be as conspicuous as a banner in the sky. I'm missing the *discreet gene* and have come to terms with it. I'm not even sure which guy this look should be shielded from. His nose is growing on me, though, that's for sure.

"Thanks for coming."

"Thanks for the invite." And then he whispers, "Rosie."

And it sounds so right that it takes my consciousness three tries to salvage my birth name from the archives in my brain.

"I think there's something you should know."

"I'm so sorry about your mom. I haven't said that yet."

"Thank you."

He spins me, pulls me closer. The proximity saves me. It would be an awkward crank of the neck to look deep into those soulful black eyes, so I speak to the space above his right shoulder.

"There are worse things a person can do than be unfaithful."

"Yeah. A person can damage someone to the point that they think that kind of behavior is acceptable."

And he released that statement as if it were an admission of understanding and allegiance. Another bold move. Touché.

"I got flowers today."

I test him.

"I had a successful day myself."

He's not combative like the other brother.

"And I'm happy for you."

"Thank you."

"What are you up to?"

Honesty and vulnerability truly confuse the shit out of me.

"I'm up to being happy for you, if you're happy. That's all."

Was that all? I'd know if I had the courage to look into his eyes, but my heavy lids help protect me from this liberty. We dance in silence. This allows me to extract any bullshit from the dialogue that just transpired (and *accurately* transcribe the exchange into my memory banks).

But all I come up with is that love is fickle and ruthless and rarely chooses to startle you with flowers. And if I think deeper on the subject, I've been surprised by flowers twice this week. And if I focus 'til it hurts, it appears there's a choice to be made. And the choice might be mine.

I wonder briefly if Billy's decoded the conversation as well, but my mind doesn't philosophize over it too long. It can't, because like eight of my more prominent erogenous zones have been taken siege by wonderfully tingly alcohol-induced sensations that carry me right into the physicality of the moment.

From head to toe I check off every body part of mine that's in contact with every part of his. To mark each spot I create this invisible spark, like the strike of a match as my focus moves from one junction to the next. Does he feel the trail of heat zigzagging its way down? Does he?

Love is meant to be beautiful, just like you. I imagine him whispering those words to me. At least I think I imagined it(?)

MP must detect that any extended merger of brother and

145

girlfriend could lead to further alliances as he approaches. Billy and I have a force in common greater than MP and me, or MP and Billy will ever have. And the genius scurrying onto the dance floor knows that force is him. Billy knows it, too. That's what's been going on here tonight.

But me? I don't realize it yet. I'm hanging out in oblivion for the time being. Oblivion? A state in which one confuses intelligence with kindness and equates kindness with weakness. If you can't imagine a place so dumb and you need me to elaborate, go to my website; AnnieOnMars.com. But do hurry; I don't anticipate it being up & running for much longer.

"Excuse me, may I have this dance?" MP beckons with a British accent that's way too cool for school.

As I pull away from Billy to dutifully dance with MP, Billy curtsies and takes his hand.

"But, of course, darling."

They twist into a tango that gyrates into a salsa of magnificently exaggerated proportions.

Billy has more grace than any woman out here. I can see why MP never let him lead. If he was in a pink, flowing dress or a dress at all (allow me to clarify), my eyes would be crazy dewy, like when you unintentionally channel surf into the final scene of *Dirty Dancing*.

After his third pirouette, Billy releases the firm yet lithe grip he had around MP.

"I've got to hit the road. Thanks, man."

"No problem."

MP shakes Billy's hand in a manner that claims responsibility for the high-spirited antics. And why not? Own it, MP. Own it while you're able.

We watch as Billy grabs his perfectly cordial date – the new guitar – from the booth we've assaulted all evening, and exits.

Upon Billy's departure, MP captures me in his arms with

force, with hunger, and without permission. A damsel ripped from the pages of a trashy romance novel that's exactly drunk enough to roll with it. I shake my head and drag along an unabashed smirk, empowered most notably by this game I entered into two years back.

But as we swivel to a Bob Marley cover song, the smirk is swallowed by sin; by the lies that define our life together.

Have you ever longed for something while you were still experiencing it? This evening's festivities would remain forever embossed in the cold cobblestone, the glossy ceramic fixtures, and in the tattered red leather seats of that dimly lit relic of a Mexican restaurant. They would not pursue us home. My arms hung loose around a pure fabrication, a character I'd conjured up that shocked me intermittently by materializing. And I dove fearlessly into those uncompromising sapphire eyes, searching for a motivation beyond my comprehension, but left them soon after unrewarded, then settled on the colorful lanterns overhead dancing from a breeze off the patio.

During the second trimester of our relationship, there was safety, maybe even love. I squandered the rest of the time as a daredevil, getting a rush from the sting that kept bouncing from throat to stomach. Only a lazy, thrill-seeking coward would pick such a volatile sphere as her comfort zone. I'd hoped too long for solace and identified now that I was a minute away from heartbreak at all times with this guy. If nothing else, I was plain exhausted.

But I'm stalling. It's technically tomorrow and Destiny is officially on pause, and for what? For another guy? An idea? A dream? An illusion? Because the good Samaritan in me says, "Don't go until the brothers are okay?" Yeah, right. Because I'm lazy? Lonely? Scared? Horny? Because my Intuition is lazy, lonely, scared and horny? That might be it.

Back home, MP readily passes out to a late-night *Larry King* recap as the bedroom comfortably awaits crazy old me. My clothes fall in little crinkly balls on top of a packed suitcase that when nudged into the corner of the closet appears exactly as it did a day ago: empty.

I consider the newness of Billy, the peripheral kindness he's shown, but have no genuine long-term faith in the idea of "us." Still, I twist and wake as I try to shake the clarity of a voice that keeps whispering about this guy I barely know, and a dream that was finally filed under "my wild imagination."

Keeping it in the Family

I'll have the western omelet with a side of rye…*and the bitch sporting the biggest camel toe west of the Sahara will have an order of the blueberry pancakes. What the fuck?*" Foster points at my crotch, drawing the attention of a mere dozen onlookers.

"Sweetie, those went out in the eighties with pin-striped jeans," Terbear lovingly explains as she spirals a finger right at it as well.

Relieved I've never been an advocate of self-respect or spokesperson for dignity, I reach into my khakis, slide the seam to the left (thereby crushing the camel toe against my right thigh) and take a seat at the table.

"Listen, I was running late, grabbed the *way wrong* pants,

and didn't have time for underwear. But thanks bunches for the subtlety."

"Oh, yeah, I know what you're saying," Shane sympathizes. "Nearly missed my own wedding because I rearranged my *entire* schedule at the last minute to fit in underwear. So, how's therapy?"

"Nice segue," Foster nearly applauds the man.

"Assholes. Not you, babe," I reassure Terbear. "Well, aside from the drugs, therapy's the worst present ever."

"No, no. The worst gift you ever got was sophomore year of college when Bobby Schinklestein gave you that card shuffler for Christmas."

There Terbear goes, cheering me the fuck up.

"*Nooo*, the card shuffler was from Tony." Foster's steel-trap memory has always been more of a nuisance than a benefit. And then she casually recollects, "All you ever got from Bobby was a yeast infection."

Casual afterthought turns main event as we curl forward in gut-clenching fits of laughter. Cousin Nuisance happens to be especially crude *and* funny today, and so she continues on point.

"And that's all he ever got from you!"

Then a third of her Mimosa spews from her nose onto Shane's Kenneth Cole's. We all ignore him. He's a guy, he can deal.

"And my car!" I scream. "He got my freaking car!"

We've officially gathered the attention of "Saturday brunch." And despite his snotty efforts, our reasonably amused waiter scatters a round of Mimosas across the table while noting the details of our goings-on, then dashes madly away to relay the gossip to a few other elite members of the "boys club."

"Okay, okay," Foster says, concerned mostly with calming herself down. "But in his defense, that was a pretty fair trade."

"Can we please talk about something more pleasant, like football or ringworm?" Shane futilely requests.

"Oh, no, cutie, it's not what you think."

"I'm thinking get me out of this conversation, *cutie*."

"The yeast infection was," Terbear clutches Shane's arm and admits earnestly, "*in his eye.*"

And stick a fork in us, We Are Done. We'll need to be resuscitated and eventually wheeled out of the joint.

"Aw, I'm eating!"

The conversation has reduced him to whining.

"Hey." I'm a pillar of self-defense. "I warned him not to head south that night." The defense rests...and continues to giggle.

Suddenly, a vital detail resurfaces and I launch an accusing finger at Foster.

"But to make matters worse, she sent a bouquet of flowers along with two – count 'em – *two* cases of Monistat to the hospital!"

"He was *hospitalized?*" Shane regurgitates, damn near literally.

Terbear strokes her hubby's arm soothingly.

"They just had to make a small incision. You know, drainage."

But then she figures, fuck Shane and his sensitive stomach, and she bursts out laughing again.

"No wonder the guy dumped you," Shane deducts.

"It had nothing to do with that. That guy – " I clear my throat, wipe a tear from the corner of my eye, "that guy was so dumb, Fos and I convinced him that I didn't give him a yeast infection in his eye, but rather, he gave me – "

"Pink eye of the vagina," Foster states tritely.

"And he *believed* you?"

"Well, the drops stung a little at first, but it was worth it."

And I squeal through this whole next statement as if *it's* the funny part; "We broke up because he fucked my roommate."

"She was such a bitch," Terbear announces solemnly.

"She had this *pirate* fetish. What are you gonna do? I bet that moron is still wearing that patch," Fos speculates.

"It got him chicks, I have to admit."

"That was the best thing that could've happened to that guy."

Foster's head hangs in defeat.

"Did he at least have the decency to thank you?" Shane honestly wonders.

And then we all pause in wonderment. *Did he ever thank me?* This gives our guts and vocal cords a small reprieve.

"You know, you're awfully cheery today, Annie. MP break a vertebra?"

A legitimate question from my man friend. Well, they've been pillars of undivided attention since the introduction of the "camel toe," so I may as well mention it.

"He kissed me."

"Who?"

"The brother."

"What? Where? Which brother?" demands Her Cuteness.

"*Not* the one I'm sleeping with."

"Yet."

Foster's got a mouth for detail.

Terbear starts clapping. She loves gossip, especially when it revolves around men and sex. Or sex and anything.

"Oh, my god! What are you going to do?"

"I don't know." What a lame response. Yet it sounds better than my already botched plan, which Fos and Lisa Marie haven't even been made privy to. "All of a sudden MP is being nicer, too."

Shane's head gyrates wildly to and fro.

"Honey pie. In order to get *nicer*, you have to start out nice. He just senses something. But I'm more than impressed you might soon be engagin' in some fornicatin' behind Master Prick's back. Although, I have to ask myself: Wouldn't it be easier if you found yourself a guy who…I don't know, had a job, a car, a home, and, say, wasn't a felon *or* the brother of the man you're currently fucking?"

"This is L.A. Where's she gonna find all that?" Foster slaps him hard on the side of the head, a move stolen from our mutual Italian grandmother. "Jesus Christ, man."

"The odds are good, but the goods are odd!" Terbear exclaims.

The pickings do seem slim out here on this sunny Southern coast. Then she turns to me and asks the most important question of the day.

"Was it good? The *kiss*?"

Was it good?

How does one describe the most surreal experience of one's life? Where are the words? I struggle for a composition that will only serve as a vague hollow playback and wish there was a system beyond language with which to draw from.

"It was…it was like at that moment I was all he was thinking about…and he had to kiss me to finish his thought."

The booth draws me into a slouch, a pensive dreamy mini-break from all that's ordinary. Shane yanks me back into Saturday brunch with one of his Perfect Man Bulletins.

"Guess what, babe? We don't all think about our mothers while we're kissing our girlfriends."

"No relationship's perfect," I half-mumble.

"Terbear leaves her shoes all over the apartment and I constantly forget to recap the toothpaste; *that's* not perfect. Your relationship is…it's beyond crazy…*beyond lesbian*."

And we all anticipate another Italian grandmother backhand, but instead Fos jerks her head toward Shane and announces, "Excellent point."

Phew. Interesting. Speaks volumes.

Our friendly waiter swaggers toward the table, a menagerie of breakfast entrées stacked along his arm.

"Egg white & avocado scramble right here, please," Terbear smiles. "All he's trying to say, is we love you and we just wish you'd start fucking somebody *you actually liked*."

"Hell, I wish you'd start fucking somebody *we actually liked*. Western omelet." Foster snatches her breakfast. "And another round of Mimosas."

"Sure, princess. Whatever."

The waiter blazes from the table with a swing and an attitude most runway models couldn't hold a candle to.

"You know what? It's fate. Fate! If you have to fuck one brother to finally fuck the other…go for it."

Leave it to Terbear; even strange, irrational, semi-incestuous relationship advice sounds adorable coming out of her mouth.

"Girls, girls, girls. Enough nonsensical speculating. How about a toast?" Shane interjects on cue. "To…"

"To keeping it in the family. Yeah!"

Terbear glows from her quickly derived pun. And Fos and I get off on her happiness, which is weird because our own happiness has never done much for either one of us.

I couldn't imagine my life without any one of these adorable goofs. And to think that a decade ago two of them didn't even exist. Now they're like family, but in a good way. They love me so nonjudgmentally that they'll allude to the obvious (i.e., leave MP) but would never give me an ultimatum. Thanks for the freedom: This is what I secretly raise my glass to. And I raise it to the three of them for handing out strength as if they've all been built with an endless supply.

The Sixteenth Chapter

We join glasses high in the air. They clink as we reiterate in flawless unison, "To keeping it in the family!"

The Little Black Dress

I hop lazily out of the Mustang and glance up at a balcony that is permeating melody. There he relaxes, striped from the sunset wrestling its way through the olive tree, strumming his guitar, singing with his eyes closed. MP was right about one thing: Billy *is* a modern day Shakespeare, words his most vital sustenance. He's a maudlin, penniless poet, lacking only the conception that the mind and the heart are two separate entities. As hard as I work not to, I keep rolling back to this same conclusion.

When I barge in sporting a Mimosa high that increases the comfort level of my pants by, like, a million, I spy Billy's nose peeking around the edge of the sliding door. The rest of his body is smashed cartoonishly up against the transparent glass itself.

The "move" was intended to make me laugh. It worked.

"Hey, Billy. What's up?"

"Oh, hey, Rosie." He casually jumps out from behind the glass, hooks his thumbs into his raggedy back pockets. "What's up? Um, a concert honoring the great musicians of the seventeenth century, I believe."

He believes. Right. Shit. The clock on the wall further validates his rightness. Looking to my attire promotes another "shit." I look back at Billy. I can do this. And nod my head repeatedly. Shit.

Billy nods back and smiles, *you can do it*. The devoted keeper of faith hangs onto enough for both of us (and only God knows why).

I barrel down the hallway.

"It's times like these that really make me miss the short-term!"

This wasn't exactly a case of pot-induced, short-term memory loss. I mean, I thought there would be no "Me & MP" by this Saturday, so I scratched the concert from the smudged, crumpled up, scribbled over piece of scrap paper inside my brain that contains all pertinent future engagements. But as far as everyone in this house is concerned, I'm still "the girlfriend," so off to concert I go.

I have five minutes. Makeup: a little shadow on the upper lids, curl lashes, apply mascara, smear gloss across lower lip and smudge lips together – done. Hair: toss fingers through scattered mess – done. Dress: might be screwed. *Gets me every time*. Ya know, if I ever bothered to reorganize between direct attacks on my wardrobe, this would be a whiz, but…shit; I can't find anything! Wait…there's the box. Shane, Terbear, and *Betsey Johnson* just saved my freakin' life. I slip into the dress: sleek and simple with just a touch of frill; an exceptional complement to my I-just-got-fucked-really-hard hairdo. My toesies jam into a pair of stare-at-my-runner's-calves heels, and then I sprint into the living room for final assistance.

I leap at Billy and spin in mid-air.

"Could you zip?"

Staring back over my shoulder through a window of curls, I watch as Billy runs his eyes down and up my bare back, forgetting to grab the zipper.

"Yoo-hoo?" I wake him. "Chop, chop."

He steps forward, reaches down for the zipper, and with gaze unbroken, raises it gradually to meet the hook, then nimbly tends to that.

"Thank you."

I shy away, notoriously familiar with that moment, then boldly dive for my purse.

A couple more spins allow me to case the place for any missing items essential to outfit. Ah, my final accessory: a crocheted family-heirloom-scarf-shawl-thingy, perfect for table and evening wear. Fists curl around its corners, a short inhale prepares me to Houdini it from under lamp and candle when Billy lifts them like clockwork.

"Thank you. Again."

Wrapping shawl around shoulders and reversing toward the door prompts (yep) another ramble.

"Okay, there's leftover chicken pesto ravs – nuke 'em for a minute thirty – they'll be fab. And, there's a nice marble rye on the counter and some pastrami and fontinella cheese inside the fridge in one of the veggie drawers – "

"Stop," he announces. I shut up. "Go," he instructs.

I wave and open the door.

"Hey."

I swivel back around. My keys dangle from his middle finger. He grins and fakes a toss. I step forward and cup my hands to catch the keys that were fake tossed. Good one (and only moderately embarrassing on my end). So I toss a cocked head, a frown, and a couple of crunched eyebrows right back at him. Billy frowns back playfully. Then he waltzes toward me all George Clooney-like (*picture that*), captures a fist from my hip and opens it palm up, hands me the keys, then cradles my hand inside both of his.

"You look amazing."

I could practically cry, but my tear ducts promised to be on restricted duty for the day. So I do nothing, nothing but log the phrase, extend the heat he's created around my hand to that of my entire body, and savor the quivers prancing down my otherwise idle limbs.

"Go," he whispers.

Our eyes remained locked until that blasted squeaky door shuts and obstructs the view.

Five blocks, three minutes, no cops or aimless pedestrians to impede my frenzied venture…and I'm successfully parked. I hop from the car. As a breeze ruffles my dress, I notice for the first time that it is truly sensational. Could definitely have gotten out of a ticket in this dress, possibly even a murder rap. Assuredly, my neck lengthens, shoulders roll back, and I begin to subtly strut toward the concert hall. MP and six of his whitest-and-tightest stand just outside the doors talking and what not. I wave, real big like. The majority bolt inside. That is to say, everyone but MP. We meet at the crest of the staircase.

"I'm sorry. I'm sorry."

"You're late."

"I made it. I'm sorry."

We walk through separate double doors.

"Where'd you get that dress?"

A sideways glance sums up his disapproval.

"The Happy Drunk Couple – Shane and Terbear. For my birthday."

He steps a pace ahead of me.

"Don't suppose you have a comb in that purse?"

While digging for a comb or clip and scurrying to keep up, it strikes me hard; we both suck (and not just a little). Individually *and* as a unit, every single minute of "us together" sucks.

"Tell me I look pretty," I blurt.

"What?"

My pace is halted in the hopes of capturing a bit of air and the same amount of courage.

"Tell me I'm beautiful."

He conceals two quickly tightening fists inside roomy pockets and faces me, feet planted firmly shoulder distance apart.

"Come on, Annie, let's go."

Under the pleasing loose drape of his *Armani pants*, his hands squirm like they've taken over the job of cringing for his face.

My feet remain on standby.

He bites his lip, exhales through flared nostrils, rolls his eyes, yet still manages to conceal the scowl burning just beneath the surface of every feature.

"What do you want from me?"

My rusty spine is put to use for the first near-sober moment in a long, long while. I stand strong, or at least steady, and think, *I want you to say one nice thing and set me free.* And then I can move on to simpler things – conquer the world if need be.

"You look..." Several frown lines accumulate across his forehead during the strain. "You look...The dress is fine. *Okay?*"

Not okay. And he recognizes this by my effort-impacted stillness, not by the tremble engulfing the leg that's supporting the majority of my weight.

"Fine. I like the dress. The dress is pretty. Can we go now?"

Feet carry me back, again and again, until my bare back meets the chilly unforgiving metal of the double doors through which we just entered.

"Hey? What are you doing?"

He speeds toward me, fingers efficiently shackle my elbow. Now, there's the guy I know, demonstrating his fondness for PDA: Public Display of Aggression.

"It took me all summer to orchestrate this event. This is *my* concert. I'm not walking in alone. Do you hear me? *I don't want to be alone.*"

My arm twists from his clutch as the weight of my body releases itself backward and eases open the rigid door.

"Neither do I."

And I vanish.

I'd speculate all evening that things would've been great with this anonymous brave chick inhabiting my body had my car turned over on the first try. But it didn't. And the little men guarding the gates at my tear ducts took a permanent leave of absence, or so it seemed. Anyway, I lost it. And this time it would be an absolute waste to bother with the radio or another useless, inner monologue in the hopes of settling the riot in my head. So I politely dismissed the brave chick, replaced her with the girl that felt pretty for one split second, and chose instead a faithful, familiar cry and a nice quiet drive along the ocean.

The Alchemist

*T*here's an added poignancy to a woman dressed like her version of a princess with swollen eyes and makeup streaked vertically about her face. The dichotomy is striking, a natural attention inducer. But muddled is how I feel, muddled and too tired to consider the impact my altered state of grace may have on the rest of the planet; i.e., Billy.

You know, I refer to myself and my people in relation to the planet quite regularly. The allusion makes me feel significant in a definitive place, rather than minuscule in an incomprehensible space. The conviction: If the edge of the world is within my eye-line, it corroborates my notion of hope.

By creating a tiny crack in the door and slithering through, body part by individual body part, I successfully eliminate the annoying squeak.

The room is dim and lonely, and enhances my somber

mood. Purse rolls off shoulder, keys drop lazily to the floor. I arch my back 'til my shoulder blades discover the door, tilt my head back, rest my eyes. I could fall asleep right here.

Billy leans into the wall that separates living room from balcony, a book in one hand, something resembling a quarter twisting amid his fingers in the other.

"Damn, I should've warned you," he scolds himself. "That Baroque music can be a real downer. Which is why I said; *'Sorry, MP, I want to be there for you man. And it's real sweet you offered me front row seats, but this right here…'*" He pats his heart and shrugs. "I had to pass."

The air hits my eyes, burns as I look at him, an echo of a laugh escapes my lips.

"Do you want to go for a walk?"

He checks the time.

"Sure."

"You don't have to – only if you want to. I interrupted you. Go back to whatever you were doing. You know, if you want to."

The quarter, which turns out to be a guitar pick, falls to the floor. I'm lulled by the slight distraction. He picks it up and places it in the center of his hand, studies it as if he's reading his own palm, then plants it regardfully in his pocket.

"Actually, I was just preparing for a walk." He references the book, "I like to read a little William Blake before lifting heavy objects or any type of physical activity. It pumps me up."

My knuckles sweep under my eyes.

Billy places the book gently on the coffee table.

"A walk sounds perfect."

"Okay."

I roll on a shoulder to face the door. My forehead rests heavy on its frame and an exhale helps to excrete any sedimentary cerebral jumble. Yes, a walk would be perfect – it's infamous even – for clearing one's head. And then I notice my feet. Huh? I'm about to go for a stroll in a pair of heels that have a half-life of like, an hour – and that's if you're not standing in them.

"I should probably go change my shoes."

As I pivot to do just that, I collide right into him. My left heel skips across both of his boots. The skirt of my dress stops mid-turn, crinkles against the roughness of his jeans. My breasts brush his chest as the tip of my nose skims his soft, warm lips. Pulling back instinctively incites him to pursue me. His lips close hot and strong over mine. This particular kiss *has* a goal. I would've lost my equilibrium and crumpled dizzy to the floor, were I not sandwiched between two very intense structures. My dress rises in disarray, rests high on my thighs. My left leg compulsively bends and clings, then loses grip from up around his hip. He slides his hands down my face, arms, waist, to beneath my ass, where he hoists me up to lock my ankles around his back.

Billy then turns and walks us to the couch. All the while we're kissing – kissing and groping. And we make so many sounds, noises that resonate as if we're suffocating from all the kissing and groping. I fall back into the spongy cushions. Billy slows the pace by tracing the seam of my dress with his eyes and fingertips, then rolls me over to unlatch the hook with which he's already been acquainted.

Holy wow, I'm about to experience sex without any clothes on whatsoever. No joke. It's been years since I've participated in long, slow sex that encompasses plenty of caressing, gazing, and hand-holding. I'm shivering from anticipation, praying memory will serve.

Memory paled in comparison.

At one point, Billy wrapped a blanket around us; my knuckles shone white from gripping it for leverage. I also re-member saying somewhere in the middle of it all, "I think

Blake's my new hero" because if that's what he meant by the book really pumping him up, that author is, in fact, my brand new god.

Tired, numb fingers combed methodically through his sleek saturated hair as I transfixed the rest of my being on the wave our bodies were creating as they raised and lowered every second or so in expert metrical precision.

I assumed he was sleeping, but then he whispers real sweet and kinda cheesy-like, "*Thou fair-haired angel of the evening.*"

"Do I have a real live poet on my hands?" A smile links my blush-stained cheeks.

"Technically, I'm on your body." His chin rests on stacked fists. "I stole that from your hero."

"Sure. I'm neither fair nor an angel."

"You should never contradict a man when he's wooing you," Billy teases.

"Are you wooing me? Am I playing hard to get?"

"No, Rosie, you're not hard to get." A kiss tickles my chin. "I get you." Then he sprinkles my jaw line with a dozen more. "But tell me something I don't know."

I didn't want his body separated from mine, but what a question.

"I make it a point not to know anything too valuable. That way if I'm ever kidnapped by spies or hooked up to a lie detector, I'll have nothing to hide."

"A person can never be too safe," he chimes in.

"Tell me about it. Nothing like safety and ignorance to keep a girl smiling."

Yes, I'm brandishing a big, fake, grin.

"Is that your motto?"

"Nah, for me it's more like…*fleeting moments of ecstasy interrupted by staggering lengths of numbness.*"

…And grin be gone.

"Sounds rather cultish for a prudent, stupid chick."

"Oh, I left the cult."

"Where to next?"

"See, that's the problem. What comes after Recovering Catholic?"

"Trapped in Limbo," he exhales hopelessly.

"Sure, if I believed in it anymore." K. That was fun. I exhale, too, then weirdly test a little realism. "What do you believe in?"

What's up with his crooked-crazy-sexy smile? His hand disappears into a bundle of lazy curls. He inches his face up to mine, and draws from his bible: *The Alchemist.*

"I believe; *if you want something bad enough, the whole Earth conspires to help you get it.*"

"Madonna just said that in her *Vanity Fair* interview! Don't you just *love* Madonna?"

Did I just say that out loud? Can't imagine what this guy thinks of me. But my body feels charged yet calm, and the dull ache vanishes when he touches me. So why don't I just announce that, too, and watch him nose-dive off the balcony? That'd make for an interesting end to this evening's follies.

I'm sensing technical difficulties; like always, the silence… is killing me. Paranoia is settling in heavy on my chest. I wish there was something clever to say. Something that's not about Madonna. I'd even take boring, if I could muster up the courage. *And what's up with his crooked-crazy-sexy smile?*

"I do. I just *love* Madonna."

Billy kisses me square on the lips as if he's done it a hundred times before. Then he lifts himself up and scans my body down to the shoes.

"You might want to go change those now."

"Okay."

I smile and dash down the hallway as fast as those heels

will take me. Maybe nothing went wrong this evening. Nothing *outside* of my head anyway.

So I lied. I wasn't *entirely* naked for the event. But sexy footwear hardly counts; it's like a Chris Isaak album, a glass of Merlot, or foreplay – existing solely to heighten the intensity of the interlude.

Thirty minutes later, I'm sitting at a faulty table for one in the far corner of this dark, outdated bar, buried behind a thick row of chunky decrepit booths and a very weathered pool table. Still, awkward comes to mind as I crouch in my seat and watch yuppies here, yuppies there, yuppies weaving everywhere. Never seen so many straight people gathered in one place in this city before. Billy's off in the corner designated "stage" (due to the strategic placement of a bar stool and standing microphone).

We don't belong here. First of all, we look and reek of sex. And these boring blondes with alligators embroidered on a boob are looking at me like I've got a knife strapped to my thigh. And they're looking at Billy like they'd kill to fuck him as long as their law student boyfriends never got word of it. Meanwhile, the law student boyfriends are placing bets on whether Billy's illiterate – money is practically exchanging hands. They're looking at him they way MP does. I hate them. Can't believe he got a job at what has to be L.A.'s last standing yuppie hangout. The good news is, there may be a few walkouts when they realize nowhere in his venue does he include any Jimmy fucking Buffett.

And I wonder: Are we that drawn to that which we loathe? Or do we merely cling to what we know? Or does one eventually become the other? At least MP's concert saves me from running into any of his flock; that's one good thing.

Billy takes a seat at the bar stool. I slide a leg underneath my butt to increase my height and get a clear view.

"This is a song about something that'll creep up on you, if you let it. So don't let it."

His audience could care less, but based on the beautiful look on his face, they're his last concern.

He starts strumming and then adds, "Oh, it's called, 'Roses.'"

> *"Lift up your veil and watch the sun rise.*
> *See all the mysteries of the world in your eyes.*
> *When I awake, it fades away,*
> *And I wrestle from the bed and start a new day.*
> *I find a picture in a drawer,*
> *I recognize that's a sweater that you wore,*
> *And I regret it to this day that I let you slip away.*
> *'Cause I almost brought you roses…*
> *Now I've awakened from my big dreams,*
> *And I'm sitting here wondering what that means.*
> *And I wonder where you are, and I find it very hard.*
> *Cause I almost brought you roses, you almost saved my life.*
> *I should have said; I love you.*
> *You should have been, you should have been my wife."*[1]

They love it. They're *in* love with it. Even the displaced gargantuan goon bartending is tearing up. And I need to stop judging the entire world because of their uniform hairstyles, matching blue and/or yellow button-downs, and sheer lack of body piercings. What if people automatically assumed I was a frantic frazzled mess of a human being just because my clothes look slept in, my hair hasn't seen a comb in weeks, and

1   Lyrics by Newton's Theorem.

my breath reeks of liquor while my eyelids droop from weed? Never mind. Bad example.

Billy plays a handful of more unique melodies, each one as enticing as the last.

I feel as if I've been taken hostage by some very kosher aliens whose purpose is to study humans at their most relaxed: while undergoing acute seduction by the almighty trinity of Man, Music, and Mood. Damn, I feel good. Whose world is this?

"Thank you very much. I'm going to take a short break."

Billy leans his guitar against the stool with the red vinyl cushion that seeps stuffing from both wear and tear, then darts across the bar to meet me with a kiss. Big scary goon sneaks up, greets him with a beer. When Billy tugs at some cash in his pocket, the guy swats at a tear, then Billy, *put your money away*, and moseys back to business. Billy sits practically on top of me at "cozy table for one" (yes, Billy's company launched the status of this table from faulty to cozy within milliseconds of his arrival).

"I – I'm…speechless."

Dumb again, natch. We stare like lovers. And not too keen on words like *lovers*, but geez, I can't think of one more suiting.

Who is this guy? Who is this guy whose kisses are so sweet and lovemaking skills so savvy? *And who writes songs like that?*

I drift to the music for three more beers, all the while pondering, have I just met "the one?" Or have I gone gaga for the first dude that's nice to me? Or is it conceivable that they're one and the same? I mean, after all these years of dating, hating, and regurgitating, have I unwittingly stumbled upon the man of my dreams? Is Billy the air mattress to my twenty-story building? Or do I need to get a freaking grip?

Could I possibly be this lucky?

Well, my mind settles on "maybe," and "gosh, that'd sure be nice." And, as it does, the billows slow their crashing in my brain, and the monsters in my tummy tame.

Star Gazers

MP's crouched over the piano composing; jazz. You know, the kind where you can't guess the next chord, and when you hear it, you rarely agree with the choice. When he completes the arrangement, yeah, yeah, it'll be divine. In the meantime, the racket is reminiscent of background music for "A Day in the Life." I think it's purposeful. He's been extra edgy since I left him at the concert. I know this *not* because we've discussed it, but because his sneers have doubled in both size and quantity the past few days.

Billy is reading. He seems to be really good at that.

Me? Pretending to read. I'm really good at *that*. It started out as a way to get What's-His-Name to fall for me. I thought if I came off as an authentic worshipper of the written word he'd have to. Right? Right. Of course, now I've grown so accustomed to *virtual* reading, I can't recall the last book I read straight through. Occasionally, yes, some of the non-life-altering-bullshit from the well-regarded crap I pseudo-read ends up retained, but most of the time I frivolously flip pages while planning a creative dinner or my next encounter with a six-pack and a fistful of Valium.

Billy stands, yawns, stretches, bares his navel.

"I'm gonna head to work."

"I'll drive you!"

I spring to my feet as if they're stapled to a pogo stick; the vaulted ceiling saves me from a sure concussion. Just watch my expertise as I dial this one down. Leaning on a hip, I twirl a curl and shrug.

"You know, if you want me to."

That was brilliantly casual. No matter. MP is too caught up in his music to notice any enthusiasms I possess toward his brother or his brother's torso.

Billy underplays as well.

"Sure, you can drive me. Whatever. MP you need anything, man?"

MP shakes his head between chords that resonate flat, as if the instrument had been abandoned in a cold, dank basement next to a dusty old rack of coats once owned by long-dead relatives.

"MP, you sure you don't need anything?"

He ignores me.

"Maybe a nice Merlot. Nothing too oaky. Or too sweet. Something French."

And the silent treatment ensues.

"Are you planning on speaking to me at all this century? Cause I was thinking of starting one of those 'goal journals,' Oprah and Tony Robbins are really into that crap. I could pencil you in between drinking and dreaming – you know, under the 'banter' section of my day."

A pin dropped, and, yes, we all heard it.

Billy finally turns.

"You ready?" He's *so* blasé. Bravo. Or maybe he really doesn't want to hang out with me. Shit. These two dudes make my existence doubly confusing.

In the twenty-two seconds it took to reach the other side of the door, I've evolved into a nervous wreck (yes, I know it's not a dicey transition). He doesn't want me with him. The other night must have been a dream. What have I done? Freak. Why does it always boil down to me being a freak? I should just dodge back inside without explanation. Smooth Freak, smooth idea.

"Um – "

Billy interrupts my "um" with a kiss that presses me hard against the door (you'll never comprehend the depths of my newfound fondness for this annoying squeaky contraption). I straddle him. Yep, it's the next natural move. My back welcomes the cool dense wood even as my tailbone stumbles jagedly up and down it. Instinctively, eyes open mid-kiss as the Greenblatts teeter toward us toting groceries.

One by one, my legs set their captor free.

"Mr. and Mrs. Greenblatt. Hi!"

Silence.

They hate me. *Fill gap with polite commentary* is a good thought.

"This is my brother, Billy."

They stand frigid and wide-eyed.

Hmm? They *really* hate me.

"No, no, that wasn't right." I take Billy's hand. "This is my boyfriend's brother Billy, not my brother, Billy. Oh, boy, you thought that I was...*with* my brother. No. Eww. This is my *boyfriend's* brother."

"Mr. and Mrs. Greenblatt, it's lovely to meet you."

Billy oozes charisma, charm; you name it – he's oozing – but the Greenblatts seem to hate him, too. They suck.

Mother always said, "Some people just suck."

They're "some people."

Then Mr. Greenblatt surprises me.

"Would you kiddies like to come in for a cocktail?"

"Fritz?!" belts the scarier counterpart.

Our apartment door flies open. MP pokes his head out, hands me a twenty. I release Billy's hand to grab it.

"Hey, grab a bottle of Merlot while you're out. Nothing too fruity. Or too oaky. Something French."

I nod…and nod. But MP just stands there, so I pop an awkward kiss onto the edge of his lips.

He vanishes. Mr. Greenblatt bares a grin that's new to me and quite possibly his own face.

"Maybe another time."

And with that, I bow my head in appreciation and tug Billy away.

On a scrambled pile of clothes and menus; wrinkled, dirty, bent, and faded, some in both categories even outdated, we lie wet and tangled in the back of the Mustang. A spattering of stars spy on us through streaks in the misty window as a serious, yet moderately innocent make out session off Beverly Glen Canyon comes to a close (compliments of *moi*). Another nail loses its life between my teeth. I stare at Billy feeling, well, weirdly guilty. He takes my finger, which happens to now be minus a fingernail but plus a bandage, and he kisses my boo-boo.

"Yeah, that's what I get for splintering a cucumber with a knife that costs five ninety-five. Five *point* nine five, that is."

"Isn't a chef without knives like a musician without a guitar?"

"Ah, my Henkel's set. You should have seen it sparkle," I get all melodramatic. "A gift from Fos. A casualty of *the firing*."

"C'mon," he says, and takes my hand.

"Eventually my mother wrote a hit…thus the college fund. But about a year after I was born, so the story goes, they weren't making a living from their music and one day he flipped – couldn't take the pressure of impending failure. Fortunately, I didn't inherit that gotta-be-the-best gene, like MP."

Billy thought it best we cool down and spark up. So we lay in our undies, sticky and sprawled out on top of the hood. I love Billy; he's chuck full of good ideas and a vat of freely dispensed background information when stoned.

"You don't know your dad at all?"

"Nope. Rumor has it he moved to Phoenix. Apparently, he remarried and opened up his own business; *Happy Meadows Yogurt Shop* or something."

Happy Meadows Yogurt Factory. Oh, my God, I knew their dad. Mike. Even liked the guy. So did Foster. Free ice cream every Sunday. What was not to like?

See, that's not fair: I know the guy and Billy doesn't.

We didn't even deserve free ice cream.

Wow, MP is nothing like his father.

I'd wager Billy was the kind of kid who deserved free ice cream.

"We should go see your dad. I mean, you should go visit him."

"MP told you about him," he groans cynically, dropping his head and picking at a stray chin hair. "That can't be good."

"No, not really. MP doesn't ever bring him up."

"He is a cold, lonely guy. Someday you'll see; men like him will become obsolete."

"You don't know him. Don't say that."

Here I go defending a complete stranger. What an ass.

"No, I don't know my father, Rosie." He flicks away the glow at the end of the joint, diffuses the remaining smoke between two moist fingers, passes me the roach for safekeeping, then confesses cautiously, "I was referring to MP."

"MP's been tortured since your mother's funeral." *And now I'm defending MP?!*

"*Tortured* wouldn't be my choice of verbiage. He hated Mom as much as he loved her. It's always been that way. He blamed her for Dad leaving and worshipped her in the same breath. I watched it for years. It takes a whole lotta "clever" to walk that line, I'll give him that."

Billy stops talking, but his mind is detectably reeling. I don't know exactly what to say, but my fingers find the courage to sweep delicately down his forearm and lightly caress the back of his hand. And my touch is about to release a secret – I feel it. He looks at me square on: I could fill the pages of a book extracting every truth he reveals with one small look. Or just as easily, relax in the "not" knowing, and allow my weary soul to crawl inside those beautiful eyes for simple sleep and safekeeping. But Billy maintains an impossibly steady gaze.

"He didn't even bother to glance in my direction the day of her funeral. But you, you looked right at me, like you already knew me. And it was strange…you almost looked like her. *Lady in Red*; her favorite color. Bold move, by the way."

And there it was.

Billy was sitting in a remote folded chair that afternoon, his hair random and reckless perfectly suiting an outfit that was dispensed in bulk – one size fits most. He was with a pudgy amiable-faced cop that looked like he carried about as much authority as a pink stuffed bear you'd win at a carnival. I assumed they were passersby and remembered feeling sad that that's how they chose to pass their time on such a hot day. And I did stare. I stared carelessly at him as if the brim of that hat was one-way glass. And I felt both pity and harmony during my slow, deep gaze. He wasn't the only one livin' behind bars.

His admission releases a sigh of instant gratification.

"I was captivated by those daring eyes. And that dress. It

was a sign. Made me want to know you; made me feel I already did. And it gave me purpose." Then he smiles as if this is small talk. He's so brave. "And Fate, I openly admit, led me to you."

I drop my head in certain shame.

"I knew you had to be someone that day. But I blocked it, decided *the day of the daisy* was more suitable for memory. I'm sorry."

"Hey. That's not why I brought it up; look at me. Look at me."

I look. And guilt sprints from my veins, buries itself deep in the canyon.

His arm draws me into the heat of his body, which conversely drops our huge confessions into the category of "a natural, everyday occurrence."

Fate? Sure, why not. A series of coincidences tied together by theme should, even by idiot standards, be construed as fate sooner or later.

Yeah, Billy, I believe in fate, but can't say with any veracity that I've ever trusted it. The way our lives have overlapped goes way beyond predestined happenstance; it's downright spooky. And no joke; I'm spooked.

To think that just a few weeks back I had fully submitted to the notion that as long as I maintained a moderate buzz, life would be perfectly tolerable. I mean, I had my health: I wasn't alone. What more could a girl ask for?

She could ask for Billy.

Maybe.

Or she could turn back into me and ask for something different.

Later that evening, I'm lying in bed, waging a stare-down with the popcorn ceiling. They died that way, clinging for life, those little balls of plaster-paint, whatever they are, drained from fighting gravity. Then they *dried* that way, suspended, incomplete, out of place. But at least their struggle was over. Did they win that battle? Trapped inside a shell, screaming under an airtight sheathe, disoriented, but not so much as to obtain too much notice. Their outcome doesn't ring of victory, these little dried globs. They look petrified.

I no longer feel like the same person. Thoughts are stirring. And I've managed to climb the ego ladder and pause to re-evaluate midway between suicide-obsessed and self-possessed, which is a small relief. Still, where will I land when *I* dry? The sheer fear of the unknown is so hard to escape.

And is the relief even in the winning? Or does it come from simply ending, from ceasing to be? The pessimist in me takes advantage of constant disorientation because what good is a little self-realization when self-sabotage has been the custom? Suspense keeps robbing me of nerve and I want it over, which begs the question: How many detours dare I tempt en route to Destiny? I'm trapped in the middle of my own board game; a maze built to confuse even its creator. In-stant gratification may defeat determination in this round. I may be hopeless.

"Michael?"

"Ugh," he grunts, annoyed that dialogue has been insti-gated in the sack.

We don't do a lot of talking here; as a rule, we try not to make any contact – physical or otherwise. The grunt is a sure prelude to a doomed conversation. Nonetheless....

"I just want to talk for a min – "

"You just uttered my full name, is what you just did. So either you're already in trouble or you're planning on get-ting yourself into a shitload of trouble in the near future and trying to save face in advance." With exaggerated effort, he rolls toward me. "What's going on in that twisted little head of yours?"

The same question twice in one night (replace "charming" with "twisted" and "Billy" with "MP").

"Billy's ready to be on his own."

"One little trip to the 7–11 and you've established all that? That's beautiful; you're not even licensed to practice."

"You should talk to him."

"He's fine. He can tough it out for a while."

"Tough what out? He's been suffering, too. If you want him to stay, that's fine, but don't use the money as an excuse to keep him here."

What am I doing? A brilliant question. I'm making sure Billy isn't hanging around for the money. Or tempting Fate.

"Now, you're saying that I want him here and I'm not giving him the money as an excuse to keep him here without letting him know that I really want him here because I would rather it be the one way, without him knowing it was the other? Because that would make me a nice guy and we all know that's not true. Is that what you're saying?"

If I had a nickel for every time this guy officially duped me, I'd be a freaking millionaire.

"I…I'm saying goodnight."

"You're something. You know that?"

And with that he rolls over and he's out like a light. So much for the theory "no rest for the wicked."

Well, that was my meager attempt to make everybody clear and free of everybody; to reinforce the power of free will, no monetary or obligatory strings attached. MP doesn't want Billy here; that's clear. But what he wants less is to listen to any of my bullshit ideologies. The globs on the ceiling will listen, though. They have to; they're trapped. I roll onto my back, stare at the abandoned droplets 'til they blur together. Tears trail into my hairline, soak in around my ears, and the room becomes a collection of foggy tints. Satisfied, I finally shut my eyes.

I sleep easily, knowing the specks of nothingness I'd given life to on my ceiling have blurred together and finally found each other. And I sleep soundly because I know Billy's just a hallway away, tucked under the gold chenille throw, a pillow snuggled tight against his chest – probably from habit, maybe for security. And I sleep deeply, dreaming of one day becoming that pillow.

Brotherly Love
and Otherly Love

*I*t's a brand new day, and with new days come new decisions. I brew a pot of coffee and arrange tasty mid-morning snacks strategically around the kitchen table, then grab my purse and keys and spy momentarily on the brothers from a distance.

They sit across from each other, delaying eye contact, distracted by the breakfast menagerie. It's encouraging to discover the powers of seduction homemade cinnamon rolls possess. Engrossed would be a mild description of the boys' reaction to the toasty pastries. Billy tears at his in an unwinding motion, a swig of coffee between each bite. MP is cutting his, dipping each piece into the bowl of excess frosting. They both ignore the fruit. And who can blame them when the apartment's been perfumed with scents of cinnamon and vanilla? Well, they're at the same table; my good deed is done. And now I shall leave them to their brotherly-ness. Good luck, boys.

MP clears his throat, a rare but nervous habit he passes off as aristocratic.

"Listen, I'm free tonight, if you want to, how should I phrase this…put this situation to bed."

Billy swallows one last morsel of cinnamon roll and grins into his bowl of fruit at the pun.

"My schedule's wide open."

"Good." MP spears a chunk of papaya. "But let me know if you need to reschedule to say, *get a life*."

Billy looks up calmly, precisely, and ready to enlighten the Enlightener himself.

"Unless you care to award me one of yours, I'm free."

"Fantastic."

MP's pride muffles anger. He hops up, refills his coffee, sits back down. Billy follows suit and refills his coffee.

"Annie's quite the cook."

"Yeah, it's the one thing she can do without getting totally distracted."

"I'm sure it's not the only thing."

"Trust me bro, it is," he snarls like the Joker.

The second to the last thing Billy wants to do is take their all-time favorite game – some good old-fashioned intellectual sparring – to another familiar yet more grueling level. But the *last* thing he wants to do is listen to his brother deface Rosie. He exchanges the jab in his tone for sincerity.

"What are you doing, man?"

"I'm doing her a favor. Like to think of it as my good deed on Earth: helping those less fortunate. Paying off some serious karma." Not convinced Billy has complete comprehension of his static state of martyrdom, MP adds, "She's a fucking Class A quack. Or haven't you noticed?"

Billy sets his fork down and tilts his chair back to study this guy in wide-screen.

MP clears his throat again, "But what woman isn't? And mine can whip up a Chateaubriand that'll get you hard. And she doesn't interfere, like the other ones have…in my private life." MP rises, flings his plate brazenly onto the counter like a Frisbee. "Tame 'em early, little brother; words of wisdom. There, now I just did *you* a favor."

MP reaches for his keys, tosses them into the air, hooks the collar of his suit jacket into a finger, lifts it from the back of the chair flings it over a shoulder, catches his keys, then walks backward toward the door.

"Oh, yeah, and she can suck a golf ball through a garden hose," he brags, sauntering smoothly away.

Billy remains still; strength of character focuses to alleviate affectation from his brother's tactically displayed arrogance. By his fifth deep breath, he finally resolves that MP's performance wasn't about him and it wasn't about Rosie. It was about a man who never outgrew the anger and resentment of being raised fatherless; a man who determinedly grew into a woman-hating prick. And all the tomfoolery and verbal trickery in the world can't hide that from his "understudy," the boy who found the good sense to flee from his doomed realm despite the fact that identity and destination were utterly indiscernible.

Peace envelops Billy as he rises to clean up their mess. He's back on his feet for good this time.

Over wine, roses, and bittersweet nostalgia, I was recently made aware of the above conversation. I'd like to add two small addenda:

In MP's defense; I'm sure he didn't use the phrase, "suck a golf ball through a garden hose." His analogy probably incorporated an ancient inventor, a medieval instrument, and a whore from biblical times. He was precisely that sharp.

In *my* defense; I didn't know squat about blowjobs until MP ridiculed my early, poorly executed endeavors. Sometimes humiliation makes perfect a lot faster than practice ever could.

I'm waltzing back in from the longest jog *ever*. My mind is what's mostly exhausted as it raced absurdly through all possible conversations that could have taken place between the brothers. So much for the mind/body cleanse. It started with: *Wow, Annie is the most amazing cook in, like, the entire Universe*. And ended somewhere around: *By the way, did you know I'm screwing her, too?* And then that was followed by a brutal bloodbath; a fight to the death for "the girl." And the final fantasy encompassed a miniscule rumble just for kicks, and a consensual agreement – complete with a pinky-swear – to mutually discard me forever.

So I'm walking into the complex feeling defeated and unwanted, when MP tiptoes past. Yes, literally. Cartoon-style.

"Hey," he whispers.

"Hey," I quietly retort.

And he's gone.

I round the corner heading left toward my place, when I hear some chick go, "Crap!" And try *so* hard to tell myself: *You heard nothing. Just keep walking.*

"Double crap!" Whines chick voice, *thee* chick voice – The Blonde.

Through gritted teeth I grumble, "Triple crap!" And not just because of the "who" who's clearly in need. But because Mr. Fancy Feet tiptoed out to avoid assisting a particularly needy member of the human race whom he also happens to be screwing. Bastard. So, with slouched shoulders I turn and swagger, bummed and almost drunk-like, up to Summer, who's kneeling and pleading into the crack of her door.

"I'm here, Buttons, Mommy's here. She just lost her keys. Don't worry, Peaches, don't worry."

Then she full-on dumps the contents of her purse and kinda starts crying.

Oh, brother.

"Hey," I say, the apparent greeting-of-the-day.

She turns, seemingly non-*nonplussed* by me.

"I locked myself out. I'm late for an audition. Buttons needs her meds. She suffers from severe anxiety, poor little – "

"Got it, got it. You don't have a spare hidden anywhere?"

"I do!" She squeals, then with equal and opposite enthusiasm exhales, "In the planter."

I look around. No planter.

"On the balcony."

I turn and walk away.

"A girl can never be too safe!" She yells. Then, "Thanks for stopping by!"

We DON'T speak each other's unspoken language, so I pop my head back around the corner, "You coming, or what?"

"Okay, up you go!" You know, I've always wondered what it would feel like to have a pair of huge bazookas (haven't used that term yet) plastered to my face. It feels just like I imagined: Sticky, squishy, not knowing for certain if air will find me... finally, she topples to the ground, possibly saving my life. I inhale in a big way.

"You okay?" she beckons, face all twisted and worried.

"Yep." And I'm on my feet. "Up you go."

I fold my hands together and...up she goes. This time she grabs a hold of the edge of the balcony, loses balance, and falls *on top of me*.

"I got an idea," I squeak, peeling a strand of her hair off my lip and sliding out from under her.

We opt for my idea.

"Up you go!" she cheers.

This is better. I grab readily onto the balcony and in one smooth sweep, pull myself up and over it.

"Cute butt," she comments sincerely.

"Ah, thanks."

Okay. So this is my first official *Out Of Body Experience*. The others, I'm certain now, were just practice runs.

The Blonde dashes around as I make my way into her home. And without trying to notice anything too much, I open the door. Buttons licks my ankle. I tug playfully at her bow-tied up-do. Then Summer and I do "the awkward dance" to get past each other.

"Hey, I already missed the audition. Would you like a spritzer?"

And my *O.O.B.E.* sails on, so I roll with it.

"You got a beer?"

There I sit with something *very berry* as Summer rips off a piece of a hot dog to lodge a pill into it for Buttons.

I down another swig of the gooey girly concoction and blurt, "*What are you feeding her?* No wonder she suffers from anxiety."

"Is this wrong?"

"*Would you eat it?*"

She drops it like she was holding a roach (not the kind you smoke). I move to the fridge, pass a bag of dry dog food along the way, ditch it into the trash. She nods in approval. Then I find some turkey and start cooking.

"First of all, you want canned food. It's pricier, but miniature dogs are like foreign cars. If something goes wrong it takes a team of ten with a tool the size of a pubic hair to figure out the problem. The key is preventative maintenance."

"Got it."

And there we sit, twenty minutes later, conversing casually over spritzers, nibbling off Buttons' plate. Yes, Buttons is *at* the table. Not the first canine I've dined with. Be cool if she were the last.

Summer may be orgasming as she sucks the life out of each and every nibble.

"My goodness, how *did* you make this?"

She grabs a pen and Post-It. She means business.

"Okay, clove of garlic – minced. Dash of white wine – it burns off. A few pieces of turkey bacon – " I spot an error on the Post-It. "Aw, that's pieces – p-i-e – "

"Excuse me?"

"Pieces is spelled i-e, not e-i. You know, I before E, except after C."

"Wow, are you like a poet or something, too?"

"I've been told I'm something." I grin and down my drink. "I gotta kick it."

"Would it be weird if I said thanks *and* sorry."

"Weird? Hunter S. Thompson once said: *When the going gets weird, the weird turn pro.*"

"Hunter from 5C?"

"What I mean is, we've entered the Olympic finals of weird. So, you're welcome *and* apology not necessary.

"Yes, it is."

"I'm no innocent."

"I started it."

"He started it."

And we're so close to a silent treaty, except she seems dissatisfied. Like I care.

Apparently, I care.

"Look, if it'll make you feel better, I can still pretend to hate you."

"That'd be great!" She exuberantly chirps, binding our verbal truce.

As I slip through the door, nostalgia and trust trails me. Don't ask.

"See ya around," she says, hopeful-like.

I wave without looking back.

Let Me Count the Ways

My knock does double-time as the sound of cats either mating or being de-skinned screech into earshot like a summer thunderstorm stampeding toward your house after midnight. Three seconds between screeches, two seconds between screeches, and…

Whew, Fos appears. She blows a quivery ring of gray smoke at my face, inspects me.

The contents in my arms: two limes balanced on a bag of Nutter Butters sitting on top three board games piled on a twelve-pack of Corona. She snatches the Nutter Butters and rips into them; the limes tumble to the ground and obediently roll straight into her kitchen. Were they built with a brain?

Does the floor tilt at an angle? Welcome to my cousin: the Eighth Wonder.

"Where's the brothers?"

"Bonding." A hasty confession escapes my lips. "Where's the Happy Drunk Couple?"

"Bond-*age*," she says, spraying me with crumbs.

"So that's the secret to their success?"

"Mm-hmm."

"But I thought…well, why do we call them *The Happy Drunk Couple*?"

"The Infertile-Cross-Dressing-Sadomasochistic-Couple just doesn't have the same ring to it."

Foster jams two more Nutter Butters into her mouth.

Another shriek. My features scramble to the center of my face. Fos grimaces, too.

"Mm-hmm. I'm so sick of hearing them screw, I'm ready to donate my uterus to get this kid-thing over with."

We contemplate the idea.

Fos? Pregnant? A somber disgust settles over us.

"Jenga?"

I brought Jenga.

So we're smoking, drinking, playing Jenga, the three of us: Fos, Lisa Marie, and me. Actually, Lisa Marie's too preoccupied with chasing second-hand smoke and high jumping for Nutter But-ters to be bothered with our Jenga extravaganza.

The bold in me removes a block near the bottom as the whiner in me…well, starts whining.

"I should switch to chicks. It's just that the thought of go-ing down there…" I literally puke in mouth. "And the thought of some chick going down on me…"

Suddenly there is no gag reflux and I'm off dreaming of the possibility of my new, interesting, amiable, orgasmic (however selfish and one-sided) lifestyle.

"Are you about to hit on me? Because despite the fact that I find you amusing in an unnerving self-deprecating sort of way, I must remind you, we *are* related."

I want to tell her about every deep, beautiful Billy-thought inhabiting my every brain cell. And that I believe destiny has crept to my door (late-night, and literally). And time served with MP is becoming obviously clear to me. But I don't.

"Thank you." I stupidly respond. "Unfortunately, I lust men."

"What's unfortunate is that you're scattered, so you end up with all these emotionally vacant nickel dicks."

Nickel dicks? Hmm? Dare I ask what she means? A dick worth a nickel? A dick the size of a nickel? (Yikes.) A dick the size of a roll of nickels? (Still yikes, and no one I know.) Well, in any case, I feel a maryjane-induced lecture coming on. Fos lives for this shit. Who am I to stop her?

My knuckles mush into my cheeks to brace the weight of my overworked brain. Getting back into thinking is a lot like getting back into running; there are shin splints to work past every damn time. Makes ya wonder if it's worth it. Or what foolish blunder made you stop in the first place. But Foster is right; I have been with my fair share of...um...nickel dicks, and I have been scattered. She knows me as the girl with a long-standing goal but no concrete path toward it. And you know what they call people with goals but no clue how to reach them? They call them dreamers, or losers, or both.

So talk, Miss Foster, talk. I'll revere what you have to say, as always. And then I'll store it away as backup. Promise.

As my path is clearing, I'm learning to listen. Life is so funny that way.

"Okay." Foster stamps out the joint, pushes the delicate rectangular tower remorselessly back into its box, looks at me intensely. "I don't give this information out to just anybody. It's

taken me a long time to come to terms with the fact that I'm
the ultimate amalgam of wit, enlightenment, and intellect. I'm
never going to find anyone who can compare, and at this stage
in the game, it doesn't even interest me. Besides, I get a kick
out of watching all these bozos stumble through life with their
thumbs up their asses. That and marijuana are two of the few
simple pleasures left in this world, and I have no intention of
denying myself either one of them any time soon."

And here she goes...

She pours us each a shot and raises her glass.

"So with that said, let's talk, love. This is for you, babe."

Foster is four years, four months, and a dozen lifetimes
older than me and most: a true voice of our time. That is, if
we (women) ever really get "a time." I raise my glass; we clink.
The liquor stings our throats, warms our tummies, and seeps
like smoke into our limbs. Then Fos proceeds to let me in on
the secret of the Universe.

She explains that there are six, and only six, types of love
in this world:

1. Romantic Love
2. Love Between Women
3. Love Between Men
4. Unconditional Love
5. Immature Love
6. Inevitable Love

Romantic Love is love between two individuals regardless of
gender, which ultimately results in sexual gratification in order
to fulfill and sustain itself.

Love Between Women is what she and I share. It's intimate,
honest, and emotionally fulfilling. It's unconditional and af-
fectionate. Love between women ranges from loaning your
girlfriend your favorite earrings for a hot date to teaching her

how to insert her first tampon (without actually inserting it for her).

Love Between Men is more boundaries-oriented. It ranges from sharing your popcorn at a Bruckheimer flick, to sharing your pitcher of beer while watching a playoff game at the local pub. It doesn't entail endless chitchat nor does it encompass conversations of the problem solving nature. Mostly you talk about sports and chicks, and if you agree enough on both subjects, you wind up maintaining a long-term superficial friendship of sorts.

Unconditional Love is love without pretense or hidden agenda. Some find it to be obligatory, as in the case of family members, but in truth, it goes beyond that. It's a sustained state of affection toward any one individual despite all the bullshit they pull to try to get you to feel otherwise. Its components are two-fold: 1) total nonjudgmental acceptance, and 2) pure undeniable honesty. This is the exact love that anyone involved in a long-term romantic relationship should strive for. But sadly, this love is also rare.

Immature Love is when you love somebody but you're too much of a fucking pussy to be able to express it. The result: You come off as an egotistical idiot capable mainly of abusing the unlucky recipient of your emotionally underdeveloped affection.

Then she said, and I quote, "There's no need, *MP*, to reference anyone, *MP*, specifically here, *MP, MP, MP*."

And finally, *Inevitable Love* occurs when you're so fucked-out-of-your-mind whacko yet you find somebody who not only appreciates the utter oddity of your existence, but contributes a sufficient amount of their own nut job mentality to the equation. It then becomes *inevitable* that you'll fall in love. Foster freely associates The Happy Drunk Couple with inevitable love and goes on to say that she believes their bond is also unconditional, as is ours.

According to Fos, there's more than one way to love a person. *Romantic Love* that also encompasses *Unconditional Love* is a beautiful thing. But a romantic relationship that's dominated by *Immature Love* is obviously not a good thing. Hi, again – hint.

When she finishes her oration, she relights the joint and gets good and baked. This allows me time to file away all this wonderfully pertinent, shrewdly relayed info.

"And there you have it, F.O.C." Fos smacks her lips together and smiles, impressed with the ease with which she can formulate any and every thought into perfect, explicative phrases. "Now, all you have to do is decide what kind of love you want in your life, Annabelle. Then stick with that decision, be *patient*, and it will come to you."

I smile, knowing that from this moment on Fos will take credit for any romantic good fortune that comes my way. And I'll be happy to let her.

She tag-teams two joints, hands me the baby one.

"Now, what do you got for me next? Shall I solve world hunger? Do you realize there are more babies born every day than there are people dying of starvation? You do the math. Or how about obesity? In Europe, people freely indulge in fat, alcohol, starches…yet obesity's not an issue. Here in America it's the number-two killer. Additives, preservatives, artificial sweeteners, and hydrogenated *whatever* are killing Americans, and nobody gives a fuck. Which topic would you like me to tackle next?"

"Um…" I'm amusingly dumbstruck; so many topics to choose from, so little time before the effects of marijuana comatose my listening skills. "Hey, how 'bout we color-code my keys? It could help me be on time for shit, you know?"

She cracks her knuckles and points a finger.

"I'll get the polish."

From philanthropist to Cover Girl in two seconds flat.

Everybody should have a Fos in their life.

Ignorance, Insight, and Singing the Blues

he song of the hour, The Calling's "Our Lives," blares from a champagne-colored Mercedes convertible stopped at the light outside the Coffee Bean. Billy, shadowed by a burgundy umbrella, watches the driver bob her head and poorly tackle the lyrics. All the same, he whimsically joins in by drumming his fingers on the table.

The light changes.

"Go, you blind bitch!" a deep voice instantly bellows from the bright yellow Hummer behind her.

"Bite me, asshole!" the Beverly Hills mom-type snaps back, then flips "hot guy in flashy Hummer" the finger (showing off a big, chunky diamond and high-maintenance manicure) and burns through the light.

The altercation interrupts Billy's beat but not his radiant mood, the pleasure of his fine company, or the subtle sweetness of his kick-ass caramel latté. And in addition to all that, abrasive catch phrases like "go, you blind bitch" and "bite, me asshole" sound more or less refreshing outside the realm of jail.

He indulges in a generous gulp, then wipes the corners of his mouth, removing the coffee smile, maintaining the perma-smile.

"Yeah, we went out. It didn't really get brought up."

Lily, prim and coifed par for the course and torn fully between concerned and beguiled, eyes him from across the table.

"Billy, half of the inheritance is rightfully yours. I thought you were moving on to *greener, more melodic pastures.* Isn't that what you told me?"

"I know. I will. *I am.*" A collection of whiskers serve as distraction; he tugs on one at a time, moving right to left along the edge of his chin. "But if I ask him for it, I'll have to leave."

"I see." Lily eagerly scoops up the opportunity to go "shrink" on him. "You and your brother are finally communicating. You're afraid the bond will be severed before it's strong enough to stand on its own."

"Um, no."

"Billy," she consoles, "separation is a common fear among siblings, particularly those who've been brought together because of a great loss – "

"It's her."

He shifts from tugging whiskers to chewing a thumbnail. "Who?"

"Oh, Lily." Billy exhales and raises his eyes to the sky, then underscores the enormity of his oncoming admission by scooting to the edge of the seat and dropping his voice to a sly whisper. "I've never met anyone like this in my life. She's everything: honest and funny and childlike, completely without ego. I don't know what she's doing with *him* – except that I know him – and I've been there." He shakes his head and concentrates until a few incisive points on the topic of "fiery dream girl" materialize. "She's like this delicate flower. I call her Rosie, but her name's Annie. She's my brother's girlfriend and...I'm in love with her." Then he falls back in his seat, throws his arms out airplane-style, turns his palms to the sky and announces, "I'm in love with her, Lily!"

Lily grins and gags on a piece of scone (not necessarily in that order), then glances at her watch.

"Oh dear, I just realized, I'm running late."

I'm pacing like a mad woman outside her office, eight minutes late, *natch*. But Lillian is late, too. Hello? I'm no scholar, but isn't that frowned upon? So much to say and now only thirty... no forty – *oh, this is ridick*. As I wind my watch back to real-people time for the *very first time*, Lillian rounds the corner.

Before she even gets a key in the lock, I'm driven by an overdue childlike need to confess everything to a woman who is but ten pounds and five Martinis shy of being my mother's clone. The irony is textbook.

As we enter her domain, back history regarding my adult-rated infantile existence flows stridently toward her.

"Hey, remember when we were discussing hate fucking and you said that while you've never been fortunate enough to experience it, you knew exactly what I was talking about?

"Ah, no."

Lily slams us in – trapped for another round of cerebral rehab.

Today, I'm up for it.

"Well, anyway, you may have been off the mark a little. Not pointing any fingers, but the sex I just had – with the brother of the man I'm living with – wasn't only very good, but *really* quite amicable. Yep, no feelings of hostility whatsoever." I pounce onto the putrid couch, cross my ankles on top of the coffee table, fold my hands behind my head. "So I was thinking; if losing your virginity has anything at all to do with connecting on an emotional level, I've lost it all over again!" I toss my hands into the air, then use them both to fan away the virtual steam rising from my body. "That'll be three times in all. Bet you can't say that," I dare, all giddy.

She shakes her head vigorously, but I detect behind that shake/shudder a definite curiosity in this twisted tale, and so I'm off.

"So, the first time I lost it was at cheerleading practice. Suzy Boucher fell off our seven-man pyramid and on her way down kicked me right in the crotch; dead center, big ole' saddle shoe, size eight and a half. And guess what? Size *does* matter."

Lillian ineffectively covers a chuckle with a cough, "I'm not sure that counts, Annie."

"No? Tell that to my mother. You should've seen her."

And suddenly we're gabbing like girlfriends as I take Lillian back to 1989 as a flock of naïve cheerleaders gape in confused horror while my rabid mother tows me by my black-and-gold sweater to our '78 Ford station wagon, tan, with veneer-paneled racing stripes. The car door's still ajar and my right foot's pressed into the pavement as she peels away. Dad's crouched in the back seat, an idle invertebrate buried behind a *Time* magazine. As soon as I've secured my body in its entirety *inside* the automobile (as opposed to under it), focus turns to the matter at hand. I bend forward and hold tight onto my crotch. I've also applied direct pressure to it here in her office, mostly because pain derived from *the-saddle-shoe-to-the-crotch-story* is exactly the kind of pain that recurs as often as you recap the saga. Sometimes it even transfers from *storyteller* to *story-tellee* during the vivid reenactment.

"So anyway, I was thirteen," (see that – bad number) "and Mother's gone berserk behind the wheel. 'Oh, my baby's been deflowered!' she's ranting. So I go, 'Mom, that doesn't count!' which was basically me taking another futile stab at self-defense when it still didn't feel entirely unnatural to do it."

That kooky statement shamelessly disrupts my pace.

"Does it feel unnatural to defend yourself now?" Lillian inquires sincerely, bridging the vulnerable space between us.

"No." Looking at her makes my defenses crumble. "Well, I don't know. I'm working on it."

"Working on it is good."

"Right." It is, isn't it? "So I'm in agony when Mother regurgitates a pun that to this day wakes me in the middle of the night. She shrills, top o' lungs, *Honey, a ripped hymen is a ripped hymen, any way you slice it!*' (Reread *that* statement with a Minnesota accent.) And then she slices into the air retracing the same imaginary "x" over and over, until that rigid hand of hers dives dramatically into her purse and emerges with a pack of Barclay's and a book of matches."

When I think of that day, I can almost feel the car swerving and jerking all the way home. Still, Dad read through it all. Anyone else would have been fully unnerved, but not Dad. He was truly, impressively, predictably, recurringly absent.

I recross my legs for added pressure.

Lillian finally crosses her legs tightly, too: universal sign that pain-induced-from-saddle-shoe-story is officially transferred.

"So I told Mom that was disgusting – because it was – and the shrew barks back 'So much for the white wedding!' Then she's convulsing and mumbling in tongues and tossing match after unstruck match over her shoulder like she's making a wish with salt (or hoping to light Dad on fire), and I'm thinkin': God, please get me outta here! Get me a block of ice shaped like a rocking horse so I can ride it into oblivion. But I'm trapped inside this mobile from Hell and stupidly resort to logic. Talking about the long-term psychological damage she's inflicting on my young, impressionable mind. Explaining that however twisted her views on sex may be, this incident is totally unrelated and so on.

"Did she comprehend any of this?"

Lillian leans forward onto her elbows, fully engrossed in my grade "A" chronicle.

"No. She continued to drive, heavy-footed behind the wheel, drunk, distraught, totally remiss of my plight." Embarrassment flushes over me. "So then I stooped to pleading. You know, something about the dawn of my adolescence and how I need to learn to love my body and sex is nothing to be ashamed of – " I inhale big for the finale. "So I'm rambling like a bastard when a faulty flying match still hinged to the book snarls itself into my hair and the Barclay's smack me right on the cheek. I look at her in shock and she barks, *'Ah, shut up and light one for your mother, will ya? She's having a real bad day.'*"

"You lit her cigarette?"

My head drops. A few ringlets fall forward, shadowing glossy eyes.

"Mm-hmm."

"I'm sorry, Annie."

"It's okay, Mom – *Doc.*" My head jerks up. I swipe away a tear that has lost its battle to gravity and downplay my *huge* verbal faux pas with a lame nonsensical remark. "Yeah, well, as luck would have it, I got my first post-coital smoke out of the deal. So that's something."

"When's the last time you spoke with your mother?"

"That day I told you about, two years ago, when she met MP."

And thank you for not addressing *huge* verbal faux pas with tedious long-winded shrink rationale. Forever indebted to Lillian at this point – forever.

"Is she still drinking?"

"Supposedly, no. Can we not talk about her any more today?"

Lillian nods.

"So, to wrap up, I then lost my virginity by way of penis, blah, blah… But last week with Billy – that's his name – I lost it for the third time. And you know what they say, 'Third time's a charm.'"

I collapse euphoric onto the Styrofoam-like cushions. Not the crescendo I was looking for, but it'll do.

"That's what they say." Lillian's thighs release the death grip they have around her crotch and her legs recross at the ankles: universal sign that pain-induced-from-saddle-shoe-story has officially faded.

And based on the history of recapping this peculiar tale, she has let go in record time. Good for her and her *awesome* letting-go skills. Damn, this woman is rapidly reaching "idol status."

"Annie, do you see how these incidents are directly related to your fear of functioning in a happy, healthy relationship?"

"I'm not afraid." Flustered maybe. And why is she turning into my shrink again when we were making such great girl-friends? "That's exactly what I want. A nice guy with a job and a dog, and a house where the sun always shines and everybody loves everybody. I told you that."

"Yes, you did. Now, why don't you tell me about the time you really lost your virginity? You know," she clears her throat, "by way of penis."

"Love to, but it's already 3:50, which is…3:50! Time's up."

Ooh, I like that. I look at my wrist again; still 3:50, which is…3:50! Wow, that was fun. Real people time is cool.

"I was late." Lillian checks her watch. "We've still got eight minutes."

My new near-idol has tricked and trapped me.

"Wow. You're good."

She smiles as if by design.

"Okay. Dang. Here goes." I rip at a nail. "Danny. His name was Danny." Danny, the true keeper of my virginity. "Just so you know, this story isn't what you think."

"I don't think anything yet."

"Right."

And I tell her about Danny.

That infamous night was abnormally humid, due to a monsoon that beat at his bedroom windows, creating this fantastical surround sound. And it was humid because Danny's body, sticky and still, save for the beating of his heart, lay gently on top of mine.

I sat at Sunday Mass the next morning, two rows behind him. It was August 18, 1992, the day after the eve of that mystical monsoon. And I prayed he'd turn and look at me. I remember my body curling into itself, alone among two hundred people.

We had joked about it for months, like that person who knows only one joke and retells it at every party, thereby saving himself from outcast. It was our standing joke, kept us interesting to each other, kept us anxious in love; our mutual virginity.

I sat in the pew, petrified from the abrupt, uncomfortable, disappointing mortal sin that took three and a half minutes to occur and has remained steady on my mind some thirteen hours later. We were sixteen and chose to be thieves, willfully stealing each others' innocence, or purchasing two direct flights to Hell, however the Catholics cared to look at it. And Danny was two rows up, slouched, shoulders stiff up by his ears, sandwiched between his parents. I willed him to turn and look. Just see me, please. One glance. That was my prayer that entire endless hour. Nothing. The congregation sang "Hallelujah." I heard murmurs between lyrics, felt four hundred eyes boring holes into my freshly damned skin.

That night, I went home and prayed until my blanched, veiny forearm developed a visibly jagged bloody mark.

There, now God and Mother wouldn't have to punish me. The lost skin from my arm settled under my fingernails, left to harden and figure its own way out.

Danny and I broke up by week's end, the third day of Junior year. After performing the deed in public, he turned from my locker and zigzagged back to class. For the next two weeks or so he walked like that – crooked, with his head hung low as if he were kicking a rock down a dirt path in the woods. And even though he would stuff his hands deep into his pockets to make himself less noticeable, I could see the blood on his arm, too, dark but not quite dry.

I burned inside my belly for Danny: lonely girl, lost, ugly, unloved, sad, hopeless, fearful, silent, sinner. I wanted forgiveness and with every new self-inflicted sting came a little of it. God couldn't hate me forever. And He surely wouldn't punish me if I beat Him to the punch. So I started sprinting toward pain, cunning and swift, anywhere I could find it.

"And that was it. Never spoke to Danny again. And that pretty much brings us up to date."

Yep, all the demons have officially come out to play; they've been revealed, released, and realized. And I've been so reckless with myself, with my soul.

A total of four nails fell victim to that story. Not bad. As I finish tearing off a cuticle, a surprising calm sweeps over me. I look up at Lillian with a shit-happens grin. She reciprocates the look, until both our smiles evolve into a laugh.

"So, what do you think?" I ask, just for fun, because I know what she thinks – that shit happens.

Traumatic tales of virginity lost, fucked-up parents, long-standing guilt, and asshole boyfriends are as widespread as the sunrise. No one can escape them. She folds her hands over her notes and looks at me sharply.

"I think you've been wavering between bliss and insanity for a very long time now. And I'm curious…which life are you ultimately going to choose?"

Excuse me? She just said that as though it's up to me, as though it's *always* been up to me. I was to blame for my life with MP. That's fine, but so was he. *Choose?* Is it really that easy? Suddenly, I feel stupid. And two things happen upon the onset of stupid. The first: need to abandon immediate area immediately. Done. Time's really up now, anyway. And the second: must cry. Assuming the first two reactions took place in chronological order, a third objective inevitably arises. As I jet efficiently (despite the double vision) toward my car, I dig for my cell and dial "happenstance number three."

"Samsu Institute of Alter – "

"Why can't I just have a normal life? A nice guy with a dog – "

"Jesus Christ, I'd rather make out with my own asshole than hear that speech one more time."

I sigh, groan, and paraphrase the best description of my life I've ever heard *in my life.* "I'm on the brink of bliss and insanity."

"Wow. I couldn't have said it better myself. Listen, your prana of circulation is freaky disturbed, but I'm jammed all day. Go home, smoke out, dab a little lavender on the temples, meditate on it, and call me in the morning. Hey, I just sounded like a real doctor!"

"My God, you've gone totally Eastern on me."

"Not my fault. Until I start my own practice, I'm surrounded by fucking Orientals." Fos redirects to a fellow employee, "Not you. You're fine." Then she moves the phone away from her ear and studies him. "Wait a minute, aren't you Mexican, *José*?" José stares at her all slanty-eyed and ethnically indistinguishable. "Fine. Fucking *Asian-Americans*," she states, patronizingly.

"It's José *Wong*," he scowls.

Fos points the phone at him. "Listen, José *Wong*, don't blame me. I didn't pick your American name. And don't be so sensitive. It takes away all the fun." Finally, it occurs to her to hang up. She presses her ear to the phone. "Look, you're twenty-eight, um...*Saturn Returns*?"

"You sound like my shrink."

Fos watches her "former" intern buddy strut brazenly away.

"Great, that'll be a hundred and twenty bucks. Look, I gotta go *José! C'mon, let's discuss this over cervezas –saki, I mean saki!* Ciao, Annabelle."

I reach my street, but can't shake the echo: *So what are you going to do now?*

An idea's brewing. I flip a bitch and head toward UCLA.

Saturn Returns

So the big mystery behind *Saturn Returns* has been uncovered: Every twenty-eight years, respectively, Saturn completes a circle around the zodiac to exactly where it was at the moment of birth, and then starts all over again, and so on. And because Saturn is the ruler of responsibility, when it comes full-circle, we become struck by an overwhelming sense of obligation to reassess our lives.

Hmm? I buy that. I mean, if I plan my social calendar around what *Cosmo's Bedside Astrologer* has to say, surely I can stop to consider some truths behind a concept that's not only thousands of years old, but manages to incorporate the entire freaking Universe. So *Saturn Returns* is basically an opportunity handed to each of us every twenty-eight years to reevaluate our circumstances, change our lives, follow our dreams, take new chances. If you feel antsy, now is the time to pay attention to your intuition. If you feel sick about a job or a relationship, use this time to fix the shit. Be bold.

Supposedly, if you ignore the "force" the first time around, you could wind up driving ninety MPH down a deserted road. Why? Because you're tailing a hooker you couldn't get it up for who stole your Rolex, the remains of your very first eight-ball, and your wallet containing three hundred bucks (a one-time hooker fee), along with a picture of your brand new grandchild. All this the result of turning fifty-six and toppling into what we less *cosmic* folk refer to as "a midlife crisis." Not pretty.

So, in addition to being jobless and working to wriggle out of lousy relationship with successful musician, and then plotting to discover lifelong happiness with his sibling – a much younger and slightly more homeless musician-type – I'm riddled with angst because one of my planets is all screwed up, or lined up, or whatever.

And then I ask myself how much reassurance can one person possibly need before they make an ultimate break toward their destiny? This one, that'd be me, clearly needs constant. And I just got that: An unavoidable life-altering phenomenon the size of, well, *a planet* has just been brought to my attention. The signs are piling up like dirty dishes in a bachelor's apartment. I should be grateful, elated.

I'm queasy as I climb the steps to the music hall and envision how peaceful my life might have been if no one had ever told me shit about shit. Determination further encourages this enlightened state of insight-induced nausea. Anonymous wasn't kidding when she or *he* said, "Ignorance is bliss." And speaking of happy-go-lucky half-wit dipshits, there's Summer and her bundles of bliss. Kidding, I'm kidding; that's my fake-hate at work. Through a tiny translucent window on the heavy soundproof door, I make out their images – MP's and hers –

side by side at the piano. Hell, they're both upright. Screw it, I'm going in.

Okay, breathe, blink, and pretend to behave yourself. And remember, this isn't about everything he's done, the affair(s), or the insults. This is about forward motion, breaking up, and moving on. This is about starting a new life in a clean and positive fashion. This isn't about vindication. Be "direct," think "amicable."

Direct.

Amicable.

I slip inside the door.

MP plays a string of melodic chords.

"Do you feel the spontaneity in both pieces? Schubert was a romantic a century before Porter and considered the most poetic musician to ever live…and then along came Porter." His fingers fondle the keys again. "Smooth, yet surprising and whimsical, with echoes of Schubert laced throughout. This is *feeling* the music."

And then he places his hand on Summer's heart/boob.

As the door snaps shut, MP's head jerks in its direction.

"Excuse me for a minute."

"I'll be right here-*ere*," she sings.

She's so silly, sexy, sleazy, tone deaf. *Kidding.*

He jogs the distance, as if I won't sense the awkward tension from twenty feet away when I've felt it from five doors down since the day The Blonde moved in.

"Hi, sweetie. I was just teaching Summer how to sing the blues."

"You're definitely the man for that job."

Well, so much for *amicable.*

Summer slips me a wave.

"Cute. What are you doing here?"

And with "Chop Sticks" as my theme song, I proceed.

"Just came from the library – "

A laugh erupts through his nose. "Did they start serving Margaritas at their book-of-the-month club?"

"Shut up. Um, I was wondering, um – " *Oh, Jesus, just say the words; it's over!* "You didn't talk to Billy did you?"

And we can kiss *direct* good-bye.

"We went out."

My hands go palms up.

"And…"

He mimes the move, says, "And it was fun."

MP's an expert diverter via two techniques: 1) long, tedious elucidations that go way beyond the point, or 2) short, choppy sentences that never quite get to the point. Decoding the dude and the situation *toute de suite* has become second nature.

As I focus and peer honestly and bravely into those steely blues, his true state of affairs busts wide open. Call me Claire Voyant. *Or* call me a sucker who's lived with this fucker long enough to read his mind.

"It's gone, isn't it?"

"What do you mean?"

"Now who's cute? Billy's share; his *college* fund. Where'd it go? Is it paying for your *PhD?* Is he going to reside clueless on our couch *indefinitely*? Is that your *plan?*"

And I am air-quoting *all* over the place.

"Your annoying sister stayed with us for a month last year and I didn't say shit."

"It's my annoying cousin, and you bitched every day for a week, then took off for three. And don't evade the point. You need to say something so he can make plans."

"You're right."

I am? Never been right before. *Who drugged this guy?*

"Have you kleptoed my Klonopin?"

"What?"

"Never mind."

"I'll talk to him tomorrow. I'm working here late tonight."

"Perfect."

Weird – I mean that. Don't care how late he works on whomever.

"Anything else?" he demands.

But I'm lost in thought, overcome by a satisfying indifference toward this foul creature in front of me.

"Hello? Is that what you came here for? To razz me about Sir William while I'm working?"

He's an ass. Decidedly not worth a break-up. And the *other* good news is that I'm already packed.

"Nope, nothing else." As I spin on a heel to go and sense a freedom-inspired groove creep into my gait, another epiphany strikes (*enough already*). I stop and turn. "MP, what are you living off of?"

"I still have my money. William's was used on my master's."

An amazingly guilt-free admission.

"No, *we* paid for your master's. Remember one for all and *all* for you?"

"Okay, that's either Foster or PMS talking, two things we could use a little less of. I paid off my bachelor's, then. Who can remember at this point?" he mutters while pivoting into his own version of a saunter.

"MP?" I call back, "Why don't you give Billy the money you're spending on my therapy? Off the record – *I be healed.*"

He chuckles.

"That's pro bono, sweetie. She was a friend of Mother's. See you later tonight."

By the time I reach the parking structure, my hands are fully cemented around my 34As while I unabashedly praise God, Fate, and quarter tosses. *Pro bono?* What kind of freak would I be if I was sporting a pair of *pro bono* C-bags?

I look back and don't even remember what came first, the move to Los Angeles or the ludicrous obsession with my breasts. Or maybe moving to this city merely unleashed a buried fixation. I think I expected that my body would turn out exactly like my mother's. I had this live-in, in-your-face-image of "woman" and didn't know I had the right to be different. They didn't give out "As" for originality in my house.

And now, I'm finally free to actually dig the little suckers. I mean, c'mon, they're just boobs. They've been very well-behaved, have never gotten in my way or upstaged me. Plus my wire-free bras (if I bother with one at all) set me back a mere $5.99 a pop.

Enough about that. My immediate needs: get to Billy, grab my shit. Go. And then on long-term list I log: make a phone call (i.e., "Hi Mom, it's me. How ya doing?") and write a letter to Dr. Lillian Schulman that reads:

Dear Doc Schulman,

Hi. Really sorry about filling your head with graphic images of a sexual nature regarding two men you must deem as sons. Understand now why you were lookin' at me funny. By the way, chose bliss.

Best Regards,

Rosie – the woman formally known as a girl named "Annie."

I put the key in the ignition, which teases me before starting, and then I turn on the radio, not paying much heed to any of it. My brain is a gymnasium of thoughts boomeranging around like acrobats. They move freely and eloquently in and out of my consciousness, politely taking turns at center stage: MP, Billy, Lillian, my cute little boobies, Mother, tequila. Haven't had any of that today…hmm?

Meanwhile, I'm driving and singing along to 98.7. "*Is it love tonight, when everyone's dreaming of a better life. In this world divided by fear, we've gotta believe that there's a reason we're here. There's a reason we're here..."*

And thinking; Venus, Mars, *Saturn*, who knew?

"'Cause these are the days worth living. These are the years we're given. These are the moments..."

The tequila's probably warm and nasty. Forego the alcohol...but my boobies, they *are* cute.

"...these are the times, let's make the best out of our lives."

God, listen, Dude; I get it. I *finally* get it, but enough of The Calling. I've heard this song six times today.

I shut off the radio but keep on singing, the lyrics dug into my brain like, well, like lyrics do.

"See the truth all around. Our faith can be broken and our hands can be bound. But open our hearts and fill up the emptiness..."

Man, that Lillian is one resilient gal. I love Billy.

"...is it not worth the risk? Yeah, is it not worth the risk?"

Yeah, Billy, you're worth the risk.

Beam me up, Lama

aiting for Billy to show up *whenever* has my insides buzzing.

"Billy, hi," I practice, while bouncing from a pile of clothes in the closet to a pile camouflaged behind a dresser to a pile oozing out from under the bed. Might as well keep packing on behalf of the impending getaway.

"Billy, hi. Guess what? I love you. I know it sounds a little whacky, due to our current living situation. Okay, that sucks. *'Cause these are the days worth living…*" But have strategically found a week's worth of my favorite undies. Wow. This guy makes me wanna wear underwear. Damn, that's progress. "*… these are the days we're given…*" And the dry-run continues. "Billy, hi. So, what do you say we fuck everything and ride off into the sunset?"

Ugh. That's romantic.

I bolt to grab bathroom necessities. "*...these are the mo-ments, these are the times, let's make the best out of our lives.*"

"Hey, Billy? Knock-knock. Who's there? Tada! It's the woman of your dreams!"

With arms spread wide, both feet planted firmly on the ground, back arched and smile broad, I study the eccentric stranger staring back at me.

A word to the wise: Don't ever tell a knock-knock joke in front of a mirror. You'll discover you're not funny. And you'll find instead a disheartened, lovesick fool who's sick to death of the sight of herself. Or more specifically: a not-so-funny, perpetually over-tired, under-nourished, mentally wavering, borderline addict who's cute but not gorgeous, fit but not flaw-less, and genial enough, sure, but not quite confident.

What am I doing? Sobriety, one whole day of it, may be causing delusions of grandeur.

A sluggish tear inches down my cheek, detours around my nose, then dwells in the groove of my upper lip. With a lick, it vanishes. Time to start recycling. The makeup bag topples from hand to floor, only to be replaced with a bottle of *my* "whitest and tightest."

I dismally dismiss the chick who wants to take-a-gamble-and-turn-her-life-around and sit on the bed yoga-style, pills propped within eye-line. Time to beckon Buddha.

"Om...Om...Om Ah Hum Varja Guru Padma Siddhi Hum...Somebody Get My Life Unfucked Up...Om Ah Hum Varja – "

Suddenly, Billy pounces onto the bed wearing a faded-blue "I ♥ NY" T-shirt and grungy Levis that ride his hips, revealing an underwear band and a string of tiny hairs that trail down and sneak behind it. His feet bob up and down, a pair of worn-out black thongs hang loose about them. The sheer look of him has sufficiently messed with my meditating.

His head finds my shoulder, while solemn black eyes plead

deliberately and a hand slips around my waist. And, I think I hear him cooing.

"Let's run away. You pack a bag, I'll get my horse. We'll ride off into the sunset."

This is conveniently surreal.

His words douse me with an original overpowering happiness. And in doing so, a crucial mistake rapidly evolves: We escape to the indiscriminate world of young-in-love, rather than to the pragmatic shelter of old beat-up Mustang (going seventy and heading east).

I'm shining like polished silver in the sun as I tease, "You don't want to run away with me. I'm a bundle – "

"Of joy."

He sprawls on top of me, mischief of the ultimate kind branded inside those dancing eyes.

"Well, I talk too much."

"Loquacious. Mmm, I love that word. *Loquacious.*"

An open kiss tickles my neck.

"And…I'm excessively emotional."

"You have a heightened sense of consciousness. We should all be so lucky."

He takes my hands, holds them above my head, distributes a generous amount of quick soft kisses on my cheeks and lips.

Wriggling away, I blurt (see "chatty" above), "I'm too flirtatious."

"Alluring. People are compelled by you."

"Compelled to slap me."

"And I revere your modesty."

I slide out from under him, prop my head in my hand.

"It's not all modesty, Billy."

New love has just taken a turn for the serious – the *seriously* insecure.

He rolls onto his side, mirrors my lean.

"Feeling sorry for someone is no reason to stay with them."

"He doesn't feel sorry for me. I might not be the most cosmopolitan chick on the planet, but I'm nobody's charity case."

Apparently I'm en route from Paradise to Paranoid. Buckle up if you're along for the ride; it might get rocky. That's all I can think, as my heart slowly sinks.

"I was referring to MP, Rosie."

Billy lies back on the bed, doubles the space between us. I watch him sullenly as he studies the lonely globs of paint on our ten-by-twelve sky.

"You know what I loathe most about him?" he says.

Is he asking for a list?

"I hate that he has the mastery to compliment and belittle a person at the same time. Like he loves them despite all their imperfections, then brainwashes them into believing they should be damned grateful for it."

Wow. A long overdue sigh escapes my mind, body, and soul.

"I've known him a few more years than you," he smirks apologetically.

I'm the one who should be apologizing.

Then he reaches into his back pocket, pulls out a slim white box garnished with a simple red ribbon, and rests it on my chest.

I open it: Two Henkel's paring knives.

"I know it's not much, just a small start – "

"It's roses," I whisper. "You brought me roses."

He nods. We really "get" each other. And he finds me charming, despite all my bullshit. I slip the gift into my half-packed bag off the side of the bed and then rest my head on his chest. His arms wrap around my shoulders. It's beyond me how I've made it to the eye of my own tornado to finally discover warmth and strength inside an embrace. I could sleep here, his heartbeat my new sedative of choice.

He sweeps a hand down to my waist.

"Billy…stop."

But he progresses until I squirm like crazy and make a bold break for it.

I slap him away playfully, catch my breath, and order, "Behave yourself!"

Then, he gets back on top of me like a good boy, shoves his tongue down my throat like a *great* boy and wrenches at my clothes like the *rock star* he was born to be.

And hooray for me. Destiny can wait fifteen more minutes. Right?

"Ah! Earring!"

"Sorry, Rosie," he giggles, yanking at my shirt.

"It's cool. I only need one ear. But seriously, stop yanking. *Untangle.*"

"Oh, okay. Right."

Shirt and earring go their separate ways while I undo his jeans. We're wild and so in sync that neither of us hears the door squeak open.

MP barges into the apartment, heads for the piano. His mission: to seize forgotten sheet music and be on his way. As he reaches for his latest composition, he picks up muffled sounds of deep scratchy chatter coming from the bedroom. Instantly, the last pliable fraction of his heart turns cold, dense, and as hard as the rest.

The noises recall a memory that's been stashed for two decades: a twelve-year-old MP marching nervously, systematically down a dim hallway to his mother's bedroom. His baby brother, Billy, grips the net of his playpen, cries out when he sees his brother breeze past him. MP pushes open the bedroom door to see his mother, Maggie, in bed with a man who is clearly *not* his father.

"Michael…" she says. *"Michael!"*

Her voice rings through his ears, shaky and piercing. She jumps from the bed, chases him a whole block before he sprints free of her. But the name echoes on, haunting him like a disreputable dutiful follower.

MP swallows the memory, angry for having had it. As he barrels down the hallway, he reminds himself that the past is a crutch for the sentimental, an excuse for the weak to stay that way. For him, there's no logical reason to hold on to any of it, especially with Mother gone.

He bolts into the bedroom to see Billy and me in a "position" that could be deemed compromising. But it's not so bad. We're dressed – mostly. I mean, it's not like I'm blowing him. Still, "awkward" and "fucked" quickly come to mind as big brother encroaches.

"Michael!" I leap up, hoping to hinder a potentially grizzly situation. But my attire – a bra and a pair of cut-off Levi's – doesn't prove to be much of a visual anesthetic.

"There's that fucking name again."

He smacks me solid across the face. I spin a hundred and eighty degrees and land hard on my knees; a burning sensation quickly sprawls across my left cheek.

Billy comes to my rescue.

"Calm down, man," he says, lunging between MP and me but making the mistake of casting the majority of his focus onto "the safety of me."

"You have to steal everything, don't you!"

And MP seizes this opportunity to nail his brother square in the jaw. Billy falls down (oops) onto me (ouch), jumps up (dizzy), punches MP (a mistake), loses his balance (foreseeable), and then topples toward the bed (phew), but lands clumsily on the floor (bummer).

"If you'll just let us explain – " he speaks to the ground on bended knees.

"Explain what? My sociopathic brother's been fucking my schizophrenic girlfriend!?"

As Billy stabilizes himself enough to rise, MP pummels him again. They fall onto the bed, punching and biting and choking each other, pulling out hair, and it's like ultimate fighting. Under vastly different circumstances, this could be wildly entertaining. Of course, due to these current and specific circumstances, my beak is freaked and the outcome's lookin' bleak.

A dresser-drawer handle helps hoist me to my feet. The idea: to assist Billy in his unmitigated losing battle. But on my first step forward, a stray heel juts backward and biffs me right in the face, the other side of my face. Small consolation. I hit the wall hard, then slink to the floor. And the cold truth is, I've always been more of a "mental anguish" kind of girl. This sort of pain is totally new. And I believe I'm seeing stars, and I'm not talking about Cruise and Pitt. The room is rapidly revolving into a darker blurry version of itself, but my hearing is holding strong.

"You treat her like shit," Billy utters, and quite audibly, considering MP's elbow is cutting off like eighty percent of his oxygen.

"This from the bastard who was cuffed at our mother's funeral!"

MP jumps off him, disgusted, falters before gaining balance.

"At least I know how to treat women – " Billy coughs, grips his throat.

"Oh, shut the fuck up! You're a kid; what do you know?" MP wipes the blood from under his nose, then deadlocks his fist with his kid brother's eye. "I knew it was a mistake to let you anywhere near my life!"

Billy's head springs back and forth on the bed, trapped between the mattress and the cold hard fist that continues to drive rhythmically into his eye like a high-speed lever attached to a power source.

Propelled by my old friend, Adrenaline, and a new, odd inhabitant of a mother-like nature, I thrust myself up from the fetal position with Billy's physical well being at heart.

"MP! Get off him! I'm sorry. I'm so sorry. Let's just go. Let's go for a ride, just you and me."

MP stops and steps back awkwardly while flexing and releasing the raw, bloodied knuckles on his right hand. He angles his eyes toward me like he's won a prize, grabs my wrist as if to claim it.

"And you can forget about your winnings, William."

A concise summation on "reunion with baby brother" finally evolves into spoken word.

We sort of drag each other from the room as I delicately mouth the words, "I'm sorry."

So I'm tragically dizzy and equally bewildered as to who just kidnapped whom. But Billy's alive, that's the main thing.

He scans the room as though he's lost something valuable. Blood runs from nose to chin and drips onto the bedspread. He wipes his hand down his whole face, then across his jeans, and stumbles to his feet, then backs out slow and steady, in the fashion of MP, but minus any trace of glory.

A couple of books and his flannel are scooped up from around the living room and shoved into his duffel bag. He strides toward the door, reaching for and sweeping his guitar over a shoulder along the way, and exits. Moments later, the door squeaks open. Billy pops his head in, reaches for a set of keys on the bookshelf, retreats.

He stands outside the apartment, sizing up the Mustang. Duffel bag and guitar tumble into the backseat as he hops into the front. The key twists in the ignition, but the car doesn't start. He waits, scans its interior, counts six different shoes, but can't spot all their matches. Notices there's a vacation's worth of clothing piled up in the backseat and based on their size and style, he notes the vacation would lean harshly toward tropical. Then he spots a leather-bound book peeking out from under his duffel bag: *an address book*. So old-school. So Rosie. He seizes the jewel. When he twists the key a second time, the engine revs, and the car speeds off.

The Semi-Done

*t*he *Semi-Done* is any relationship that should be over but isn't because either one or both of its constituents are too scared, too cheap, or too fucking lazy to actually end the goddamned thing. MP and I have been in a semi-done since the day we began. No lie. For starters, he's a Pisces and I'm a Libra. That spells doom right there. Won't even tell you his birth date; it hit me like a karate chop to the larynx. Feel free to surmise it (think of my least favorite number *ever* and toss it into a month/day format). Anyway, I figure half of all existing relationships are in The Semi-Done. The other half? Divorced.

I look around through two swollen eyes that are rapidly turning Japanese and refuse to come into focus. MP's driving like a bastard and has reached the 405 in under five, a new record for all of us. It's 6:00 P.M. and we're going seventy. It's 6:00

P.M. and we're going seventy on a Friday on the 405! This is apocalyptic. I mean, I hope not, but if someone from one of the other cars whizzed past and screamed, "Run for your freaking life, this is the Apocalypse!" after today's string of events, I'd buy it.

MP is dangerously silent, and from his profile the blue and whites of his eyes blend together, making them even more *empty*. I sit contemplative and creeped-out.

In the time it takes to order dinner, tie your shoes, or take a pee, an already floundering relationship was forever severed; that's what really just went down. My own selfish tendencies, combined with capricious dallying, destroyed any chance Billy and MP ever had of reconciliation. Plus, they strongly increased Billy's chances of an unexpected yet prolonged stay – *hospital* stay, that is.

I had planned this so differently in my mind – the big getaway. Envisioned the horse, Billy dressed in velvet garb from another century, while scarves of magenta and violet swam away from my gown, teasing the autumn air as we galloped toward our sunset. And MP...well, he was nowhere near my fantasy, but off contentedly educating his latest muse – The Blonde. Today's follies have instead been a stark example of the startling variation between "virtual" and "actual." Another mentally mapped-out experience foiled by the authenticity of fruition. Because, you see, when it was played out in my mind, "virtually" everyone won and no one was hurt. But in "actuality," history is unfolding quite differently and viciously: One man has been drained of any trace of compassion while another has been raped of dignity and (most likely) a straight nose. And both have lost any future chance at *a brother*.

Now I'm slumped – all sticky in the black leather bucket seat – consumed with a guilt so powerful that the numbness in my cheeks has traveled to my legs, rendering them use-less (otherwise, yes, Yours Truly would have no qualms about jumping out of a moving vehicle driven by What's-His-Name, even at seventy MPH).

But this is horrible, and so, so wrong. MP is neither a nice nor faithful companion, but now I, too, fall into that squalid category. And with his brother! My crime was the superior, or so it felt upon disclosure.

People make mistakes, accept them, and move on un-der the try-and-try-again postulate. But guilt, lust, and reck-lessness create a toxic blend of emotions that hinder natural forward motion. Guilt feeds on the soul like a virus without a deadline for departure. Its twisted logic generates a series of slow, suffocating choices that seem practical, but in truth, smother the voice of unblemished desire that makes life not only worth experiencing but, at the very least – tolerable. The intent of guilt is to banish sin, but it only buries it, triggering all future motivations to be driven by self-loathing, resentful cynicism.

I'm blanketed by that very emotion, too distraught to brood over my next best move. All I know is that for once in my life, the responsibility of this situation is mine to bear. And I can't let a lifetime of well-maneuvered, too familiar brain-washing dictate any more reactions.

MP finally glances over. And in a rehearsed condescending demeanor, he asks, "Does it hurt?"

I flip down the visor to inspect my red, inflamed eyes.

"Not too bad," the liar in me replies.

"But it hurts a little, right?"

"You're a funny guy."

"All in the name of making you laugh."

"Oh, I'm laughing…on the inside." Then I rotate my body to see him. "Could we please break up now?"

He twists his neck to display the full-frontal version of a wry smile: *This* is his reply.

"What are we doing?"

"Going for a drive."

"MP, I'm serious."

He continues cruising along a deserted freeway that's generally considered more of a parking lot. But not today. The cards haven't been played that way.

"I think we should end this like, um…adults."

"Are you an adult now, sweetie?"

He muffles a laugh.

"I don't know, I'm thinking about it."

"Well, think about this; William has always wanted what I've got. It's all a competition with him. He loathes losing but loves using."

I watch with my less-bad eye as he trails off, impressively convincing himself of his own bullshit. He goes so far as to cite specific childhood incidents where Billy duped and deceived him. And then he explains the whole karma-thing to me, for the hundredth time this year.

"So steer clear," is his advice.

And his stories would be quite convincing if one didn't bother to consider the age difference *or* ever meet Billy. But it's impossible to imagine an eight-year-old regularly exploiting his eighteen-year-old brother, particularly when Billy and MP are the eight and eighteen-year-olds in the aforementioned scenario. In therapy, MP's spiel would be referred to as "transference." See, I've been listening.

For the life of me, I can't figure out where he's going with this. But fear, fatigue, foresight, one month of therapy, and two ballooning cheek bones tell me to remain calm, kind, kinda clever, and above all, candid.

"MP, you and I both know that "together" we're a train wreck. And this whole thing with Billy and me is insignificant. We're like the smoke that settles after the disaster; we're "weightless" by comparison.

I realize all this quiet logic, which is way out of character, must be confusing to him. Surely, though, he has to agree. Yet he's eyeing me as if I'm speaking Cantonese and he's *not* fluent in it. And I detect the onset of a smile or snarl, with him, it's hard to distinguish. And I'm sort of getting the impression he has no intention of ending our erroneous affair, and sees this *joy* ride as an opportunity to gloat in the victory of the latest "unmentionable interlude."

The silence is too alarming. And knowing MP, this is a perfect opportunity for me to get him to realize he's the one who doesn't want me – which he doesn't – and should realize.

"What do you see in me anyway?"

"You remind me of her," he whispers.

His mother? To my surprise, I'm traumatized. That is the sweetest thing he's ever said since the day we met. A lump rapidly forms in my throat, mostly on behalf of the sad futility of the overdue admission.

And he continues like the quiet philosopher.

"It's like this: you're her rough cut, sweetie. You know, before she discovered her talent and grace."

And the lump efficiently vanishes.

But his enthusiasm and stylized speech escalate with each new insult.

"It's like if my mother were the *Venus de Milo*, you'd be the chunk of alabaster they carved her from. Like if my mother were a painting, say the *Mona Lisa*, you'd be – "

"Yeah, yeah, I get it. I'd be the blank canvas."

"More like a mediocre Picasso rip-off. But my point is there's hope for you."

I'm beyond tears and it hurts to smile, so laughing is definitely out of the question. But I am aghast, wondering how my life ever got so far from center.

"Plus, you kind of look like her, you know, when she was in her thirties," he adds, matter-of-factly.

"I'm twenty-eight."

"I know."

Welcome to my freak show. In a frenzy of panic this was my solution? *Talking to the guy?*

You know, Mother once told me: *Reasoning with a narcissist is like playing chess with yourself. If you ever get to the end of the game, it's only because you lost.* Wish I had thought of that two years ago.

"MP, look, this isn't easy. I know about Summer, okay? And I'm really, really sorry about Billy. I never meant to hurt you, but this has to – "

"Wait a minute; are you breaking up with me?"

"No. No." I keep my voice low and level. "I think we should break up with each other. I mean for starters, we're both dating other people."

He hovers over me as if he's forgotten he's driving.

"You can't break up with me! I settled for you! Besides, I'm in mourning."

"Bad timing, I know," barely maintaining, "but for two years now my ego's been buried under your insults." And now I'm pointing and shaking and having another *O.O.B.E.* "You want to talk about karma? Someday you'll find real love. The kind that makes you forget to eat and steals your sleep. And when you do, if she reels you in and then slowly whittles at your soul, ridiculing the essence of who you are until you speak in choppy banal sentence fragments and can't recall the last time you touched a piano…*that, my friend, will be karma catching up with you.*"

I'm livid, fearless, and queasy, too, as tears of anger and regret erupt begrudgingly. There's the "truth" and there's "brutal honesty." The latter, even in times of necessity, rarely resolves anything. The latter just possessed my body.

Here's what happened next: MP got off at the closest exit and jumped back on the freeway heading south.

"What are you doing?"

"We're going back home, sweetie. I'm taking you to Sir William, the man who makes you forget to eat and…what was that – steals your sleep? Good one, by the way, very prosaic – I mean poetic. Did I say *prosaic?*" He laughs coldly. "You're a regular Elizabeth Barrett Browning…*How do I love thee…*"

And he's doubled over in hysterics, wrapped around the wheel while veering in and out of our lane.

"It's over, MP. You and me: We're over. You know that."

"We'll see," he responds with eerie confidence. "I bet he won't even be there. Care to wager?" And he chuckles some more. "Bet ya five bucks."

Fortunately, the inflammation in my face is doing a fine job of masking any added disdain I'm developing for the creature beside me. I concentrate on the road, knowing that shortly I'll be traveling down it alone. My kinship will be with patience, focus, and faith this evening, and I'll be just fine.

Not a word is spoken for the next fifteen minutes. I fight off a serious case of "baby-head" near journey's end and there's but one thought inhibiting a hasty jaunt into Never-Never-Land: Is all this, this mess of catastrophic proportions, a chain reaction to my reaction to some guy grabbing my ass on a day I wasn't particularly in the mood to have it grabbed?

Is this the single trivial isolated incident responsible for unraveling my entire world? For blood shed, excess tears, for ending family ties?

Or, is all this a direct result of burning and yearning to seize the day without having a goddamned clue how to do it? Is the destruction surrounding me a result of being doggedly proactive yet utterly ignorant? I sure hope so. All I know is that I've made a mess of things. Still, I must sacrifice everything to chase, as Lillian put it, my bliss.

On the Brink of Bliss and Insanity

I'm so very, very tired. But that's just unbridled anxiety coupled with a few heavy blows to the head talking. Because I'm outta here. I'm off to chase my rainbow, where I pray Billy will be waiting, guitar slung over one shoulder, leaning earnestly against the edge of it.

Happy Halloween

The most highly regarded, widely celebrated holiday in the greater Los Angeles area has at long last rolled around again: it's Halloween, baby! Well, technically, it's the Friday before Halloween. But here in HELL.A., the festivities start early and wind down about a week later. It's a beautiful thing.

Foster's costume seamlessly defines her from the core out. The proud title of "Brazen Bitch" she's worked incessantly to validate finally has a bona fide visual counterpart, rending any "biting commentary" fully optional on her part. Terbear's *dominatrix outfit* is a little too small in the tits and hips, but in her case works to augment the effect the ensemble has on the innocent onlooker.

As she applies a third coat of scarlet lipstick, a hasty series of knocks assault her door. She struts over, opens it, strikes a menacing pose and glares suspiciously at a freshly bloodied, soon to be bruised Billy.

And Billy's sufficiently spooked. He's heard rumors. Also, he's forgotten about Halloween with the whole love triangle/ damsel in distress thing looming over his head.

"You *must* be Billy," Foster knowingly surmises in her best sinister tone.

"I can't help it; I've fallen in love with her."

When his mind's in anarchy, his heart does the talking. And to Foster's chagrin, Billy just unwittingly quoted Elvis, turning five extraneous seconds in the company of this dude into several grueling hours, inclusive of medical attention and a viable rescue mission.

Foster shakes her head, extends an arm, crumples up the "I ❤ NY" part of his T-shirt inside a fist, and jerks him inside, where he's enthusiastically greeted by a gender-iffy Wonder Woman and an espresso-overloaded, private school "girl." Terbear's got the knee-highs, the short pleated skirt, the ponytails... but she doesn't look sixteen. She looks like a centerfold – surging her fuckability-factor through the roof while diminishing the hugability trait to just "a means to an end."

"Wow! Hi, I'm Terbear! It's so fabulous to finally meet you!"

She gives him a quick, cute hug.

"Hey, buddy! Shane, good to meet you." And as they grip hands and shake heartily like "men," rays of light deflect off Shane's gold bracelet.

Holy Fright Night is the only phrase Billy's mind conjures up, and it keeps reverberating: *Holy Fright Night, Holy Mother of Fright Night*, and so on.

"Great costume!" Terbear says, charmingly.

Billy smiles but lacks riposte, mostly cause he doesn't realize she means him.

But as the awkward urgency of the moment reveals itself,

that is, when Shane and Terbear realize Billy's outfit isn't a costume, and the blood on his face, shirt, knuckles, jeans, etc., didn't come out of a kit, they decide to give him and Foster a moment in private.

Shane wraps his arms around Terbear, carries her out.

"We'll be next door playing *hide the smokin' soy sausage.* Knock if you need us."

"Baby!" She slaps him jokingly and yells, "I don't eat meat!" explaining Shane's esoteric vegetarian penis reference.

Billy and Foster are left alone, knowing all they got in common is their disinterest in penis references. Well, there's *that…* and Annie. He gently sets his bag and guitar on the floor, trying not to disrupt her noticeable intensity.

Foster opens what should be the silverware drawer and pulls out a vat of pot-smoking paraphernalia, then rolls a joint and smokes it. Then she rolls another one – smokes that.

Billy stands quietly and uncomfortably – qualities Foster really looks for in a guy. Well, to rephrase: if Foster gave a shit about *any* traits a member of the XY Club might possess, "quiet" and "uncomfortable" would definitely be at the top of her list.

Billy can't tell whether the smoke in the room is preventing him from seeing the whites of her eyes or whether there is no "white" in her eyes. He vaguely makes out Lisa Marie nibbling on his sock. He squats to pet him, then stands back up, leans against the stove, and spots the ceramic Elvis salt-and-pepper shakers. They're simply one of those novelty items that have to be touched sooner or later, so he reaches over and nabs one.

"Don't touch that! Put that back." Foster vehemently barks.

"Sorry." Billy nearly fumbles the object, but regains composure and grip, and places it carefully back on the stove. "Sorry. I didn't know."

"You can touch Jesse if you want to. Just not Elvis." She

pauses, then continues condescendingly, "You do know Elvis had a twin? *Jesse.* Died at birth."

"Yeah, of course. Who doesn't?" Billy lies, afraid of the consequences that might result from ignorance on the subject of unusual Elvis trivia.

"So go ahead, touch him," she orders.

"Okay."

Billy reluctantly but obediently reaches for the other shaker, holds it securely between both hands. A drop of sweat crawls down the edge of his face, then another.

All of a sudden (like a hundred hours later) Fos breaks out pad and pen and…more rolling papers.

"I have a plan," she announces, and proceeds to rigorously roll another joint, light it, draw a bunch of diagrams, smoke it, and rattle out some kind of scheme.

He listens intently, incorporating all the behaviors that ultimately prevent him from being booted from the room, until he's totally overwhelmed.

"I'm not so sure that this is the most rational solution."

Foster stops mid-drag, and through the focused inhalation of a professional smoke-aholic, she states, "Of course it's not rational. It's relative." Then she exhales a healthy clump of smoke right into his face. "But trust me, at this point, it's the only plausible cure to the condition we've politely dubbed 'Annie's Fucked-up Existence.'"

"I don't know, Foster. I told you they're not even there. He dragged her out and drove off."

"And I told you, they'll be back. I give 'em an hour, tops."

Behind fresh blood, dried blood, and swelling, Fos perceives his trepidations.

"Hey, you asked for my help. I'm giving it to you."

She reaches into a drawer reserved for things like tape, scissors, and paperclips, and pulls out a gun.

"What are you doing with that?!" Billy screeches, discovering a whole new octave.

"Boy, quit asking me stupid questions," she says, pointing the gun at him. "You're not going to muck this up, are you?"

Foster fires a flame from the gun/lighter and laughs like Satan. Or, like Billy imagines Satan would laugh, if he was a woman, which apparently he is. Then she jumps onto a chair and starts pounding under a vent on the kitchen wall.

Billy heard the shrieks earlier from what he assumed was the "undead," but wishes desperately that Fos would pick a better time to correspond.

"Hey, time for the dismount people! You have five minutes to get off your ride and into mine. The Happy Drunk Couple *will* be joining us." She jumps off the chair. "What are you doing?"

Billy has rummaged through his duffel bag and put on the ski mask.

"I don't want to be recognized."

"You know, every day I wake up in this city it becomes increasingly apparent that I'm an endangered fucking species."

"What's that supposed to mean?"

She creeps ever closer and yanks off the mask.

"It means, don't make me hurt you." Then she chucks the mask back at him and mumbles, "Broad freaking daylight?"

"It's Halloween."

"Shut up."

"Look at you!"

"What *about* me?"

They face each other, eye to silver-studded nipple caps (she's an Amazon in those five-inch thigh-highs).

"I'm just saying – " Billy catches himself slouching, then cautiously re-erects.

Foster nudges him, steps back.

"And perk up, will ya? We'll get ya your girl."

Shane and Terbear barge in, both their makeup is smudged everywhere, and, of course, they reek. Billy moves aside to clear himself of sniffing distance, then waits for Fos to implement Part 1 of Plan A.

Billy watches warily. As Fos reviews "The Plan," he discreetly examines "The Clan."

"You know what? You two ride with him." Fos points to Billy. "I need some breathing room."

Billy's driving with thoughts bouncing equally between Rosie's well-being and Shane's shiny, blue, shrink-wrapped balls taunting him through the rearview mirror.

"So, what do you two do?"

"We teach over at Carpenter Avenue Elementary. Off Laurel Canyon," the sweet little vixen riding shotgun chirps.

"Right. Know the place. Progressive." Billy nods directly to Shane's balls.

"I like your hair. Here, you have a twig or something." Terbear leans over, rips a dried-blood-hairball-like concoction from above his ear. "Oh. *Sorry.*"

Then she hands it to him. Billy gives it a strange once-over, rubs his head, tosses it out the window.

"Litter bug," Terbear sings, then slaps him and smiles. "Kidding!"

"So you don't think my hair's too shaggy?" Billy inquires.

"No, it's sexy."

"Yeah, man, it's hot." Wonder Woman adds. "I mean, I'm way too conservative to pull it off, but chicks dig that sort of thing."

Billy glances back through the rearview mirror (again).

"Thanks, man. Ballsy costume, by the way. No pun intended."

"Thanks."

Shane readjusts his balls. And he's not the only one.

The Slip Knot

MP parallel-parks in front of the apartment. The three of us get out and go upstairs – Me, MP, and MP's goddamned giddy Ego, who's got a smirk from ear to ear and a saunter just as queer.

Two minutes later, Fos pulls up to the curb and screeches to a halt in front of MP's Beamer, nearly side-swiping the mirror.

Two minutes after that, Billy rounds the corner in the Mustang and parks behind the Beamer.

The Dominatrix, Wonder Woman, and Playmate of the Year race into the building for a much anticipated assault on a door labeled 3D.

And two minutes after that, MP's giving my patience, focus, and faith a run for their money as he blocks the path to the bedroom. To my suitcase. To my freedom. Or so he thinks.

"And he took your car!" Then he buckles over, propping his waxed ass against one wall, while his hands grip his abs to prevent the guttural fits of laughter from exploding right through them. "He took your car! Too perfect!"

Finally he stands, wipes tears of triumph from the corners of his eyes, and steps aside, sweeping his arm in a motion that gives me permission to pass.

"I don't care about my car. I'll leave on foot."

I brush past him.

"Oh, okay. Bu-bye!"

He waves like a baby, cracking himself up again.

Two minutes after that, Summer pops opens her door. She's face to face with a gun and three oddballs.

"Eww!" she jumps, like she just rolled onto the wet spot. Or at least *not* like she's freaked about being abducted at gunpoint.

Foster covers her mouth (primarily because she's hot, secondarily for ceremony), shoves her inside and instructs, "I need you to make a phone call and nobody gets hurt."

"Yeah, nobody." Terbear points a petite finger right in The Blonde's face.

Ooh.

"Do I know you from somewhere?" Summer casually inquires, looking Foster up and down.

"You wish. *What the hell is that?*"

Foster points the gun at a pink sweater-vest-clad Pomeranian licking her pleather-ridden ankles.

"That's my Buttons!" She picks up the pup. "Please don't hurt her. She's all I've got. Aren't you, Buttons, my Buttons?" And they smooch and lick and smooch some more – Buttons and The Blonde.

Fos is a sucker for dogs and chicks with big tits, so this really mellows her shit.

"Don't worry. Your Buttons are safe with me." She finds the phone, clutches the hard cylindrical object briefly, then thrusts it at The Blonde. "Now call MP. Tell him to come over. And make it sound urgent."

Shane checks his hair/wig in the foyer mirror.

Terbear searches the refrigerator for a cherry wine cooler, and, to her glee, finds one. The Blonde takes the phone and dials MP's number. But before hitting the "call" button, she brushes her finger languidly along the length of the gun.

"Is that a real gun?"

She is a fearless fusion of heavy breathing and eye batting.

Foster reddens (who knew)?

"We'll talk later."

The Blonde teasingly bites into the air between them.

"You know, he's on his way over anyways."

"Oh, he is, is he?"

That's what Foster said, but what she was thinking was, *I'd like to take you to dinner, then bend you over one knee and lick apple pie a là mode off your ass. How would you feel about that, sugar?*

"Why, yes. Yes, he is," The Blonde responds, all boobs, all breath.

But what *she* was thinking was, *Ooh, yes, but make it something with bananas. I just luv a good banana.*

They gaze curiously, dubiously, dramatically. There's enough fire between the two of them to scorch the dog and melt the phone. Without breaking eye contact, The Blonde pushes the little green "call" button and places the phone to her ear.

It's taken me about (you know it) two minutes to pee. As I exit the bathroom to grab my suitcase, the phone rings. MP answers it.

"I know. I got tied up."

Click.

"I'll be back later. But if you're gone, well, then, bu-bye."

And his obnoxious cackle is finally stifled as that squeaky door shuts it out of my life for good.

With suitcase in hand and cell phone in pocket, I've got all I need. I mean, I want Billy, and I love him, and will find him one day, and maybe that day will even be tomorrow, but for now the goal is *leave*.

I don't even bother to close our obnoxious door. My old life and all its junk is up for grabs. Already, even the length of the hallway serves as my first finish line, the stairs my second, and the door to the outside world – the third. I feel as if a record has been broken, and sense an inner harmony resonate throughout my body, like all my molecules finally jive.

Meanwhile, with ski mask over his head, duct tape slung around his wrist, the aid of that charming olive tree, and the theme song to *Mission Impossible* buzzing through his brain, Billy has scaled the building and toppled onto the balcony of the apartment. He bounces up off the cement, scans the joint – no sign of MP – then runs zippity-split into the bedroom.

I'm strolling along, wondering vaguely where the hell I'm headed but not really caring, when I notice a piece-of-shit Mustang that looks a lot like the version of a car I once knew a few hours back in a former life. There's a guitar shoved indifferently on top of some kind of old army bag mingled with weeks of dirty laundry. That's funny. And it's funny I never noticed this Mustang on the block before and...*and I jam my suitcase in amongst the clutter.*

"I'm coming, Billy!" I scream to the sky.

And spring wildly back into the apartment.

"I'm coming!" I repeat while zooming down the hallway just as Summer's door flies open and a gruesome transvestite pops his head out to gawk (or be gawked at), then slams the door shut again.

Whatever. My plans are big. *Huge.* Can't be bothered with transvestites tonight.

Billy dodges from an empty bedroom toward the door and all he can think is; *Please tell me I didn't screw up the plan and miss her, and damn, this mask must be made of wool, I'm sweating like a bastard.*

I fly through the door, still reciting my new mantra and *slam* right into Dude in Ski Mask who's traveling at an equal if not greater velocity. I flip backward, bang my head on the Greenblatt's door. Billy bounces onto the coffee table. It breaks in half, which looks really cool, but oh, so painful.

Budging is not an option, but speaking seems viable.

"Hi," I utter.

"Hi," he politely groans back.

Mrs. Greenblatt opens her door; my head hits the ground.

"Fritz. Fritz! Call the police!"

"No, Mrs. Greenblatt, it's okay." A trickle of blood slithers out my nose, into my hairline. "That's Billy."

Billy rolls up the ski mask, streaking fresh blood from his lip up the length of his cheek.

"Hi, Mrs. Greenblatt. Would you be so kind as to get us some ice?"

Mrs. Greenblatt shuts her door in a huff.

In the fashion of a crab, I crawl over to Billy.

"You came back."

"The truth is," he says through breaths interrupted by other breaths, "I came here to kidnap you."

"Shut up!"

That's too weird. It must run in the family.

"No, I swear. Even have tape. See?"

He holds up the arm bearing the ring of tape, but exhaustion drops it swiftly back onto the floor.

"Foster?"

"Foster."

"Don't you just *love* her?"

He can feign love for Madonna, but Foster? While Billy tries to figure out how to smartly evade *that* question, Mrs. Greenblatt opens her door.

"Here!" Mrs. Greenblatt pitches two packs of frozen vegetables at us as if it's bottom of the ninth and her team, Team Haven't-Gotten-Any-in-Thirty-Years-and-When-They-Did-it-Lasted-Twelve-Fucking-Seconds is up by two, but the bases are loaded. Anyhoo, Billy gets plowed in the face with one bag, while the more injured of my two knees is lambasted by the other. He inspects his package.

"I hate brussels sprouts."

I switch bags with him because that's the kind of love we share. He smiles gratefully and lays the frozen broccoli on the right side of his eye/nose/lip. Together we almost have one injury-free face. Holy shit, there's that optimist again.

"Billy?"

"Rosie?"

There's that beautiful name. I'm overjoyed, exuberant, and I'd get up and dance if I could do it without answering "eleven" to the question: *On a scale of one to ten, exactly how much pain are you experiencing?*

"What were her plans for MP?"

He tilts the broccoli off his face and leans on an elbow.

"Shit. Let's get the hell outta here."

And we scat like cats, like fat, matted, injured, limping cats.

So the getaway is proving to be more and more anticlimactic as we sit in a beat-up Mustang that refuses to start. How dare it blow our grand finale. Billy works feverishly, twisting the key gently, speaking in sweet urging affirmations, and pausing every so often to caress the dash.

I transfix on the license plate in front of us: "MPM" with musical notes and blah, blah – *bingo*.

"I think you ought to leave with what you came for."

He reaches over, squeezes my hand.

"I am."

Then he plants a delicate, warm kiss on my bruising cheek-bone. "But I see your point."

And we lunge dramatically through our designated doors.

Do You, Billy...

I hang up my cell phone.

"And?" Billy inquires.

"And of course we can crash there."

"And…"

"And she's dying to meet you."

"Told you."

"Yes, you did."

My face is painted with a pure delight it just can't shake, and also a couple of serious black eyes which will fade long before the other, is my prediction.

"You know, rumor has it that Phoenix is considered the yogurt capital of the world."

"Oh? Well, it's not very L.A. of me, but I am a big fan of dairy."

"Yeah, I sensed that about you. Rebel. We're going to have to check that out someday soon."

I hope he meant that.

"Hey, Billy?" I say, mood-spoiler that I am. "Do you think we have anything to worry about?"

I'm referencing the BMW. He knows it just like he knows me.

"Grab the envelope out of my duffel bag when you get a chance."

I seize the chance. Rummage. Find it. The title to the car: *William R. Meadows*. It almost makes the most sense of all.

"Mom never pegged me for the college type," he says through that crooked-crazy-smile and entwines his fingers into mine.

A perfect fit.

I gaze at a diminishing Las Vegas through a lipstick-smeared back window that reads: "ᴊᴜꜱᴛ ᴍᴀʀʀɪᴇᴅ," and all I feel is happy.

Ya know, it's a pretty big deal when someone sees you for who you really are and wants to be with you anyway. Never worked that way on Planet Annie before. Natch, I hold Saturn personally responsible. My only obstacle: trying to figure out how to maintain a constant and growing respect for the dude who actually wants to spend *for better or worse for all the days of his freaking life with moi*. Screw it. It's been an interesting start, a fresh start, and I'll work it out as we go.

Where Are They Now?

So, sweet cousin Fos made her career vision a reality and opened "Doc Fos' Clinic for Alternative Healing."

The clinic comes complete with a covert greenhouse brimming with a variety of seriously smokin' medicinal herbs. And as an added touch, she employed a nice and naughty assistant who resembles more of a recovering porn star in her itty-bitty white lab coat than a therapeutic healer. But rumor has it she drums up tons of business, takes instruction very well, never talks back, and can toss both feet behind her head in one fell swoop.

Lisa Marie finally got the companion he always longed for, too. And wouldn't you know it; she is just cute as a Button.

The Happy Drunk Couple…well, they aren't so drunk anymore.

Can you say, "In vitro, baby!" And then can you say, *"Quads, ALL boys, no sleep, no sex, no money, no life."*

They replaced whips, chains, pom-poms, and pleather with bottles, diapers, noisy toys, and words without "l." But to this day, they are very, very happy, and very much in *wuv.*

"Someday soon" really did come *someday soon* for Billy. He started working with his dad at *Happy Meadows Yogurt Factory* within two weeks. Now, he never did master "the swirl technique." But one fine day, he placed one of his infamous snaky-lookin' masterpieces inadvertently into the hands of a heavy hitter in the music biz, and they started chatting. By year's end, "Roses" had hit the charts.

And me? Well, didn't realize that crazy day I ran away with Billy would be the last I ever saw of MP, smug and satisfied, hidden behind some cruel false victory. I never dreamed we'd end so obscurely. And I bet MP never imagined that on that fateful night four years back he'd wind up tied to a tree in Laurel Canyon dressed as one very brawny Wonder Woman 'til someone called the cops during rush-hour the next morning.

But as time has passed, I've grown up. And with the evolution of the mind and spirit being constant and ongoing, I've also learned not to persistently ask why. Why did he treat me that way? Why did I allow it? Why did we stay together through insolence and infidelity? Comfort has come from honoring responsibility to self-scrutiny, to truth, and to letting go. So wherever he is, above all else, I certainly wish him Hell – I mean *well.* Well. I wish him well.

But as for the rest of the world – mine and anybody else's – I do have a piece of advice that I've earned the right to relay: If you make only one worthwhile decision in your entire infinitesimal existence, decide to never mess with an eleven-year-old girl. Don't be her first bad day, her first tear, her first swear word, her first drink. Don't be the moment she realizes her parents don't know what the fuck they're talking about. And do not be the alpha ghost that for the first time rises from that happily dormant corner in her mind to tell her that she's shit.

Don't let a passing fancy, a perversion, or a dark uncovered flashing fantasy turn into decades of drama and trauma for a girl who fell simply and quite accidentally into your path one casual afternoon.

Okay.

So, would I play the lead all over again in the black comedy that was once my life? To stumble upon my prince? You bet I would.

And that's the story of my fairytale romance. It may not seem like a fairytale, and it might not be all that romantic. But it's mine, my story, my life. And though you might not call me Cinderella…you just might call me *blessed*.

Now if you'll excuse me, it's August, it's hot, and it's dusk – and I'm off to dance in the Arizona rain with the man I love.

Acknowledgments

We all know "Life" is far more interesting than "Fiction." And behind every fable lies deep truth. For that, I'd like to thank all the "characters" in my life who have filled it with light, love, *drink*, wonder, tears, and too many laughs for any one person to fully deserve. You have inspired and obliged me to sprinkle pieces of each of you into these wonderfully rich, endearingly flawed, geniusly original, intense characters. So thank you, Bethany (DeMeuse) Rankin, Cory L. Schuelke, Sarah Blom, Tracie and Sean Madden, Roberta Renaud, Rick Cerasoli, Lora Cerasoli, and J. David Newton.

A million thanks to Sandra Siegal for having a "sick" amount of faith in me since the moment we met in the spring of '96. You embody an optimist whose honest, energetic spirit cannot be rivaled in this industry (or on this planet). To this day, I can't believe I'm not your only client. I often think of that thing you once said regarding your work ethic: "Never mistake kindness for weakness." You're a brilliant businesswoman with a heart of platinum.

Thank you, Ken Atchity, of Atchity Entertainment International, Inc. for suggesting I turn my screenplay, *On the Brink of Bliss and Insanity,* into a novel. When I said I didn't know how to write a novel, you tossed me one and replied, *"Here's a book: Do it like that."* You're awesome. I'm beyond thrilled you squeezed me into your highly successful schedule and taught me through "tough love" editing how to pull this off. And thank you, Andrea Mckeown of AEI, Inc. for your expertise and innumerable phone calls throughout the editing and revision process. You have a really cool phone voice (which always helps when one is getting critiqued...over and over and over).

Special thanks to Newton for the use of your song, "Roses." I can't wait for the whole wide world to be blessed with your unique, eclectic, soul-touching tunes. You've been a rock star in my eyes for years: an inspirational talent. And William Potter, thank you for your time, friendship and artistic genius. Your concept for this cover brought it to where it is today – perfect.

Five Star Publications, Inc.; I am blown away by your energy, efficiency, excitement, and accessibility. Gary Anderson, you were speedy and insightful throughout our editing process. And Sue Defabis, thanks for the info, emails, that keen proofreading eye, and "laughing out loud" while reading this on the plane. Linda Radke, your enthusiasm toward your company and clients is contagious. You work around the clock and are a bounty of fresh marketing ideas. Plus, your company has accommodated my artistic whims beyond my imagination. And speaking of beyond "imagination" and "expectation," the cover of this novel is exactly that. *Wow*. Thank you, Kris Taft Miller. When I saw your creation, it was "love at first sight."

And lastly but not "leastly," thanks to Peter Weaver, my funny, cool, sexy, perceptive, patient hubby. You must be sick of reading my shit...*but you just keep on doing it*. There's a writer inside you that has let me snag some really great ideas, characters, and plot points. Thanks, Babe. And, Mom, Sherie Cerasoli, you rock on a number of emotional (and financial) levels. Where would an artist "like me" be without a mom "like you?" Thanks baby sis (Lora), baby bro (Rick), Brock Weaver, Grandma Nori Cerasoli, Jazzlyn Jo Weaver (my favorite every-thing), and my late father, Dick Cerasoli. You had a dream two weeks before you died that "*They'd be fighting over this.*"

Dad; I'll keep you posted.

About the Author

L isa Cerasoli spent nearly a decade in Los Angeles as an actor before discovering her true passion; writing. She was a series regular on *General Hospital*, portraying the quirky character, "V." Then she appeared in numerous nighttime series, including recurring roles on *The Pretender* as Zoe, and *Boomtown*.

She now lives with her husband, their young daughter, his teenage son, and her eighty-seven year old grandmother near her hometown of Iron Mountain, Michigan.

"Life is definitely interesting up here in the "woods." I keep inviting my mother *and* my stepson's mom to join our near-commune-style, *blissfully-insane* abode, but they haven't taken me up on it yet!"

I tried reading it, but the language and sexual content threw me for a bit of a "loop." Now I did read Lisa's *Grey's Anatomy* speculation script last spring, and that was just fantastic!

Sherie Cerasoli – THE AUTHOR'S MOTHER

My first thought was...*I have to read this book again!*

Kristine Leonard – THE AUTHOR'S FRIEND
AND PSEUDO MOTHER-IN-LAW

Reading *On the Brink*...was like spending eight hours in a car with Lisa.   *Rose Loeks* – THE AUTHOR'S FRIEND

I have read this book AT LEAST fifty times...and still find myself laughing out loud, crying quietly, and thanking God for making me way less screwed up than Annie.

Lisa Cerasoli – THE AUTHOR